THE SAINT RETURNS!

The headline screamed at him:
Turista Inglese Trovato Assassinato
James Euston of London. . .

So the Saint pledged himself to a vendetta which took him to Sicily, a land particularly suited to that ancient bloody custom.

From then on, except for an interlude with a luscious Italian pasta named Gina, it was all-out, heel-stomping war, with the Robin Hood of Modern Crime pitted against the arch-evil, centuries-old traditions of the Mafia!

VENDETTA FOR THE SAINT

BY LESLIE CHARTERIS

CHARTER
NEW YORK

A DIVISION OF CHARTER COMMUNICATIONS INC.
A GROSSET & DUNLAP COMPANY

VENDETTA FOR THE SAINT

Charter Books
A Division of Charter Communications Inc.
A Grosset & Dunlap Company
360 Park Avenue South
New York, New York 10010

2 4 6 8 0 9 7 5 3 1
Manufactured in the United States of America

There is no doubt that the Mafia is one of the principal causes of the misery weighing on the population in Sicily. Whenever there is an offense to the law, one hears repeated: 'That is an affair of the Mafia.'

The Mafia is that mysterious feeling of fear which a man celebrated for crime and strength imparts to the weak. The *mafioso* can do what he likes because, out of fear, no one will denounce him. He carries forbidden weapons, incites to duels, stabs from behind, pretends to forgive offenses so as to settle them later. The first canon of the Mafia is personal vengeance.

We must note that there are families in which the traditions of the Mafia are passed on from father to son, as in the physical order congenital illnesses are inherited. Also, there are *mafiosi* in every walk of life, from the baron to the worker in the sulphur mines.

Luigi Berti
Prefect of Agrigento
1875

I

How Simon Templar's Lunch was Delayed and his Wardrobe suffered for It

It was the pleasant pause after the *antipasto* when the healthy appetite, only slightly assuaged by the opening course, rests in happy anticipation of good things to come. The *Rosa del Vesuvio* was cool and light on Simon Templar's tongue, and for a few rare minutes in his adventurous life he prepared to surrender to whatever gastronomic pleasures Naples might provide, and tried not to think of certain other distractions for which that city is also somewhat notorious. Somewhere behind him, in the cavernous depths of Le Arcate, the restaurant where he sat, a lobster was leaving the humble ranks of the crustacea and being ushered into the realm of great art in the guise of *Aragosta alla Vesuvio*. This was a moment to be savored and treasured to the full.

Therefore the loud and angry voice which suddenly disturbed his peaceful mood was a gross and egregious intrusion.

"Go away!" it snarled. "I don't know you!"

Simon turned a little in his chair for better ob-

servation of the tableau, which he had quite disinterestedly noticed as it developed.

The source of the grating voice sat a couple of
tables away, a man in at least his late fifties, whose
paunchy build was well masked by some superb
tailoring in pearl-gray raw silk. Under the coat was
a shirt of the finest chambray, clinched at the
throat with a hand-painted tie nailed by a diamond
pin and at the wrists with cuff-links of ten-carat
star sapphires. On one highly manicured finger he
wore a massive gold ring, which served to frame a
cabochon emerald the size of a pigeon's egg. But in
spite of all this expensive elegance, his face was
completely nondescript, looking as if it had been
roughly thrown together in clay by a rather un-
skillful sculptor as a base to model a proper
portrait on. All its features were untidy except the
lipless slit of the mouth and the sparse border of
carefully barbered hair plastered down around the
gleamingly bald dome.

His companion was perhaps twenty years
younger and dressed at less than one-twentieth the
cost, with broad shoulders and curly black hair and
the looks of any untravelled spinster's conception
of a Venetian gondolier, somewhat gone to seed.
Intellectually they seemed to have even less in common, for they had hardly exchanged half a dozen
words while they were under Simon's indifferent
attention. They had finished their meal and were
sipping coffee when the third of the *dramatis per-
sonae* had arrived.

This one was as obviously English as he was a
gentleman. His flannel bags and Harris tweed
jacket were of unmistakable origin, and the act of
wearing them in Naples in mid-summer proved

that their owner, conditioned by damper and chillier climes, stubbornly regarded them as the only correct holiday wear for any country. The cut and texture of the cloth, as well as the hand-rubbed glaze on the conservatively laced shoes, indicated a man of means and good taste within rigidly traditional limits. Yet this was the individual who had, apparently, committed the frightfully un-British solecism of annoying a total stranger.

He had been strolling past the terrace, gazing all around like any tourist, when he had had a delayed reaction, stopped, turned, stared, hesitated, and finally turned in to address the putty-faced plutocrat who had responded so uncivilly.

"But, Dino!" stammered the tourist, with acute embarrassment heightening the color of his naturally ruddy complexion. "I know it's a long time ago, but don't you remember me?"

"What is this Dino?" The answering growl had an American accent that was incurably Italian at the same time. "I don't know no Dino. Don't bother me."

"I'm Jimmy Euston," persisted the Englishman, struggling to hold on to his temper and his dignity. "Have you forgotten Palermo? The bank? And that scar on your chin—"

The seated man's fingers moved involuntarily to an inconspicuous white cicatrice on the side of his jaw.

"You're crazy with the heat," he said. "Beat it, before I get mad!"

"Now look here, Dino—"

The response was no more than a flicker of a finger, a fractional movement of the head, but it brought the other man at the table smoothly to his feet. He grasped the Englishman by the arm, and what happened next would have been missed by any spectator but Simon.

Euston's mouth opened soundlessly, and his red face became white. He bent forward, attacked by a sudden spasm. Simon, to whom such tactics were as familiar as elementary drill to a sergeant, recognized at once what had happened: under cover of the victim's body and his own, the curly-haired one had delivered a short wicked jab to the solar plexus.

There was more to come. The goon's arm drew back again, and the cheap striped suiting wrinkled over a bulge of powerful muscles. Once more the contraction came that would send the arm forward again with enough force to crack a rib.

Except that this time the conclusion failed to materialize. If a steel vise anchored to a stone pillar had suddenly appeared and clamped home around the elbow, the arm would have been no more firmly fixed. With shocked incredulity the goondolier turned and gaped at the browned fingers that locked casually on his arm and rendered it immobile. From there his gaze travelled up over the broad chest and sinewy neck to the intruder's face, the tanned face of a buccaneer with blue eyes that laughed and yet were colder than an arctic sea.

"That's very naughty," Simon remarked.

If it had not been for the tenseness of imminent explosion, they would have made an almost comic trio, joined arm to arm like three convivial friends about to burst into song. But there was a far from convivial expression in the yellowed and bloodshot stare of the man whom Simon held, a darkening menace that brought a hopeful smile to Simon's lips.

"Try it on me, chum," he invited softly. "Try anything—and I promise you'll wake up in hospital."

"*Basta*!" grumbled the man who denied being Dino. "They must be from the same nut-house. Let's get outa here."

In an instant the threatened eruption was dissipated. Obediently the bodyguard released Euston, and turned to pull the table aside for his patron. Simon let him go, a trifle reluctantly, but reflecting that what might have been a delightful brawl would probably have been broken up by spoilsport policemen and very likely resulted in his *Aragosta* getting cold while they conducted the post-mortem.

A banknote fluttered down between the coffee cups, and the foppish slob turned his back and walked away, followed by his two-legged dog; and Simon shrugged and looked at Mr. Euston again. The elderly Englishman's face was still blanched, and beaded with perspiration from the effects of the single cruel blow he had taken.

"Sit down at my table for a minute," Simon said, guiding him in that direction even while he spoke. "Have a drop of wine." He poured a glass. "Or something stronger, if you feel like it. That was quite a dirty poke you took."

"Thank you. I'll be all right in a jiffy."

Color returned slowly to the other's face while he sipped—a little too much, perhaps, Simon realized, as it ripened towards the masculine cousin of a blush. Mr. Euston had not only suffered a public humiliation, but he found himself indebted to someone to whom he had not even been introduced.

"My name's Euston," he mumbled unnecessarily. "Jolly decent of you to come to the rescue, Mr.—"

Alternative replies flashed through the circuits of Simon Templar's mind with an electronic speed developed from much similar experience, to be weighed and compared and chosen from according to the circumstances. He could give his real name, and risk a recognitive "Not the chap they call The Saint? The Robin Hood of Modern Crime? Well, bless my soul!"—and so forth. Or he could give one of the aliases to which he had become sentimentally attached—so much so that even some of them ran a fifty-fifty chance of recognition in certain circles. Or he could improvise a new identity— a creative effort which the present situation might hardly justify...So quickly that no one would even have noticed any hesitation, he selected the middle course.

"Tombs," he said, and won the toss-up gamble. "Sebastian Tombs." It struck no spark from James Euston. "Think nothing of it. But next time you make a mistaken identification, it might be a good idea not to insist on it too hard."

"But it wasn't a mistake," Euston said, mopping his brow. "I'll swear he was Dino Cartelli, a chap I worked with in Sicily before the war. I was training for the foreign department of the City and Continental then, and a year at their branch in Palermo was part of the course. Dino worked next to me, and we were fairly good friends. Except for the time when he got that scar."

"How did that happen?"

"I gave it to him. It was a difference of opinion, Latin temperament and all that, over some girl. He opened a knife and I had to hit him. I wasn't an amateur champion or anything like that, but my signet ring cut him."

Simon's interested regard took a quizzical slant.

"Well, that might account for why he didn't see you as a long-lost buddy."

"Oh, no, we didn't start a vendetta. The girl ran off with somebody else and left us both feeling silly. We apologized to each other and made up, and we were still good friends again when I was sent to another post. And yet now he not only pretends he doesn't know me, but he—or the fellow with him— they behave like gangsters!"

"They did seem to have some of the mannerisms," Simon admitted thoughtfully. "Are you absolutely certain you couldn't have been wrong?"

"Absolutely."

"After all those years, even a thing like a small scar—"

"I'm positive it was Cartelli, and still more so after hearing his voice. I used to tease him about sounding like a frog instead of a Caruso. No; it only shows you," said Mr. Euston, taking a brooding refuge in one of the cardinal tenets of a true-blue Briton, "you never really know where you are with foreigners."

This line of thought was punctuated by the arrival of the lobster that Simon had been awaiting, mounted on a wheeled trolley, attended by a retinue of waiters, and trailing clouds of elysian fragrance. He made a hospitable gesture.

"Would you care to join me? We can share this while they fix another one."

Mr. Euston, however, seemed to feel that he had already shared more than enough confidences for such an informal acquaintance. He pushed his chair back and climbed hurriedly to his feet.

"It's very kind of you, Mr. Tombs, but I've already imposed on you too much. Besides, I don't think I could eat anything for a while." He pulled out his wallet and extracted a card. "If you're ever in London and I can do anything for you, please give me a ring. And again, thanks awfully for your help."

He pumped Simon's hand vigorously, turned, and marched firmly away and out of Simon's world for ever; and with a shrug Simon dismissed the encounter from his mind and devoted to the *aragosta* the whole-hearted attention which it deserved. Mr. Euston's enlargements on the theme of the nasty surprises which could befall anyone who ventured outside the counties and clans of Albion might have provided a fascinating accompaniment to lunch, but not so much that to be deprived of it would impair his appetite. As for the incident that had brought them together, Simon was still half inclined to write it off as a simple case of human error. The most interesting feature of it was that Euston had had the bad luck to pick on a character who had all the earmarks of having spent some time in the USA in associations which are not highly approved of by the Immigration Service.

That is, he thought so until the next morning.

Breakfasting in his room, he was trying to utilize the exercise of reading an Italian newspaper to divert his attention from the vile taste of the coffee, without much success in spite of the normal quota of international crises and local scandals. Until he reached a small item low down on the second page.

TURISTA INGLESE TROVATO ASSASSINATO, said the headline.

A silent relay closed in his brain, setting off a peal of soundless alarm bells in his inner ear, even before he came to the second paragraph, where the murdered man was identified as James Euston, of London.

2

A number of reasons have been suggested at different times for Simon Templar's superficially incongruous title of The Saint, and there may be a kernel of truth in all of them, while not one is the complete answer. The sobriquet is a derivative and outgrowth of so many contributory and contradictory factors attempting to crystallize the supreme paradox of the man himself. But one truly sanctified quality which had never been imputed to him was a forgiving disposition.

James Euston had never been his friend, and probably never could have been. With all his possibly sterling virtues, Mr. Euston had the essential ingredients of a crashing bore. His demise would be no great loss to anyone, except perhaps his nearest kin, if he had any. And Simon had no personal obligation to protect him, beyond a basic civilized responsibility which he had already more than fulfilled. Yet by not taking the Englishman's earnestness seriously enough, and blithely ascribing the gangsterish reflexes of Not-Dino and his bully boy to an almost amusing coincidence, he had let Euston go bumbling off to a death which might easily have been averted. He had been made an accomplice, however unwittingly, in the slaughter of a harmless innocent; and even if his

involvement had been unintentional, he could not
forgive his own blindness. And therefore he could
not forgive the men who had profited by it.

Which meant especially the one who must after
all have been Dino Cartelli.

That at least was a viable assumption. In the
light of what Simon had witnessed the day before,
it seemed as if James Euston's vacation could only
have been so violently terminated because he had
identified Cartelli. If it had only been an accidental
and unfounded resemblance, Euston would not
have had to be killed. The newspaper, of course,
gave robbery as the obvious motive. Euston's
corpse, with its head beaten in and its clothing
emptied of cash, had been found in an alley a few
blocks from his hotel: it seemed self-evident that he
had had the bad luck to be waylaid by footpads on
his way home. And such a coincidence could not be
ruled out—though all the Saint's instincts, belatedly sharpened as they had now become, rejected it
with hoots of derision. To him, the aroma of
double-distilled skulduggery had been unmistakably added to the other noisome and om-
niprevalent effluvia of Naples.

Simon settled on those conclusions while he
showered and dressed, and when he walked out
into the furnace blast of Neapolitan heat it was not
for a sightseeing stroll.

It was still too early for lunch, a meal which in
Italy never begins before one o'clock and when
combined with a necessary nap to aid digestion of
the *pasta* and *vino* can extend into the late afternoon. But at Le Arcate some torpid waiters were
sweeping and dusting and setting out arrays of silver and napery in readiness for the activity to

come. Without too much prompting, one of them was persuaded to retire to the gloomy back quarters in search of the head waiter.

In a soiled collarless shirt with sleeves rolled up to the elbows, and still in need of his first shave, this was a much less august personage than he appeared on duty, but he accepted the off-hour summons with professionally reserved aplomb. He shook hands easily when Simon extended his, and there was no change of expression when he felt the folded bill in his palm. The paper vanished with the dexterity of many such passings, and he tilted his head with grave attention to learn what small service had been purchased.

"If you remember, I had lunch here yesterday," Simon began.

"*Sissignore.* I remember."

"At the same time, there was a man here named Dino Cartelli."

"The man who sat down with you for a few minutes? I thought he was English."

"He was. I'm talking about another customer."

The head waiter's forehead wrinkled above a perfectly blank face.

"Cartelli? I do not know that name."

Unless the man was a consummate actor, he must have been telling the truth; and the Saint would usually back his own judgment against any modern electronic substitute. If it was not letting him down, then, Cartelli had not merely been reluctant to be recognized: he had a new name now and did not even want to be reminded of the old.

"An Italian," Simon said. "In a light gray suit. Heavy, almost bald, with a deep rough voice. He was sitting with a younger man at that table there."

This time he had even less need of a lie detector, as the man's eyes swivelled in the direction of the pointing finger and swivelled back again to focus on the Saint with a pronounced diminution of cordiality.

"I do not remember such a man, *signore*. You realize, Napoli is a big city, and this is a busy restaurant. It is impossible to know everyone. *Mi rincresce molto.*"

He escorted Simon to the door, multiplying his protestations of regret, but not saddened enough by his inability to help to be moved to refund the money that had already settled in his pocket.

He would need absolution for perjury before he partook of another Mass, but Simon realized that it would have been a waste of time to discuss this with him.

Outside, the doorman, not yet gorgeous in his coat of office, was stolidly sweeping the night's débris from the stretch of sidewalk over which he reigned. The Saint approached him and said: "Do you remember a man who was here for lunch yesterday—rather stout, bald, with a grating voice, in a gray suit?"

Folding money between Simon's fingertips promised gratitude in advance, and the doorman's hand started an automatic move towards it before the full import of the question drilled into his head. With comprehension came reaction, and his fingers jerked back as if from the touch of a hot iron. He glanced apprehensively over his shoulder, and a drowned-fish expression washed over his face.

"*Non mi ricordo,*" he gabbled. "We have so many customers, I forget all of them."

He returned to his sweeping with far more industrious concentration than he had shown before.

Simon looked where the doorman's eyes had swerved, and saw the head waiter still lurking in the doorway. With a shrug of resignation, he turned and strode away.

The visual impression that he had given up lasted only until he rounded the next corner. Then immediately his stride lengthened and quickened as he circled the block to approach the restaurant from the opposite side. This was somewhat easier begun than accomplished, for there are few such things as "blocks" in the American sense in any Italian city—there are only chunks and gobbets of buildings of all ages and stages of decrepitude, intersected by a completely haphazard network of streets and stairways that would seem to have been laid out by a jigsaw puzzle fan rather than a cartographer. Calling upon his sense of direction for a prodigious effort, the Saint managed to achieve his purpose with an accuracy which, in the Africa of H. Rider Haggard, might have earned him the cognomen of Lord of the Labyrinths, or He-Who-Finds-All-Crooked-Paths. In a surprisingly short time he had completed the meandering detour and was leaning against the wall of the adjacent building, out of sight of anyone who did not step all the way out of the restaurant, as the doorman pushed his broom towards that side with the normal apathy which it had not taken long to restore.

"*Amico*," said the Saint softly, "would you like to try your memory again?"

His voice froze the pavement sanitizer into immobility. Then, with painful slowness, the man's eyes travelled all the way up the Saint's figure from the shoes to the smiling face.

"Now don't go and have a stroke," Simon urged him kindly. "Nobody inside can see me, and they need never know I came back. Just prod those brain cells and try to make them give out the name of the gentleman I was asking about."

"Non capisco," said the doorman hoarsely, and resumed a pretense of sweeping that would scarcely have convinced a five-year-old microcephalic.

The axiom that money talks has its exceptions, but something told the Saint that he had found one individual who would not be permanently deaf to sufficient shouting. This time it was a 10,000-*lire* note that he produced and unfolded to the size of a small bedsheet; it shone goldenly in the sun. He refolded it to a small wad and let it drop. The doorman's eyes followed it covetously as it fell, until Simon's foot covered it.

"Do you understand that?" Simon asked. "It would be so easy for you to sweep it up."

"No!" was the mechanical answer, but the emphasis was dwindling.

"At least you might tell me somewhere else to ask. The hotel where he stays, perhaps. The driver of the taxi they took from here might have told me that, if I found the right driver. No one will know it was you."

Beads of sweat broke out on the man's swarthy face as fear fought with avarice. Simon took out a second 10,000-*lire* bill and folded it carefully like the first.

"Excelsior!" gasped the doorman huskily.

Simon gazed at him for a long moment, and, when the man failed to unfurl a banner with a strange device and head for the nearest mountain, it became clear that the speaker was not planning to emulate the eccentric youth in the poem but was simply uttering the name of the plushest hotel in Naples.

"Grazie," said the Saint, releasing the second bill, and turned away without waiting to watch it and its predecessor being raked briskly into the little pile of jetsam that the *portinaio* had been maneuvering towards the frontage of the establishment next door.

To some investors it might have seemed inadequate yield for the outlay, since it would not have taken any Sherlock Holmes to deduce that a citizen dressed and bedecked like Cartelli would not be likely to bunk in some obscure *pensione;* but to the Saint it was worth it for the time that could be saved from canvassing alternative *palazzi*— not to mention eliminating the possibility that he resided in an apartment or house of his own. Now, provided the information was true, Simon could make a more positive move.

A green and black cab followed after him when he turned into the Via A Falcone, while the driver expounded the advantages of his cool upholstery and dazzling speed over the dusty travail of walking under the noonday sun. Simon succumbed with only token resistance and climbed in; but he was not so blinded by the shady interior that he failed to notice the 300 *lire* already registered on the meter, nor too proud to draw the driver's attention to the undoubted oversight. After a brief verbal brannigan during which certain special charges were mentioned, so special indeed that they could not be found in the quadrilingual list of complicated tariffs posted inside the cab, a decision was reached that perhaps the meter should be

readjusted ; and the chauffeur launched his vehicle
through the lunatic traffic with an emotional abandon which suggested that only homicide or suicide
would salve his injured feelings.

Simon called a premature halt to the ride at a
leather-goods shop which he spotted within sight
of the Hotel Excelsior. There he bought a handsome gold-bound pigskin cigar case, making no
more attempt to stint on quality than a man with
his quarry's evident tastes would have done. To
him it was only another investment, like the solvent
which had opened the doorman's impermanently
sealed lips.

He took the case and the same attitude to the
Sale e Tabacchi a few doors farther on. On some
other occasion it might have amused him to engage
the tobacconist in a long and profound debate over
the selection of a package of salt, which for reasons
which may remain eternally obscure to non-Ital-
ians is a monopoly of the same government-
licensed stores. But that morning he was driven by
too much impatience to waste time on anything but
the purchase of two of the very best cigars, and the
shopkeeper who sold them at the inflated official
price never knew what torment he had been spared.

Simon put the cigars in the case and kept the
case in his hand as he entered the ornate lobby of
the Excelsior, and located the desk of the concierge.

"I believe this belongs to one of your guests," he
said. "Would you see that he gets it?"

The attendant examined the case which Simon
had laid on the counter, with the olympian detachment befitting his office, which is believed by all
concierges to be only slightly inferior to that of the
managing director.

"Do you know which one?" he inquired, with a subtle suggestion that his responsibility covered not merely thousands but tens of thousands, and that anyone who did not realize it was probably a peasant.

Simon shook his head.

"I'm afraid I don't. I just happened to see him getting into a cab, and heard him tell the driver to come here, and then I saw the case on the ground. I picked it up and yelled at him, but the cab was driving off and he didn't hear."

"What did he look like?"

"Heavy set—about sixty—a little gray hair, but mostly bald—wearing a very fancy gray silk suit—diamond pin in his tie—star sapphire cuff-links—a gold ring with a huge emerald . . ."

The functionary, who like all his brethren of that unique European order could be counted on to know everyone who had a room in the caravanserai during his tenure, and almost as much about their activities as God, listened with a concentration that progressed from the condescendingly labored to the tentatively perspicacious to the final flash of connection.

"Ah yes! I think you mean Signore Destamio."

The Saint's pause was imperceptible.

"Not—Carlo Destamio?"

"No. The name is Alessandro Destamio." The case disappeared under the counter. "I will take care of it for him."

"Now, just a minute," Simon said amiably. "Why not call his room and ask if he did lose a cigar case? I didn't actually *see* him drop it, you know. It might have been lying there all the time."

"I cannot ask him at once, sir. He left yesterday afternoon."

"Oh, did he?" Simon did not bat an eyelid. "That's too bad. It was yesterday when I picked it up, of course, but I've been too busy to come by before this. Where did he go?"

"He did not tell me, sir."

It was apparent that the concierge did not warm to that type of interrogation, from the darkening of his face which was quickly masked with a sneer.

"I will ask him when he comes back, sir. He is not a tourist—he keeps his suite here all the time. If you would like to leave your name and address, I will send you back the case if it does not belong to him."

And, the impeccable manner implied, if there's any question of a reward, don't worry, I'll see that you get it; you probably need it.

"Don't bother," said the Saint airily. "If it turns out not to be his, you keep it. Just be careful how you light the cigars, in case some practical joker planted the whole thing."

It was not, he felt, an entirely discreditable exit; and it left interesting vistas for future speculation.

Besides which, the visit had produced all that he had any right to expect, if not more: a name.

Alessandro Destamio.

3

A hard core of literate Americans who can still read the printed word when they get their eyes un-gummed from the nearest television set would be capable of distinguishing the name of Alessandro Destamio from all the synonyms who have gone down in windrows before the movie cameras. It was a name that had become familiar through

much repitition in news reports and popular
articles, even to a vast number of people who still
had only the vaguest idea of what he actually did.
Al Destamio was a member of "The Syndicate", a
nebulous and to most readers still semi-mythical
organization which controlled all the lucrative
rackets in the United States and a shocking percen-
tage of local politicians. He had not been one of its
chief executives, at the rarified elevation of a Lu-
ciano or a Costello, but he was at least what might
be called a minor cabinet minister—one of those
names which can be regularly flagellated by colum-
nists without fear of libel suits, which are intermit-
tently rousted by federal officers, and which nevertheless appear seldom or never on a roster of peni-
tentiary inmates, and when they do it is usually because of some technical flaw in their income tax
returns.

Al Destamio, Simon clearly recalled, had been
one of those unlucky ones a few years before, and
had been deported back to his native land after a
year's cure in Leavenworth which only cost the US
Government a few thousand dollars more than he
was already alleged to have short-changed them.

And yet, back here at home, he was apparently
suffering from no shortage of pin-money, and his
aura could still inspire terror or loyal compliance
among restaurant and hotel employees. An unap-
preciative Uncle Sam might have given Alessandro
the boot, but back in his homeland he was man-
ifestly not washed up. Far from it. In fact, he
seemed to command a respect which might have
been envied by the Prodigal Son.

At this point the Saint felt that some reliable local briefing on such mysteries might be helpful.

Unfortunately there was not a single resident of
that city in his slim but strategically indexed address book. Then he recollected that his old friend
Giulio Trapani kept a villa at Sorrento, which
couldn't be more than a couple of hours away, to
which he retreated for a vacation every summer.
Simon could find nothing in the telephone book
which he consulted in his garage, and decided at
once it would be faster to drive there and conduct
inquiries on the spot than to do battle with the Information Service of the Italian telephone system.
In less time than he could have initiated a phone
call, he was in his car and heading for the famous
Amalfi Drive.

But in this case it made no difference. He was
able to track down the villa without too much trouble, but *il padrone* had not yet arrived. No doubt he
was still skimming the cream of the expense-ac-
count crop in the Thames Valley. And good luck to
him—but Simon wished only gastritis on the bene-
ficiaries.

He lunched regally on *zuppa di pesce* and
calamaretti, laved with a bottle of Antinori Classi-
co, on the terrace of La Minervetta overlooking the
blinding blue sea, and later swam off the rocks
below in the same translucent element, and finally
drove back to Naples refreshed and recharged but
no wiser than he had been when he left.

Thanks to the recommendation of a well-meaning friend, the Saint had made his reservation at a
more modest hotel than the Excelsior, a short distance farther along the sea front on the Via
Partenope. It had turned out to be considerably
less luxurious than the class of hostelry which Simon Templar usually chose at that period of his

life; but it had been late at night when he arrived, and his room looked clean and comfortable enough, and it had not seemed worth the trouble to go searching for other accommodation for the two or three days which were all he had planned to stay. Its only vital disadvantage as against the more populous and busily serviced competition was one which had not occurred to him at the time and might never have been brought home to him if he had not impulsively befriended the late Mr. Euston.

He helped himself to his key from behind the all-purpose desk which was tended at various hours by the manageress, the porter, the floor waiter, or any chambermaid who was not otherwise occupied, and in between their shifts by a bell with a mechanical button which could be thumped for eventual attention, and took the self-service elevator to his floor. He had just stepped out when a man came running down the corridor in a frantic sprint to catch a ride before the conveyance went down again; and the Saint turned and stared at him with instant curiosity.

Readers of this chronicle who wonder why a man running for a lift should be such an arresting spectacle are only betraying their own limited horizons. If they had taken advantage of the eight-country, twenty-two city, fifteen-day excursion rates offered by the philanthropic airlines, they would know that on the Mediterranean littoral, in summer, nobody, but nobody, runs for an elevator or anything else. Wherefore the Saint took extra note of the pointed face, the rodent teeth, the pencil-line mustache, the awning-striped suit, and a wealth of other trivia not worth recording, before the febrile eccentric squeezed into the lazy-box and disappeared from view.

It had all taken perhaps three seconds, and it was over before a possible signifance to the incident could penetrate through his first superficial astonishment. And by the time Simon reached his room, further speculation became unnecessary.

The door was not quite shut, and he only used his key to push it open.

To say that the room had been searched would be rather like describing a hurricane as a stiff breeze; and in fact a hurricane could have gone through it without doing much more damage. Whoever had been there—and Simon no longer had any doubt that it had been the rat-faced man in a hurry—had efficiently and enthusiastically taken it to pieces. Not content with spilling everything from drawers and suitcases, the intruder had hacked open the shoulders and split the seams of some of the finest tailoring of Savile Row. The same blade had slit the linings of valises and playfully pried the heels from shoes, besides exposing the stuffing of the mattress.

Only a person who knew the Saint's fastidious habits would have appreciated the calm with which he surveyed the wreckage and flicked the dead ash from his cigarette on to the midden heap before him.

"*Che cosa fa?*" gasped a voice behind him, and he turned and saw a gaping chambermaid staring in from the corridor.

"If someone stayed on the job downstairs, it might not have happened," he said coldly. "Please get it cleaned up. The clothes that are worth repairing you can give to your husband, or your lover, wherever they will do the most good. And if the manager has any comments, he can find me in the bar."

Fortunately there was Peter Dawson in that dispensary, and a double measure with plenty of ice and just a little water helped to soothe the most savage edge of his anger as well as slaking the thirst which he had incubated on the drive back.

The vandalizing of his wardrobe was only a temporary inconvenience, after all: a telegram to London would have replacements under way at once, and meanwhile there were excellent tailors in Italy and some of the world's best shoemakers. On the plus side, the last vestige of possibility that Euston's death was coincidental had been removed. And Cartelli, or Destamio, had been concerned enough about Simon Templar's intervention to have ordered a complete check-up on him and a search which could only have had the object of discovering any concealed official—or criminal —association.

A revelation that might have daunted anyone but the Saint was the speed and apparent ease with which he had been found, which indicated an organization of impressive size and competence. He seriously doubted whether even the local police, with all their authority and facilities, could have done as well. But a sober respect for the opposition and the odds had never done anything to Simon Templar except to make the game seem more exciting.

The manager, or the husband of the manageress, eventually made an appearance. He dutifully wrung his hands over the catastrophe, and then said: "You are worried, of course, about the damage done to the bed. Do not think any more about it. I have put in a new bed, and we will just charge it in the bill."

"How nice of you," said the Saint. "I hate to sound ungracious, but as a matter of fact I was more worried about the damage to my belongings, which happened because you make it so easy for robbers to get into the rooms."

The manager's hands, shoulders, and eyebrows spread out simultaneously in a graphic explosion of incredulity, indignation, reproach, and dismay.

"But, *signore,* I am not responsible if you have friends who perhaps do such things for a bad joke!"

"You have an argument there," Simon conceded. "So it might be simpler not to give me a bill at all. Otherwise I might recommend some other playful friends to come here, and they might do the same things in all your rooms." He turned over the bar check. "Oh, and thanks for the drink."

He felt better for the rest of the evening; though he was careful to dine at a corner table and to examine his wine bottle carefully before it was uncorked. The fact that some back-stage Borgia might have spiked anything he ate was a risk he had to take; but in calculating it he had noted that for some abstruse reason posion had never been an accepted weapon of the fraternity of which Al Destamio was such a distinguished member. Simon had often wondered why. It would have seemed so much easier and slicker than the technique of the gun. He had never been able to decide whether the answer was in some code of twisted chivalry, calling for the actual confrontation of the enemy before his extinction, or merely because a spectacular artillery mow-down made more awesome headlines with which to keep other hesitants in line.

But nothing even mildly disturbing happened to him that night, and when the next move came in the morning it was totally different from anything he had anticipated.

When he came downstairs after breakfast and handed his key over the desk, a slight saturnine man in chauffeur's uniform who had been standing near by approached him with a deferential bow.

"Excuse me sir," he said in passable English. "Mr. Destamio would like to meet you, and sent me with his car. He did not want to risk waking you up by telephoning, so I was told to wait here until you came down."

The Saint regarded him expressionlessly.

"And suppose I had some other plans?" he said. "Such as going shopping for some new clothes, for instance?"

"Mr. Destamio hoped you would talk to him before you do anything else," said the chauffeur, with equal inscrutability. "He told me to promise you will not be sorry. The car is outside. Will you come?"

A latinate flip of the hand repeated both the invitation and the direction; and yet no threat was implied by gesture, intonation, or innuendo. Having delivered his message, the chauffeur waited without a sign of impatience for Simon to make his own decision.

Well, Simon thought, some day he would almost inevitably have to guess wrong, fatally wrong. But he didn't think this was the day. And anyhow, the opportunity of making a proper acquaintance with such a personage as Mr. Destamio was too great a temptation to resist.

"Okay," he said recklessly. "I'll take a chance."

He did not have to look around for the car. There was a Cadillac berthed in the street outside which was the only conceivable vehicle, even before the chauffeur opened the door with a certain possessive pride. It was black, high-finned, gigantic, polished to the brilliance of a jewel, and completely out of place in the constricted antiquity of the street. Without hesitation Simon climbed into the cavernous interior, and was not surprised to find himself alone. Whatever Destamio might have in mind for the future, he would hardly be so idiotic as to have the Saint killed in his own car in the center of Naples. The windows were closed and an air conditioner whispered softly. Simon settled back into the deep upholstery and prepared to enjoy the ride.

4

It was not a very long journey, but it was impressive enough. Under the driver's skillful touch, the car slid into the traffic like a leviathan into the deep. On all sides rushed schools of tiny cars, battling and honking through swarms of slow-moving pedestrians, small children, and animals. The din that arose from all this came to Simon only as the gentlest of murmurs through the thick glass and padded metal. Cool breezes laved him and wafted away his cigarette smoke even as he exhaled it.

Leviathan ploughed a majestic path through the small fry and rushed towards the bay. Without slowing, they swept through the gates of the port, and the guards saluted respectfully. The Saint looked out at the portholed flanks of the ships— only liners here, the smaller ferries were outside the fence in the public port—and had momentary qualms of a shanghaiing, until the car came to a smooth halt next to a modernistic concrete structure something like a giant's pool table on spindly legs. It had been built since his last visit to the city, and for a few seconds it puzzled him. Then he heard the roar of rotors overhead, and the pieces clicked into place.

"Ischia or Capri?" he asked the chauffeur, as he stepped reluctantly out into the steam-bath of untreated atmosphere.

"Capri, sir. This way, please."

The two island resorts of fun and sun are eighteen miles from the city, at the outer edge of the vast bay. They are normally reached by a varied collection of yachts, ferries, and converted fishing boats, in a voyage that takes from one to four hours depending on the prospective passenger's ability to translate the misleading notices. Prosperity and technology have now changed this for the well-heeled few and supplied a helicopter service that covers the same distance in a few minutes. There was one that seemed to have been waiting only for the Saint: as soon as he was on board, the door shut and he was lifted as smoothly as in an elevator.

They swung out over the incredibly blue waters of the bay, giving him what he had to admit was a marvelous panorama, much as he thought it had been over-written in the travel brochures. The vertical rock walls of Capri jutting dramatically from

the sea were as impressive from the air as when
seen from the more usual approach. The pilot
turned in over Marina Grande, circled the top of
Monte Solaro so that his passenger could appreciate the best parts of the view, then dropped
lightly on to the painted circle of the heliport.

This is located on the site of Damecuta, one of
the many palaces which the Emperor Tiberius scat-
tered over his favorite island, on the cliff edge just
as far out of town as it is possible to get on dry
land, and as Simon climbed down he wondered
what transportation would be provided for the last
lap of the journey. He felt sure it would be no less
sumptuous than the preceding conveyances.

Something appeared wearing the minimal shorts
and halter which pass for clothing on that insular
lido, and the Saint leisurely surveyed the large
areas of skin which they made no attempt to cover,
confident in the wisdom of his years that people
who undressed like that expected to be looked at.
The vision of long tanned legs and golden hair
floated towards him with a rotary motion that displayed its other accessories to great affect. "Mr.
Templar?" it asked, in a low and throbbingly warm
voice.

"None other," he said happily. "How did you
find me in all this crowd?"

The helicopter pilot and a single airport attendant—the only audience—watched appreciatively,
waiting for the reverse view when the vision would
retreat and in so doing display the remainder of her
delectable curves. She ignored the Saint's plea-
santry and merely gestured towards the parking
space.

Since the roads on Capri are barely wide enough

for two beamy baby-buggies to brush past each other, only the smallest cars are used and even the buses are minuscule. Therefore he was not expecting another Cadillac; but the little cream-colored Alfa-Romeo which he boarded, with its sensationally displayed chauffeuse, was a worthy substitute.

So was her driving style, which shot it off like a compact bomb and forced it to claw its way around the turns that wound up the face of the mountain with an abandon which made the Saint hope devoutly that she knew what she was doing. He stole several dubious glances at her; but her lips were heavily painted and unmoving, while the upper part of her face was so hidden by immense flower-wreathed sunglasses that her eyes and any expression around them were completely concealed. Her attention seemed to concentrate entirely on the road; and Simon felt too gentlemanly at the time to force his attentions on her. Particularly since they were skirting the edge of vertical drops so high that the boats below looked like toys in a pond.

Fortunately for his nervous stamina, there was quite a short limit to the maximum mileage at her disposal on the island, and she had not even reached third gear when they arrived at their destination, a villa overlooking the beaches and coves of Marina Piccola.

His alertness involuntarily tautened again as he strolled up the flagged path. Now he had helped to deliver himself unresistingly exactly where Destamio wanted him, it would not be much longer before he was shown just how foolhardy he had been. He was not even ashamed to be relieved when the Vision with the legs rang the door-bell herself, thus sparing him any concern over the per-

ils of the bell mechanism. More than once in the
past it had been demonstrated to him how lethal
such commonplace fixtures could be made. But
this time the button activated no poisoned needles,
sprays of gas, hidden guns, or bombs; if anything,
the opening of the door was quite anticlimactic. Instead of unleashing mayhem, it projected only the
prominent belly of Signore Destamio, dressed in a
cerise shirt and purple shorts which did considerably less for his pear-shaped figure than the
fancy tailoring in which Simon had first seen him.

"Well, Mr. Templar! Nice of you to come," the
remembered voice rasped. Destamio put out his
hand and drew Simon into the house. "I been
wanting to talk to you, and I figured this spot was
as good as any, better than most. Right?"

"It could be," said the Saint guardedly.

He was observing all the corners and interesting
angles of the interior without appearing to do so.
But there were no other thugs in sight, and the situation looked transparently innocuous so far.

"Come on and let's sit out on the balcony, nice
and cool with a great view, and Lily is gonna bring
us some drinks and then she'll get lost."

If Lily took offense at this rude dismissal she
gave no sign of it. As soon as Destamio and the
Saint were settled on either side of a glass and
wrought-iron table she wheeled up a bar wagon
and left. Simon heard a door close deep inside the
house.

"Help yourself," Destamio said. "And pour me
a brandy and ginger ale while you're there."

As Simon selected two clean glasses and a bottle,
he admird the neat and tactful way in which anxie-
ty about a possibly-doctored drink had been

eliminated. Nevertheless, he took the extra precaution of pouring both drinks from the same bottle. The cognac was Jules Robin, he noted approvingly, though he would not normally have chosen to drink it before lunch.

"You by any chance working for those bastards at the Bureau of Internal Revenue these days, Saint?" Destamio asked, with no change in his conversational tone.

He stared fixedly at Simon as he spoke and afterwards, his expression controlledly empty, yet not completely hiding glints of menace deep within the eyes.

The Saint sipped his drink and was externally just as calm—while his brain was whirring like an IBM machine. The mention of the income tax department nudged out a file card that had been waiting for hours to drop into the hopper.

"Gopher," he said dreamily. "Gopher Destamio —isn't that what they called you?"

"My friends call me Al," growled the other. "And that's what I wanna know about you: whose side you on?"

"Do I have to take sides?" drawled the Saint. "I hate paying taxes as much as anyone, so I can't help having a sort of sneaking sympathy for anyone who's had your kind of trouble with the Internal Revenue Service. But tax evasion isn't the worst crime you've been accused of, is it?"

"You heard all about me, then."

Al "Gopher" Destamio pulled from his pocket a wilted package from which he extracted an object that might be humorously described as a cigar, but in fact resembled nothing so much as a piece of decomposing rope that had been soaked in tar and

buried for a number of years. He sawed the thing in
two with a pocket-knife and offered the Saint half
of it. Simon shook his head politely, and watched
in fascination as Destamio pulled a yellowed straw
from the interior of one half and applied a lighted
match to the truncated end. After warming it thoroughly, he raised the revolting article to his lips
and proceeded to puff it to life. Simon moved his
chair back a bit, out of the direct drift of the
smoke, having had previous experience of the
asphyxiating potency of the infamous Tuscan
cheroot.

"Everyone's heard all about me," Destamio
said, apparently unconscious of the destructive effect of the fumes on throat and lungs. "That's the
trouble. They believe all them lies printed in the
papers, and think I got no more right than a mad
dog. Me, I'm a peaceful man. I just wanna be let
alone."

"I guess none of the other guys in the Syndicate
wants much more than that," Simon agreed com-
miseratingly.

"Lies, all lies," Destamio grumbled without
much show of heat.

He went on in a monotone, as if reciting a story
that had been told too many times, to reporters,
police officers, and the more inquisitive members
of the judiciary: "I go from Italy to the States with
a few bucks and invest it in the trucking business,
and I make a little dough. I make a little more
dough because I like playing the ponies, and I'm
lucky. So maybe I make a mistake not reporting
some of my winnings, and they make out I got
more money than I can account for earning. It's
discrimination, that's what it is. Just because I'm

Italian and some guys in the rackets are Italian, they call me a racketeer. I love America, but they give me a dirty deal."

The record ground to a halt, and Destamio lowered the level of liquid in his glass by a full inch.

Simon recalled the rest of the story now, including some details that Gopher Destamio had neglected to include. The early record was vague, but included two or three arrests on minor charges and a short term spent in jail for assault with a deadly weapon before Destamio had graduated to the upper ranks of the Syndicate. Thereafter his presence had been reported at mysterious assemblies in remote mountain cabins, and his name regularly cropped up in popular magazine articles about the unpunished aristocracy of the underworld. Although, like others similarly mentioned, he exhibited extraordinary restraint in not suing such calumniators for libel, no one seemed able to prove anything positive against him until the accountants of the Justice Department found enough discrepancies in his financial records to build a case around.

The legal duels that followed were expensive both for the Government and for Gopher, and as usual only the lawyers showed a profit. Uncle Sam was able to lay hands on less than a tenth of the amounts claimed for liabilities and penalties, and could only retaliate by depriving Destamio of his newly acquired citizenship and deporting him back to the land of his birth. What Italy thought about this was not reported, and indeed the Italians never seemed to have been asked if they wanted him.

"So you know all about me, Saint," Destamio

said. "And I know a lot about you. What I don't know is why you get so interested in me all at once. Why?"

The question was thrown in a conversational, almost offhand manner. But Simon knew that this was the bonger, the $64,000 question, the whole and sole reason why he had been brought there with such ambiguous courtesy. Many things might hang upon his reply, among them perhaps the further duration of his own life.

Yet the Saint seemed even more casual and indifferent than his host, and the hand holding his cigarette was so steady that the smoke rose in an unwavering column through the still air. He answered truthfully as well, having decided a little while ago that that would be the most uncomplicated and productive policy. Also he wanted Destamio's reaction when a certain name was mentioned again.

"I'm still wondering," he said, "what happened to Dino Cartelli."

II

How Alessandro Destamio made a Bid, and Marco Ponti told Stories

If the Saint had expected some pyrotechnically dramatic response, he would have been disappointed. Either the name meant nothing to Destamio, or he had been waiting for the question and knew in advance how he would field it. The racketeer only grunted and shook his head.

"Cartelli? Don't know him. Why ask me? What makes you so nosey about me, anyhow? All the time I get reports how you're asking questions about me. A man in my position don't like that. Lotta people would like to see me in trouble, and I gotta take precautions."

"Like having my clothes cut up?" Simon inquired icily.

Destamio grunted again—a porcine reflex that seemed to be his opening gambit to all conversation.

"Maybe. Somg guys get too nosey, they get worse than that cut up. You ain't answered my question: why should I know about this Cartelli?"

"Because that's what a man called you at the

Arcate the other night. He seemed certain that you were Dino Cartelli. I heard him."

Simon waited for the grunt, and it was more explosive than ever.

"Is that all you got on your mind? The guy was nuts. The world's full of nuts." Destamio snapped his fingers and squinted at the Saint. "Say—now I recognize you! You were the guy at the next table who gave Rocco the squeeze. I didn't recognize you till now. I pulled out because I try to stay outa trouble here. I got enough trouble." He sat back and chewed the black and dreadful stump of his cigar, staring at the Saint with piggy eyes. "You swear that's all the interest you got in my affairs? Because some nut calls me by a wrong name?"

"That's all," Simon told him calmly. "Because this nut, as you call him, was murdered that night. So he may have known something that would make a lot more trouble for you."

For a long silent moment Destamio rolled the cigar between his fingers, glaring coldly at the Saint.

"And you think I bumped him to shut him up," he said finally. He flicked ashes over the balcony rail, towards the sea far below, and suddenly laughed. "Hell, is that all? You know, Saint, I believe you. Maybe I'm nuts, but I believe you. So you thought you had to do something to get justice for that poor dope! What's your first name— Simon? Call me Al, Simon—all my friends call me Al. And pour us another drink."

He was relaxed now, almost genial in a crude way.

"Then your name never was Dino Cartelli?" Simon persisted, obviously unimpressed by the other's abrupt change of manner.

"Never was and never will be. And I didn't knock that nut off, neither. You let coincidence make a sucker outa you. Here, let me show you something."

Destamio heaved himself up and led the way back into the living room. He pointed to what at first appeared to be a decorative panel on the wall.

"Lotta bums go to the States change their names and don't care, because their names never meant nothing. But I'm Alessandro Leonardo Destamio and I'm proud of it. My family goes as far back as they ever had names, and I think the old king was an eighty-second cousin or something. Look for yourself!"

Simon realized that the panel was a genealogical chart complete with coats of arms and many branchings and linkings. The scrolls of names climbed and intertwined like cognominal foliage on a flowering tree of which the final fruit bore the glorious label of Lorenzo Michele Destamio.

"That was my papa. He was always proud of the family. And there's my birth certificate."

Destamio stabbed a thick thumb at another frame which held a beribboned and sealing-waxed document which proclaimed that the offspring of Lorenzo Michele Destamio would go through life hailed as Alessandro Leonardo. It looked authentic enough—as a document.

"And you've no idea why this man, what was his name—William Charing-Cross—should have been killed?" Simon asked.

"No idea," Destamio said blandly. "I never saw him before. Wouldn't have known his name unless you told me. But if you're worried about him, I can

ask a few questions around. Find out if anyone
knows anything. Anything to make you happy . . .
Hey!" He snapped his fingers as he was reminded
of something else. "I was forgetting what the boys
did. Be right back."

He walked into an adjoining room, and after a
while Simon heard the unmistakable thunk of a
safe door closing. Destamio came back with a thick
wad of currency in his hand.

"Here," he said, holding it out. "Some guys
working here get too enthusiastic. That wasn't my
idea, all they did to your stuff. So take this and buy
some more. If it ain't enough, let me know."

Simon took the offering. On top of the stack was
an American hundred-dollar bill, and when he
flicked his finger across the edges other hundreds
flashed by in a twinkling parade of zeros.

"Thank you," he said without shame, and put
the money in his pocket.

Destamio smiled benevolently, and chewed another half-inch from his mangled cigar.

"Let's eat," he said, waving a pudgy hand towards a table already decked with silver and crystal
in another alcove. "And we can talk about things.
A guy can go crazy here with no one to talk to."

He sat down and shook a small hand bell noisily,
and the service began even before the ornamental
Lily arrived to join them.

Al Destamio did most of the talking, and Simon
Templar was quite content to listen. Whatever
Lily's other talents might have been, aside from her
hair-raising ways with a car, they were obviously
not conversational. She applied herself to the food
with a ravenous concentration which proved that

her svelte figure could only be a metabolic miracle;
and Simon had to summon some self-control not
to emulate her, for in spite of his grossness
Destamio employed an exceptional cook.

There was only one topic of conversation, or
monologue to describe it more accurately, and that
was the depravity of the US Department of Justice
and its vicious persecution of innocent immigrants
who succeeded in rising above the status of common laborers. But about all that Destamio revealed of himself was his remarkable mastery of
the ramifications of the income tax laws, which
seemed a trifle inconsistent with his claim to have
only violated them through well-meaning ignorance. Simon was not called upon to do more
than eat, drink, and occasionally make some life-
like sounds to show that he was paying attention,
since the oracle was clearly entranced enough with
the gargled splendor of his own voice.

Hence the Saint was able to disguise an occasional unfocusing of the eyes, when his mind wandered underneath the monotonous discourse, groping for another missing item of information which
he felt might provide a key to some of the riddles of
the past two days, but which kept eluding him as
exasperatingly as an itch that could not be
scratched.

At last the coffee wound up the repast, and
Destamio yawned and belched and announced his
readiness for a siesta. Simon took this as his cue for
an exit, and was given no argument.

"Glad I could get to know you, Saint,"
Destamio said, pumping his hand with the heart-
iness of a professional politician. "You have any

more problems, you come to me. Don't try to be a big shot by yourself."

The incredibly discreet Lily appeared once more in the role of chauffeuse, now wearing a cashmere sweater and Capri pants so tight that if she had been tattooed the mark would have shown through. Simon was delighted to observe that she was not tattooed.

As she resumed her attempts to make the Alfa-Romeo behave like a scared mountain goat, he felt that he had to make one parting effort to discover whether she ever talked at all.

"Do you live here or are you just visiting?" he queried chattily.

"Yes."

He gazed at her for quite a long time, figuring this out, but what could be seen of her face gave him no help. He decided to try again.

"Do you ever get away?"

"Sometimes."

That was a little better. Perhaps it only required perseverance.

"I hope I'll see you again somewhere."

"Why?"

"I'd like to know what your face looks like. Would I recognize you without glasses?"

"No."

Always the same pulse-stirring voice, vibrantly disinterested in everything.

"Is Al a jealous type?"

"I don't know."

The Saint sighed. Perhaps after all his charm was not absolutely irresistible. It was a solemn thought. At any rate, she was evidently capable of holding

out for the duration of the short ride to the
heliport. But he had to keep on talking, because the
other haunting hint of knowledge that he had been
seeking had suddenly given up its evasive tactics
and dropped out of the recess where it had been
hiding.

"Do you know why he was called 'Gopher'?" he
asked.

"No."

"Well, I won't burden your mind with it. When
you go back just tell him that I know. I suddenly
remembered. Will you do that?"

"Yes."

They were at the heliport, and a flight was about
to leave, the vanes of the 'copter swishing lazily
around. But the Saint wanted to be sure that his
message would get through. As he levered himself
out of the bucket seat, he stopped with the door
still open and pulled out the sheaf of crisp greenery
that Destamio had given him, fanning the leaves
under her nose while he ostentatiously peeled off
one of them.

"Tell him, I liked these samples. The only thing
wrong is, there weren't enough of them. Show him
this so he knows what you're talking about. Tell
him it's going to cost a lot more now, because of
the 'Gopher' business. Do you think you'll get that
straight?"

She nodded placidly.

"Congratulations," said the Saint.

He shut the car door, and leaned over it. There
was one final touch he could not forego, vain as it
might seem. Although it should certainly help to
make his point.

"And if you want to find out whether he's jealous, tell him I did this," he said.

He bent further and kissed her on the lips. They tasted like warm paint.

2

The helicopter leaped skywards, and Simon's spirits soared with it. What had begun as the most trivial happenstance, sharpened by a curt sequel in the newspaper, had grown into the adumbration of a full-scale intrigue.

He had some of the sensations of an angler who was expecting to play with a sardine and instead has hooked a tuna. What he would do with the tuna on such a flimsy thread was something else again; and no one but Simon Templar would have made such a point of setting the barb so solidly. But it was one of the elementary tricks of fishing to make the fish work for you, and the Saint felt cheefully confident that his fish would not waste much time sulking on the bottom. As soon as the 'Gopher' barb sank in . . .

To share that optimism, some readers may have to overcome the limitations of a sheltered life, and be informed of its connotations in some circles where they may not ordinarily revolve. In some of the far-fetched variations of American slang, a gopher (aside from his primitive zoological determination to be a small rodent of retiring but horticulturally destructive habits) can also be a bumpkin, a ruffian, or a toady. These are general terms, not confined to the so-called "under"-world with which Destamio must have had some illustrious connections. But in the idiom of that nether clique, a 'gopher' is either an iron or steel safe, or the technician who specializes in blowing open such containers in order to obtain illegal possession of their contents.

This was the idiomatic detail which gave the lie to everything Destamio had tried to sell him, and which had to connect with the sudden deimise of James Euston, Esquire, a former bank clerk. And the certainty of it added no little brilliance to Simon's esthetic appreciation of the golden afternoon clouds gathering behind Ischia.

When the helicopter landed at the Naples harbor station, he remained in his seat until the pilot came and said courteously: "This is the destination of your ticket, *signore.*"

"I've decided to go on to Capodichino."

"Then there is an extra charge."

"How much?" Simon asked carelessly.

He was not nearly so concerned about being branded an arrogant plutocrat, which he could survive, as about being caught in an even swifter riposte by Al Destamio, which he might not. Even in the few minutes for which he had been airborne, Lily could have returned to the villa, Destamio could have picked up a telephone and contacted henchmen on the mainland, and the Naples heliport might be no safer than a booby-trapped quagmire.

On the other hand, an arrival at Capodichino might confuse the Ungodly still more, and possibly leave them standing flatfooted.

Once he had decided on that detour, Simon realized that he had no need to return to Naples at all. His baggage had been rendered practically worthless anyhow, and from a phone booth at the airport he promised to come back later for whatever was worth salvaging. There was anguished disbelief in the manager's voice when Simon guaranteed that he would take care of the bill at the same time; but the Saint allowed his heart to be hardened by the thought of how much more joyfully surprised that entrepreneur would be when the payment actually arrived.

A kiosk sold him a book about the glories of Sicily, after some argument, for very little more than the price printed on the cover, and left him just enough time to catch the evening plane to Palermo.

Palermo was even hotter than Naples, and there are few airconditioned hotel rooms in Sicily, despite the suffocating need for them; but by a combination of seasoned instinct, determination, good luck, and extravagant bribery, the Saint succeeded in securing one. This involved staying at a hotel with the hideously inappropriate name of The Jolly, which was anything but. However, it gave him a restful night, and he was able to console himself for the cost with the reflection that it only made a small dent in Al Destamio's advance donation.

In the morning, after a leisurely breakfast, a shave with a cut-throat razor borrowed from the valet, and in relatively clean and spruce linen by courtesy of the ingenious manufacturers of wash-and-wear synthetics, he strolled over to the local office of the City & Continental Bank (Foreign Division) Limited, to which the hotel porter had only been able to direct him after his memory was refreshed by a reasonable honorarium. In fact it was such a modest building, evidently maintained principally as a convenience for touring clients, that there was barely room for its impressive name to spread across the frontage.

A dark-haired girl with Botticelli eyes smiled up at him from behind the counter and asked what she could do for him, and it required some discipline not to give her a truthful answer.

"I'm trying to contact one of your employees," he said. "It's several years since he worked here, so he may have been transferred."

"And his name?"

"Dino Cartelli."

"Madre mia!" the girl gasped, rolling her doe eyes and turning pale. "One moment—"

She went over and spoke to a man working at another desk, who dropped his pen without even noticing the splotch of ink it made on his ledger. He gave Simon a startled suspicious look, and hurried behind a partition at the rear of the office. In another minute he came back to the Saint.

"Would you like to speak to the manager, sir?"

Simon wanted nothing more. He followed the clerk to the inner sanctum, where he was left to repeat his question, feeling rather like the man in the Parisian story who has a note in French that no one will read to him. This time the reaction was less exaggerated, except for the altitude to which it raised the manager's eyebrows.

"Did you know Dino Cartelli well, sir?"

"I never even met him," Simon admitted cheerfully. "An old friend of his, James Euston, whom you might remember, told me to look him up when I was in Sicily."

"Ah, Yes. Mr. Euston. Perhaps that explains it."

The manager stared gloomily at his hands folded

on the desk. He was a very old man, with wispy gray hair and a face that had almost abdicated in favor of his skull.

"That was so long ago," he said. "He couldn't have known."

"*What* couldn't who have known?" Simon demanded, feeling more and more like the man with the mysterious note.

"Dino Cartelli is dead. Heroically dead," said the manager, in the professionally hushed voice of an undertaker.

"How did he do that?"

"It happened one night in the winter of 1949. A tragic night I shall never forget. Dino was alone in the bank, working late, getting his books in order for the following day. The bank inspectors were coming then, and everything had to be brought up to date. He was a very conscientious chap. And he died for the bank, even though it was to no avail."

"Do you mean he died from overwork?"

"No, no. He was murdered."

"Would you mind telling me exactly what happened?" Simon asked patiently.

The manager lowered his head for a moment of silence.

"No one will ever know exactly. He was dead when I found him in the morning, with ghastly wounds on his hands and face. I shall never forget the sight. And the vault was blown open, and everything of value gone. The way the police reconstructed it, he must have been surprised by the thieves. He knew the combination to the vault, but he did not give it to them. Instead, he must have tried to grab their gun—a shotgun—and that was when his hands were blown to shreds. But even that didn't stop poor Dino. He must have gone on struggling with them, until they shot him in the face and he died."

"And how much did they get?"

"New and used lira notes, to the value of about a hundred thousand pounds, as well as some negotiable bonds and other things. Some of it has turned up since then, but most of it was never traced. And the criminals have never been caught."

Simon asked a few more questions, but elicited nothing more that was important or relevant. As soon as he found that he had exhausted all the useful information that that source could give him, he thanked the manager and excused himself.

"Please give Euston my regards," the manager said. "I'm afraid he will be shocked to hear the story. He and Dino were quite good friends."

"If Dino hasn't told him already," said the Saint, "I wouldn't quite know how to get the news to him."

The manager looked painfully blank.

"Esuton is dead too," Simon explained. "He got himself murdered in Naples the other night."

"Dear me!" The manager was stunned. "What a tragic coincidence—there couldn't be any connection, of course?"

"Of course," said the Saint, who saw no point in wasting time discussing his nebulous suspicions with this interlocutor.

Outside, the heat of the day was already filling the street, but Simon hardly noticed it. His brain was too busy with the new thread that had been added to the tangled web.

At least one detail had been confirmed: the large parcel of boodle about which he had theorized had now become a historical fact and could be identified as the proceeds of the bank robbery. The question remained whether it had been dispersed or whether it was still hidden somewhere. But in exchange, another part of the puzzle became more obscure: if Destamio was not Cartelli, how did he fit into the picture?

"Scusi, signore—ha un fiammifero?"

A thin man stopped him at the mouth of a narrow passageway leading off the main street, holding up an unlit cigarette in one hand. The other hand was inside his jacket as he gave a small polite bow. The everyday bustle of the street flowed around them as Simon took out his lighter.

"Will this do?"

He flicked the lighter into flame and held it, almost unthinkingly, his mind still occupied with other things. The man bent forward with his cigarette, and at the same time brought his other hand out and plunged a knife straight into Simon's midriff.

Or rather, that was his intention, and anyone but the Saint would have been dying with six inches of steel in his stomach. But Simon had not been unthinking for quite long enough, and the significance of the thin man's concealed hand sparked his lightning reflexes in the nick of time to twist aside from the slashing blade. Even so, it was so close that the point caught in his coat and tore a long gash.

Simon Templar would not often have gone berserk over a little damage to a garment, but it must be remembered what had so recently happened to the rest of his wardrobe. Now he was wearing his only remaining suit, and this too had been wrecked, leaving him with literally nothing

but rags to his name. Combined with a natural resentment towards strangers who took advantage of
his kindly instincts to try to stick daggers into his
digestive apparatus, it was the last straw.

But instead of blinding him, anger only made his
actions more precise. He grasped the wrist of the
knife hand as it went by, and pivoted, locking the
thin man's arm under his own. He held that position with cold calculation, just long enough to
make sure that an adequate quorum of witnesses
had stopped and stared and thoroughly registered
the fact of which one was holding the knife; and
then he made another swift sharp movement that
resulted in a crack of breaking bone and a short
scream from his victim. The stiletto fell to the pavement.

Without releasing his grip on the thin man's
wrist, Simon freed his other hand, carefully adjusted the position of his target, and put all his
weight into a piston stroke that planted his left fist
squarely in the center of the other's face. Under the
impact, nose and face gave way with a most satisfying crunch, but the man went down without another vocal sound, and lay still. All things considered, Simon decided, as his fury subsided as
quickly as it had flared, it had been only a humane
anesthetic for a fractured ulna.

The whole incident had taken only a few seconds. Looking around warily for any possible second assault wave, he saw a small Fiat standing at
the other end of the alley where it connected with
the next parallel street. The door on the near side
was open, and a blue-chinned bandit sat at the
wheel, staring towards the Saint with his jaw still
sagging. Then he suddenly came to life, slammed

the door, and stepped frantically on the gas.

Simon picked up the fallen stiletto, ignoring the gathering crowd which gesticulated and jabbered around him but kept a safe distance. It was perfectly balanced, the blade honed to a shaving edge, a deadly tool in the hands of an expert. The Saint was not sorry to think that at least one such virtuoso would not be working for some time.

A policeman finally came pushing through the mob, one hand on his holstered pistol, and Simon coolly tendered him the hilt of the souvenir.

"This is what I was attacked with," he said, taking none of the risks of undue diffidence. "All these people saw me disarm him. I shall be happy to help you take him to the police station and sign the charges against him."

3

The policeman swivelled a coldly professional eye over the crowd, whose members immediately began a circulatory movement as the spectators in front were stirred by a sudden desire to be in the rear. Simon saw his witnesses rapidly evaporating; but before the last law-shy personality could melt away the *polizie,* inured to coping with the evasiveness inspired by his vocation, had stepped forward and collared two of them—a pimply youth with an acute case of strabismus, and a portly matron bedizened with bangles like an animated junk stall.

The only things they had in common were their observation of the knifing attempt and a profound reluctance to admit this to the constabulary. Nevertheless, the policeman quarried from them a grudging admission that they had seen some of the events which had occurred; though the ocular abnormality of the younger one might have cast doubts on the value of his testimony. He then appropriated their identity cards, which they could redeem only by appearing at the police station to make depositions. Dismissed, they retired gratefully into the background; and the policeman brought his functionally jaundiced scrutiny back to the Saint.

"Why did you kill him?" he asked, looking gloomily from the knife in his hand to the recumbent figure on the sidewalk.

"I didn't kill him," Simon insisted patiently. "He tried to murder me, but I didn't feel like letting him. So I disarmed him and knocked him out. The knife you're holding is his, not mine."

The policeman examined the weapon once more, flicking open the mechanism of the blade with his thumb nail. He closed it again with one hand and pushed the safety button into place with an automatic motion which revealed long familiarity with such devices.

Behind him, two more police officers appeared, causing the crowd to lose all further interest and disperse. The one who had been first on the scene saluted the more lavishly gold-braided of the newcomers and mumbled an explanation in dialect. His superior stared at the Saint darkly, but showed no inclination to discuss the crime further in the public street. Simon accepted their glum detachment with seraphic indifference, and even allowed himself to be jammed into the rear of an undersized police car without further protest. Whatever consequences were to develop next would have to reveal themselves at the *questura*.

Once inside that ancient building, the recording and annotating of the fracas proceeded with ponderous solemnity. There was an incredible amount of laborious writing on multiple forms, and the continual thumping of rubber stamps accompanied it like a symbolic drum-roll of bureaucracy. The only ripple in the remorseless impersonality of the routine occurred when the Saint presented his passport for examination, and raised eyebrows and knowing glances informed him that his reputation was not entirely unknown even there.

When the knife-wielding citizen was brought in, Simon saw that his injuries had been partly patched up by a police sugeon: one splinted arm hung in a sling, and a large wad of gauze was taped over his nose. From behind the edges of it, a pair of bloodshot eyes glared hatred at the Saint, who responded with a beatific smile.

With the preliminary recordings completed, another door opened and the *maresciallo dei carabinieri* made his impressive entrance.

His elaborately decorated and braided jacket and cap, worn even in the heat of the office, left no doubt of the eminence of his rank. His head was nobly Roman and graying at the temples, not unlike the average man's mental picture of a Caesar; though the softness of the lower lip suggested Nero rather than Julius.

He stared coldly down the straight length of his nose at Simon; then swivelled his eyes, like the black orifices of cannons coming to bear, towards the bandaged knife-wielder.

"Well, Tonio," he said stolidly, "you were not out of trouble very long this time."

"I did nothing, *maresciallo,* nothing! I swear on my mother's tomb. It was this *fannullone"*—the man called Tonio jerked the thumb of his good hand towards Simon—"who caused the trouble. He is a madman, perhaps. He comes up to me on the street, insults me, pulls out a knife. I had done nothing!"

The *maresciallo* glanced through the papers which had been written up, and turned his imperial gaze on Simon.

"What have you to say about this?"

"Nothing—except that Tonio must have very little respect for his mother," said the Saint calmly. "There were a dozen people around when he attacked me with the knife. They all saw me disarm him. Some of them may also have noticed his accomplice waiting near by in a car, who left rather hurriedly when Tonio was detained. If that is not enough, ask him how my coat was cut if I was trying to stab him, or why I did not use the knife on him instead of my hands. After that, you might ask him who hired him to kill me."

The *maresciallo* heard the words with pursed lips and mask-like impassibility. He poked at Simon's passport on the desk before him.

"We do not like international criminals who pose as simple tourists," he said. "Who come here and attack people."

Simon Templar's eyes widened for an instant as he took the shock. Then they narrowed into chips of blue ice as cold as the edge that crept into his voice.

"Are you suggesting that there is one grain of truth in that creature's story, or that there is one shred of evidence to support it?"

Under the pressure of the challenge the *maresciallo's* imperial manner slipped a bit. He squirmed inside his gorgeous jacket and seemed to find it a relief to switch his gaze to Tonio at frequent intervals.

"That is not the point. I mean to say, this is an investigation, and we must consider all possibilities. There is some doubt among the witnesses as to exactly what happened. And you must admit, Signor Templar, that your reputation is not spotless."

Simon glanced around at the *carabinieri,* who stared stolidly back, registering neither approval nor disapproval of their officer's attitude. The Saint had never cherished any childlike faith in the impartiality of the police, but he did not have to be excessively cynical to realize that there was something more here than a normal suspiciousness of his honesty and respectable intentions. And an insubstantial but chilling draught seemed to touch his spine as it dawned on him that something more dangerous to him than any knifeman's blade might lie beneath the surface of that impersonal hostility.

Then yet another man came in, in ordinary clothes but with a subtle air of authority that invisibly outranked the *maresciallo's* gold-encrusted magnificence, and the tension that had begun to build up dissolved as if it had all been an illusion.

He was a man of medium build, flat-bellied, with the gray eyes and curly blond hair that are native only to northern Italy. His browned features seemed almost boyish at first, until one discovered the intermingled lines etched among them by twenty years more than was suggested by their youthful contours. But he walked with an athletic spring in

his step which again belied those skin-deep fore-
shadowings of middle age.

He stopped in front of Tonio, studying him
carefully, and said: "I am glad to see someone has
worked on your ugly face, piece of filth."

He added some more vivid epithets which would
have invited a duel to the death in any tavern in
Sicily, but the wounded Tonio only glowered and
kept his lips buttoned.

No one else spoke either as the newcomer turned
to the *maresciallo's* desk and flicked through the
papers on it.

"Simon Templar!" he said, looking up and
laughing. "We seem to have landed a big one this
time."

He came towards Simon and offered his hand.

"Let me introduce myself, Signor Saint: my
name is Marco Ponti. I am the *agente investigativo*
here, what you would call a police detective. Now
you know all about me, because I am sure you
know all about detectives. But I also know something about you. And since you are here, it is my
business to ask what brings you to Sicily?"

"Only the same attractions that bring thousands
of other tourists here," answered the Saint, relax-
ing guardedly. "Which of course did not include
having one of your problem *paisani* try to knife
me."

"Ah, poor Italy—and poorer Sicily! Many are in
want here and turn to crime to fill their stomachs.
Though of course that is no excuse. Be assured that
justice will be done. We ask you only to be available to support your charges."

"With pleasure. But there seems to be some difficulty."

"Difficulty?" Ponti's eyebrows lifted elaborately. He turned back to the desk and riffled through the papers again. "Everything looks in order to me —is that not right, *maresciallo?*"

The officer shrugged.

"No difficulties. I was only asking a few questions."

"Ebbene! Then I suggest that you, Signor Templar, give us the name of your hotel—but you have already done that, I see in your statement. That is all we need for now. We will notify you when the case appears before the *giudice instruttore,* the magistrate. Unless the *maresciallo* has anything more to ask?"

The *maresciallo* could not have lost interest more completely. A gesture that combined a shrug, a small throwing-away motion of the hands, and a regal tilt of the head, conveyed that he was finished, bored, and only wished to be spared further tedium.

"And you, Signor Templar, have nothing more to say here?"

Ponti's eyes looked directly into the Saint's, and for an instant the engaging boyishness no longer seemed to be the dominant characteristic of his face. Instead, there was only an intense and urgent seriousness. As clearly as if the lines in his forehead had spelt it out in capital letters, it changed his words, for Simon's reception only, from a question to a command.

"Nothing more," said the Saint steadily.

His acceptance of the silent order was instinctive. Whatever had been going wrong before, Ponti's arrival had temporarily diverted it, and Simon Templar was not one to scorn a lifeboat until unfathomed waters closed over his head. Besides which, he sensed an essential difference between Ponti's implied warning and the kind that had menaced him a little earlier. But the questions which it raised would have to wait. For the present, the opportunity to leave the police station was satisfaction enough. He was already suffering some of the feeling of claustrophobia which was inclined to afflict him in places that had a direct connection with prisons.

Ponti's ready smile returned as he retrieved Simon's passport and handed it to him.

"I'm sorry we have kept you so long," he said. "It must be already past your accustomed lunch hour. I hope it will only improve your appetite for our Sicilian cooking."

"Where would you recommend me to try it?" Simon asked.

"The Caprice is near by, and they have the first eggplant of the season. You should not leave Palermo without trying their *caponata di melanzane*. And a bottle of Ciclope dell'Etna."

"I can taste it already," Simon said.

They shook hands again, and one of the stoical *carabinieri* opened the door for him.

After the suffocating atmosphere of the police station the fresh air was revivifying, even as redolent as it was of the rich effluvia of Palermo. The Caprice, which Simon found without much difficulty, was a cool cavern of refuge from the cascade of glare and heat outside, and he entered its depths gratefully, selecting a strategically located table with a wall behind and an unobstructed vista in front.

"The *signore* would like an *aperitivo?*" queried

the nonagenarian waiter.

"Campari-soda. With plenty of ice and a twist of lemon."

"And afterwards?"

"I will order presently. I am waiting for a friend."

The Saint was as sure of this as he could be of anything. He could not imagine for a moment that Investigator Marco Ponti had taken the trouble to recommend this restaurant for no reason but pure gastronomic enthusiasm. And as he sipped the astringent coolness of his drink, he hoped that this private meeting would throw some light on the knife attack and the peculiar antipathy of the *maresciallo*.

Very shortly the street door opened again; but it was not the expected form of the detective that stepped in. This, however, proved to be no disappointment to the Saint at all.

It was a girl . . . if the writer may perpetrate one of the most inadequate statements in contemporary literature.

There seems to be a balance of nature in Italy which compensates in advance with extraordinary youthful beauty for the excessive deterioration which awaits most of her women in later years. Long before middle age, most of them have succumbed to superabundant flesh expanded in the dropsical mould that follows uncontrolled motherhood, and for which their tent-like black dresses are perhaps the only decent covering; and their faces tend to develop hirsute adornments which would be envied by many a junior Guards officer. But the perfection of face and form which a compassionate fate may grant them before that has been observed by most modern movie-goers. And this specimen was astounding proof that the nets of pandering producers had by no means scooped all the cream of the crop.

Her hair was stygian midnight, a shining metallic black that wreathed a delicate oval face with the texture of magnolias, full-lipped and kohl-eyed. The simple silk confection that she wore offered more emphasis than concealment to the form it covered but could scarcely contain. It was obvious that no trickery of supporting garments was needed or was used to exploit the burgeoning figure, rounded almost to excess in the breasts above and the flanks below, yet bisected by a waist of wasp-like delicacy. To complete the entrancing inventory, Simon allowed his gaze to slide down the sweet length of leg to the small sandalled feet and drift appreciatively back up again.

Whereupon he received a glance of withering disdain of the kind that had obviously had much practice in shrivelling the presumptuous and freezing the extremities of the lecherous, and which made it depressingly apparent that like many other beautiful Italian girls she was also impregnably respectable. Only the Saint's unjustified faith in the purity of his admiration enabled him to meet the snub with a smile of seraphic impenitence until it was she who looked away.

The cashier nodded to her in beaming recognition, and after a brief exchange of words picked up the telephone. Simon realized with regret that the girl had not come in to eat, but to ask for a taxi to be called—a common enough method in those parts where the quest for a public phone can be a major project.

After another word of thanks she started out again, and an entering customer stood aside and held the door for her. She swept past him, accepting the service as if it were hers by divine right, and he had to content himself for reward with the pleasure of watching her all the way into the cab, which providentially was an old-fashioned one with a high step. It was only after Simon had shared this treat with him, and the man finally let the door close and came towards him, that the Saint noticed who it was.

"Marco Ponti—what a surprise," he murmured, with no visible sign of that reaction. "Will you join me in a mess of eggplant? Although I can't compete as an attraction with what you were just leering at."

Ponti made the classic gesture, hands spread at shoulder level, palms up, with which an Italian can say practically anything—in this case, combined with a slight upward roll of the eyes, it signified "Who wouldn't leer at something like that? But what a waste of time"—and sat down.

"I fear the Swiss convent where she has been receiving her final polish has chilled her southern blood for a while," he said. "But one day it will be warmed again. I have been hoping to make her acquaintance since she returned, but Gina Destamio and I do not rotate in the same social circles."

"*What* did you call her?" Simon asked with unconcealed astonishment.

"The name means something to you?"

"Only if she is related to a certain Al Destamio, whose dubious hospitality I enjoyed on Capri yesterday."

The detective's smile was mask-like again, but behind it Simon could sense a stony grimness.

"She is his niece," Ponti said.

4

The Saint had received so many shocks lately that he was becoming habituated to absorbing them without expression.

"After all, it's a small country," he remarked. He looked down into the rhodamine effervescence of his aperitif, and beckoned the waiter. "Would you like one of these before we eat?"

"With your permission, I will have a brandy. Buton Vecchio, since that is their most expensive— as an underpaid public servant I have few opportunities to enjoy such extravagance." Ponti waited until the waiter had shuffled off before he said: "What was your business with Destamio?"

The question was asked in the same casual tone, but his eyes bored into the Saint unblinkingly.

"I've been wondering about that myself," Simon replied coolly. "We met completely by chance the other day, and we seem to have rather quickly developed some differences of opinion. So radical, in fact, that I wouldn't be surprised if he was responsible for Tonio's attack on me this morning."

The other considered this carefully, before his smile flashed on again.

"I have heard many stories about you, Saint, some undoubtedly false and perhaps some of them true. But in all of them I have heard nothing to suggest that your relations with these people would be likely to be cordial. But it would have been interesting to hear precisely what the differences were that you refer to."

At this moment the waiter tottered back with the brandy. Before he could escape again, Simon seized the opportunity to order their lunch, or rather to let Ponti order it, for he was quite content to follow the lead of the counsellor who had directed him here.

By the time the waiter had retired again out of earshot, the Saint was conveniently able to forget the last implied question and resume the conversation with one of his own.

"Would you mind telling me just what you meant by *'these people'?"* he asked.

"The Mafia," Ponti said calmly.

This time, Simon allowed himself to blink.

"You mean Tonio was hired from them?"

"That *cretino* is one of them, of course. A small one. But I am sure that Al Destamio is a big one, though I cannot prove it."

"That," said the Saint, "makes it really interesting."

Ponti sipped his brandy.

"Do you know anything about the Mafia?"

"Only what I've read in the papers, like everyone else. And some more fanciful enlargements in paperback novels. But on the factual side, I don't even know what *mafia* means."

"It is a very old word, and no one can be quite sure where it came from. One legend says that it originated here in Palermo in the thirteenth century, when the French ruled the Two Sicilies. The story is that a young man was leaving the church after his wedding, and was separated from his bride for a few minutes while he talked to the priest. In that time she was seized by a drunken French sergeant, who dragged her away and assaulted her—and when she tried to escape, killed her. The bridegroom arrived too late to save her, but he attacked and killed the sergeant, shouting '*Morte alla Francia!*—Death to France!' Palermo had suffered cruelly during the occupation, and this was all that the people needed to hear. A revolt started, and in a few days all the French in the city had been hunted down and slain. '*Morte alla Francia, Italia anela!*' was the battle-cry: Italy wishes death to France! Of course, soon after, the French came back and killed most of the rebels, and the survivors fled into the mountains. But they kept the initials of their battle-cry, M-A-F-I-A, as their name . . . At least, that is one explanation."

"It's hard to think of the Mafia as a sort of thirteenth-century Resistance movement."

"It is, now; but that is truly what they were like in the beginning. Right up to the unification of Italy, the Mafia was usually on the side of the oppressed. Only after that it turned to extortion and murder."

"I seem to have heard that something like that happened to the original Knights Templar," said the Saint reflectively. "But aside from that, I don't see why you should connect them with me."

Ponti waited while the *caponata di melanzane* was served and the wine poured. Then he answered as if there had been no interruption.

"It is very simple. Whether you knew what you were doing or not, you have become involved with the Mafia. A little while ago I told you that justice would be done to Tonio. But if he was under the orders of Destamio, and not merely defending himself because you caught him picking your pocket, I should not be so optimistic. Witnesses will be found to swear that it was you who attacked him. And nothing will make him confess that he even knows Destamio. That is the *omerta,* the noble silence. He will die before he speaks. Not for a noble reason, perhaps, but because if he talked there would be no place for him to hide, no place in the world. There are no traitors to the Mafia—live traitors, that is—and the death that comes to them is not an easy one."

Simon tasted the Ciclope dell'Etna. It was light and faintly acid, but a cool and refreshing accompaniment to the highly seasoned eggplant.

"At the *questura,*" he said, "Tonio already seemed to be in better standing than I was. Does the Mafia's long arm reach even into the ranks of the incorruptible police on this island?"

"Such things are possible," Ponti said with great equanimity. "The Mafia is very strong on this impoverished island. That is why I gave you the hint in the *questura* that if you had any more to say to me we should talk elsewhere."

"And I am supposed to know that you are the one member of the police who is above suspicion."

The detective took no umbrage, but only dispensed with his smile, so that Simon was aware again of what an effective mask it was, behind which anything could be hidden.

"Let me tell you another story, Signor Templar, which is not a legend. It is about a man who came from Bergamo, in the north, to open a shop on this sunny island. It was difficult at first, but after a time he had a business that kept his family in modest comfort. Then the mafia came to demand tribute, and through ignorance or pride he refused to pay. When they sent an enforcer to beat him with a club in his own shop, he took away the club and beat the enforcer. But he was a little too strong and angry, and the enforcer died. There is only one thing that happens then: the *vendetta* and murder. The man and his wife and daughter were killed, and only the little son escaped because he had been sent to visit his grandparents in Bergamo, and when they heard what had happened they gave him to friends who took him to another town and pretended he was their own. But the boy knew all the story, and he grew up with a hatred strong enough to start a *vendetta* against all the Mafia. But when he was old enough to do anything he knew that that was not the way."

"And so he joined the police to try to do something legally?"

"A poorly paid job, as I said before, and a dangerous one if it is done honestly. But do you think a man with such memories could be on the side of those murderers?"

"But if your police station is a nest of *mafiosi*, how can you get anything done? That two-faced *maresciallo* almost had me convicted of attempting to murder myself, before you came in. Then everything changed. Do they suspect that you may be investigating them too?"

"Not yet. They think I am a happy fool who bumbles into the wrong places—an honest fool who refuses bribes and reports any offer of one. Men in my job are always being transferred, and so they hide what they can from me and wait patiently for me to be transferred again. But being from the north, it has taken me many years and much pulling of strings to get here, and I have no intention of being moved again before I have achieved some of my purpose."

If ever the Saint had heard and seen sincerity, he had to feel that he was in the presence of it now.

"So you want to hear what I can tell you," he said slowly. "But knowing my reputation, would you believe me? And aren't you a bit interested in the chance that I might incriminate myself?"

"I am not playing a game, *signore,*" the detective said harshly. "I do not ask for any of your other secrets. You can tell me you have murdered thirteen wives, if you like, and it would mean nothing to me if you helped in the one other thing that matters more to me than life."

Perhaps the first commandment of any outlaw should be, *Thou shalt keep thy trap shut at all times;* but on the other hand he would not be plying his lonely trade if he were not a breaker of rules, and this sometimes means his own rules as well. Simon knew that this was one time when he had to gamble.

"All right," he said. "Let's see what you make of this . . ."

He related the events of the past few days with eidetic objectiveness. He left nothing out and drew no conclusions, waiting to see what Ponti would make of it.

"It is as clear as *minestrone,*" said the detective, at the end of the recital. "You thought the Englishman Euston was killed in Naples because he recognized Destamio as being someone named Dino Cartelli. Yet Destamio showed you proof of his identity, and you learned here in Palermo that

Cartelli has been dead for many years. That seems to show that you are—as the Americans say—woofing up the wrong tree."

"Perhaps." Simon finished his meal and his wine. "But in that case how do you explain the coincidence of Euston's murder, Destamio's sudden interest in me, the money he gave me, and the attempt to kill me?"

"If you assume there is a connection, only two explanations are possible. Either Destamio was Cartelli, or Cartelli is Destamio."

"Exactly."

"But an imposter could not take the place of Destamio, one of the chieftains of the Mafia. And if the man who died in the bank was not Cartelli, who was he?"

"Those are the puzzles I have to solve, and I intend to keep digging until I do."

"Or until someone else digs for you—a grave," Ponti snorted, then puffed explosively on a cigarette.

Simon smiled, and ordered coffee.

"For me it is very good that you get involved," Ponti said after a pause. "You stir things up, and in the stirring things may come to the surface which may be valuable to me. In my position, I am forced to be too careful. You are not careful enough. Perhaps you do not believe how powerful and vicious these people are, though I do not think that would make any difference to you. But I will help you as much as I can. In return, I ask you to tell me everythng you learn that concerns the Mafia."

"With pleasure," Simon said.

He did not think it worth while to mention a small mental reservation, that while he would be glad to share any facts he gleaned, he would consider any substantial booty he stumbled upon to be a privateer's legitimate perquisite.

"You could start by telling me how much you know about Destamio," he said.

"Not much that is any use. It is all guessing and association. Everyone here is either a member of the Mafia or too frightened of them to talk. But I am forced to deduce, from the people he meets, and where he goes, and the money he can spend, and the awe that he inspires, that he must be in the upper councils of the organization. The rest of his family does not seem to be involved, which is unusual; but I keep an eye on them."

"After seeing the niece, Gina, I can understand about that eye of yours. What others are there?"

"His sister, Donna Maria, a real *faccia tosta*. And an ancient uncle well gone into senility. They have a country house outside the town, an old baronial mansion, very grim and run down."

"You must tell me how to get there."

"You would like to see Gina again?" Ponti asked, with a knowing Latin grin.

"I might have better luck than you," said the Saint brazenly. "And that seems the most logical place to start probing into Al's family background and past life. Besides which, think how excited he'll be when he hears I have been calling at his ancestral home and getting to know his folks."

Ponti looked at him long and soberly.

"One of us is mad, or perhaps both," he said. "But I will draw you a map to show you how to get there."

III

How Simon Templar hired a Museum Piece, and Gina Destamio became Available

His decision made, Simon Templar intended to pay his call on the Destamio manor with the least possible delay—figuring that the faster he kept moving, the more he would keep Destamio off balance, and thus gain the more advantage for himself. But to make himself suitably presentable, his slashed jacket first had to be repaired.

The cashier directed him to the nearest *sartoria*, where the proprietor was just unlocking after the three-hour midday break. After much energetic and colorful discussion, a price was agreed on that made allowance for the unseemly speed demanded, yet was still a little less than the cost of a new coat. Half an hour was finally set as the time for completion; and the Saint, knowing that he would be lucky to get it in three times that period, proceeded in search of his next requisite.

The tailor directed him around the next corner to where a welcoming sign announced *Servizio Eccellento di Autonoleggio*. But for once in the history of advertising, the auto rental service may truly

have been so excellent that all its cars had been
taken. At any rate, perhaps with some help from
the sheer numbers of seasonal tourists, the entire
fleet of vehicles seemed to be gone. The only one
left in sight was an antique and battered Fiat 500
that had been largely dismembered by the single
mechanic who crawled from its oily entrails and
wiped his hands on a piece of cotton waste as
Simon approached.

"You have cars to rent?" said the Saint.

"Sissignore." The man's sapient eye took in his
patently un-Italian appearance. "I guess mebbe
you like-a rent-a one?"

"I guess I would," said the Saint, patiently resigning himself to haggling down a price that
would be automatically doubled now that the entrepreneur had identified him as a visiting foreigner.

"We got-a plenty cars, but all-a rent-a now,
gahdam, except-a dis sonovabitch."

It was evident that the mechanic's English had
been acquired from the ubiquitous font of
linguistic elegance, the enlisted ranks of the American armed services.

"You mean that's your very last machine?" Simon asked, nodding at the disembowelled Fiat.

"Sissignore. Cute-a little turista, she built like a
brick-a *gabinetto.* I 'ave 'er all-a ready dis evening."

"I wouldn't want her, even if you do get her put
together again. Not that I want to hurt her feelings,
but she just wasn't built to fit me. So could you
perhaps tell me where I might find something my
size?"

"Mebbe you like-a drive-a da rich car, Alfa-

Romeo or mebbe Ferrari?"

There was a trace of a sneer in the question which Simon chose to ignore in the hope of saving time in his search.

"I have driven them. Also Bentleys, Lagondas, Jaguars, and in the good old days a Hirondel."

"You drive-a da Hirondel, eh? How she go, gahdam?"

"Like a sonovabitch," said the Saint gravely. "But that has nothing to do with the present problem. I still need a car."

"You like-a see sumping gahdam especial, make-a you forget Hirondel?"

"That I would like to see."

"Come-a wid me."

The man led the way to a door at the rear of the garage, and out into the dusty yard behind. Apart from the piles of rusty parts and old threadbare tires, there was a large amorphous object shrouded in a tarpaulin. With an air of reverence more usually reserved for the lifting of a bride's veil preparatory to the nuptial kiss, he untied the binding cords and gently drew back the canvas. Sunlight struck upon blood-red coachwork and chromed fittings; and the Saint permitted himself the uncommon luxury of a surprised whistle.

"Is that what I think it is?" he said.

"It gahdam-a sure is," the mechanic replied, with his eyes half closed in ecstatic contemplation. "You're-a look at a Bugatti!"

"And if I'm not mistaken, a type 41 Royale."

"Say, *professore,* you know all about-a dese bastards," said the man, giving Simon the title of respect due to his erudition.

There was once a body of *aficionados* who

looked upon motoring as a sport, and not an airconditioned power-assisted mechanical aid to
bringing home the groceries, and among their ever-
dwindling survivors there are still some purists who
maintain that only in the golden years between
1919 and 1930 were any real automobiles constructed, and who dismiss all cars before or after
that era as contemptible rubbish. The Saint was
not quite such a fanatic, but he had an artist's respect for the masterpieces of that great decade.

He was now looking at one of the best of them.
The name of Ettore Bugatti has the same magic to
the motoring enthusiast as do those of Annie
Besant or Karl Marx to other circles of believers.
Bugatti was an eccentric genius who designed cars
to suit himself and paid no attention to what other
designers were doing. In 1911, when all racing cars
were lumbering behemoths, a gigantic Fiat snorted
to victory in the Grand Prix. This was expected;
but what was totally unexpected was the second-
placing of Bugatti's first racer, looking like a
mouse beside an elephant, with an engine only one-
eighth the size of the monstrous winner. Bugatti
continued to pull mechanical miracles like that.
Then, in 1927, when everyone else was building
small cars, he brought out the juggernaut on which
Simon was now feasting his eyes.

"Dey build only seven," the owner crooned,
carefully flicking a speck of dust from the glisten-
ing fender. "Bugatti 'imself bust-a one up in a
wreck, and now dey only six sonovabitch in 'ole
gahdam-a world."

Immense is an ineffective word for such a car.
Over a wheel-base of more than fourteen feet, the
rounded box of the coupé-de-ville shrank in per-

spective when seen along the unobstructed length of the brobdingnagian hood. The front fenders rose high, then swept far back to form a running-board.

"And-a look-a dis—"

The mechanic was manipulating the intricate locks and handles that secured the hood, and with no small effort he threw it open. He pointed with uncontainable pride to the spotless engine, which resembled the power plant of a locomotive rather than that of an automobile. It must have been more than five feet long.

"I have heard," Simon said, "that if a Bugatti starts at all, it will start with just one pull on the crank."

"Dat's-a-right. *Sono raffinate*—what you call, 'igh-strung like-a race 'orse—but when she fix-a right, she always start. I show you!"

The man turned on the ignition, adjusted the hand throttle and the spark, and slipped the gleaming brass crank-handle into its socket. Then he waved the Saint to it with an operatic gesture.

"You try it yourself, *professore!*"

Simon stepped up, grasped the handle and engaged it carefully, and with a single coordinated effort gave it a crisp turn through a half-circle. Without a cough or a choke, the engine burst into responsive life, with a roar which did not entirely drown out a strangely pleasing metallic trill not unlike a battery of sewing machines in full stitch.

"That," said the Saint, raising his voice slightly, "would give me a lot of fun for a few days."

"No, no," protested the owner. "Dat sonovabitch not-a for rent. Much-a too valuable, should-a be in museum. I only show you . . "

His voice ran down as he stared at the currency which the Saint was peeling off the roll in his hand. The sum at which Simon stopped was perhaps wantonly extravagant, but to the Saint it did not seem too high to pay for the fun of having such a historic toy to play with. And after all, he reflected, it was only Al Destamio's money.

Thus, in due course, having gone back to collect his jacket while the rental paper-work was being prepared, after signing the necessary forms and being checked out on the controls, the Saint seated himself at the wheel, engaged first gear, and let up gently on the clutch. With a tremor of joy the mighty monster gathered itself and sprang through the open gates into the alley behind while its owner waved a dramatic and emotional farewell.

For a motorist of refined perceptions, driving a Bugatti is an experience like hearing the definitive performance of a classical symphony. Dynamic efficiency and supreme road-holding were the qualities that Bugatti wanted before anything else; and since he was a man incapable of compromise, that was what he obtained. The steering wheel vibrated delicately in the Saint's fingers, like a live member, sensitive to his lightest touch; guidance was like cutting butter with a hot knife. There was a little more difficulty with slowing up, since Bugatti always intended his cars to go rather than stop, but this could be overcome by adroit down-shifting and extra assistance from the hand brake. Simon happily sounded the horn, which gave out a rich tuneful note like a trombone, as he passed groups of cheering urchins and gaping adults on his way out of the town. The engine boomed with delight, and the great length of the red hood surged forth into the countryside.

Only too quickly the details of Ponti's sketch map spun by until at a last turning he saw the Destamio manse before him. With some reluctance he turned off the pavement and parked under the shade of a tree.

A high wall, topped with an unfriendly crest of broken bottles and shards of tile, surrounded the grounds and hid all of the house except the roof. He pressed a button beside a pair of massive iron-bound wooden doors, and waited patiently until at long last a medieval lock grated open and a smaller door set in one of the vast ones creaked open. A short swarthy woman in a maid's apron peered out suspiciously.

"*Buona sera,*" he said pleasantly. "My name is Templar, to see Donna Maria."

He stepped forward confidently, and the maid let him pass through. His first strategy was to give the impression that he was expected, and to go as far as he could on that momentum, but this was not enough to get him into the house. On the balustraded terrace which ran across the full width of the building, the maid waved him towards a group of porch furniture.

"Wait here, if you please, *signore.* I will tell Donna Maria. What was the name?"

Simon repeated it, and remained standing while he surveyed the house, a typically forbidding and cumbersome box-like structure of chipped and fading pink plaster with shutters that badly needed repainting, a shabby contrast with the well-kept and ordered brilliance of the garden. He had transferred his attention to that more agreeable scene when he heard a measured and heavy tread behind him, and turned again.

"Donna Maria?" he said, with his most engaging smile, proffering his hand. "My name is Simon Templar. I am an old friend of your brother Alessandro. When he heard that I was coming to Palermo, he insisted that I should come and see you."

2

The woman stood unmoving, except to glance down at his hand as if it were a long-dead fish. This expression perfectly fitted the lines around her mouth and flared nostrils, and was obviously one that she used a great deal. Her straggly mustache was black; but the mass of her hair, pulled back into a tight bun, was a dull steel gray. She was a head shorter than the Saint, but at least twice his diameter, and this bulk was encased in a corset of such strength and inelasticity that there was little human about the resultant shape. In the traditionally characterless black dress outside it, she reminded him of a piano-legged barrel draped for mourning.

"I never see my brother's friends," she said. "He keeps his business separate from his family life."

Just as no ornament relieved the drabness of her robe, no trace of cordiality tempered the chill of her words. Only a person with the Saint's self-assurance and ulterior motives could have survived that reception; but his smile was brazenly unshaken.

"That shows you how much he values our friendship. We were in the same business in America, where I come from—almost partners. So when I was at his villa in Capri the other day, for lunch, he made me promise to call on you."

"Why?"

The question was a challenge and almost a rebuttal in advance. It was clear that Al Destamio did not send his friends to the ancestral demesne out of spontaneous good-fellowship—if he ever sent them at all. Simon realized that he would have to improve his excuse, and quickly, or in a few seconds he would be outside again with nothing achieved but a glimpse of the unprepossessing facades of Donna Maria and her lair.

"Alessandro insisted that I should get to know you," he said, allowing a rather sinister frigidity to creep into his own voice. "He told me what a good sister you were, and how he wanted to be sure that in any time of trouble you would know which of his friends to turn to."

The ambiguity reached a mark of some kind: at least, there was an instant's uncertainty in the woman's basilisk gaze, and afterwards a very fractional unbending in her adamantine reserve.

"It has been a hot day, and you will enjoy a cold drink before you leave."

"You are much too hospitable," said the Saint, achieving the miracle of keeping all sarcasm out of his reading.

She made a sign to the maid, who had been pointedly waiting within range, and lowered herself stiffly into one of the chairs.

Simon turned to choose a seat for himself, and in so doing was confronted by a vision which almost equalled his wildest expectations.

Approaching through an archway of rambler roses, from a hedged area of the garden where she had apparently been taking a sunbath, was Gina Destamio, clad only in a bikini of such minuscule proportions that its two elements concealed little more of her than did her sunglasses. Her skin was a light golden-brown in the last rays of sunlight, and the ultimate details of her figure more than fulfilled every exquisite promise they had made under the dress in which he had last seen her. It was a sight to make even a hardened old pirate like Simon Templar toy with the idea of writing just one more sonnet.

Not so Donna Maria, who sucked in her breath like an asthmatic vacuum cleaner, then let it whoosh out in a single explosive sentence, crackling with lightning and rumbling with volcanic tension. It was in dialect, of which Simon understood hardly a word, but its themes were abundantly clear from the intonation: shamelessness, disgracing a respectable family before a total stranger, and the basic depravity of the new generation. The thunderbolts sizzled around Gina's tousled head, and she only smiled. Whatever other effect the Swiss finishing school might have had, it had certainly finished her awe of matriarchal dragons.

She turned the same smile on the Saint, and he basked in it.

"You must excuse me," she said. "I did not know we had a visitor."

"You must excuse me for being here," he replied. "But I refuse to say I am sorry."

She slipped leisurely into the cotton jacket which she had carried over her arm, while Donna Maria

painfully forced herself to perform a belated introduction.

"My niece, Gina. This is Signor Templar from
America."

"Haven't I seen you before?" Gina asked innocently, in perfect English.

"I didn't think you'd recognize me," he answered in the same language. "You looked right
through me to the wall behind, as if I were a rather
dirty window that somebody had forgotten to
wash."

"I'm sorry. But our rules here are very old-
fashioned. It's scandalous enough that I sometimes
go into town alone. If I let myself smile back at
anyone who hadn't been properly introduced, I
should be ruined for life. And even a nice Sicilian
would get the wrong ideas. But now I'm glad that
we have another chance."

"Non capisco!" Donna Maria hissed.

"My aunt doesn't speak English," Gina said,
and reverted to Italian. "Are you here for business
or pleasure?"

"I was beginning to think it was all business, but
since your uncle sent me here it has suddenly become a pleasure."

"Not Uncle Alessandro? I am glad you know
him. He has been so good to us here—"

"Gina," interrupted the chatelaine, her voice as
gentle as a buzz-saw cutting metal, "I am sure the
gentleman is not interested in our family affairs.
He is only having a little drink before he leaves."

The maid returned from the house, opportunely,
with a tray on which were bottles of vermouth, a
bowl of ice, a siphon, and glasses.

"How nice," Gina said. "I am ready for one myself. Let me pour them."

Her aunt shot her a venomous glance which openly expressed a bitter regret that her niece was no longer at an age when she could be bent over a knee and disciplined properly. But the girl seemed quite oblivious to it, and the Dragon Queen could only glower at her back as she proceeded to pour and mix with quite sophisticated efficiency.

"Have you seen much of Palermo yet?" Gina asked, as if seeking a neutral topic out of respect for her guardian's blood-pressure.

"Nothing much," Simon said. "What do you think I should see?"

"Everything! The Cathedral, the Palatine Chapel, Zisa, Casa Professa—and you should drive out to Monreale, it is only a few kilometers, and see the Norman cathedral and cloisters."

"I must do that," said the Saint, with surprising enthusiasm for one who, in spite of his sobriquet, seldom included cathedrals and cloisters among his sightseeing objectives. "Perhaps you could come with me and tell me all about them."

"I would like to—"

"My niece cannot accompany you," Donna Maria rasped. "There are professional guides to do that."

Gina opened her mouth as if to protest, then seemed to think better of it. Apparently she knew from experience that such battles could not be won by direct opposition. But she gazed thoughtfully at the Saint, biting her lip, as though inviting him to think of some way to get around or over the interdiction.

Simon raised his glass to the chaperone with a courteous *"Salute!"* and sipped it, wishing there had been more choice of beverage. His palate would never learn to accept the two vermouths as drinks in their own right, instead of as mere ghostly flavorings added to gin or bourbon respectively.

"I did not want to cause any trouble," he said. "But it was Alessandro's suggestion that Gina might like to show me around."

Donna Maria glared at him sullenly—he could not decide whether she was more resentful at having to control an impulse to call him a liar, or at a disconcerting possibility that he might be telling the truth.

"I must look in my diary and see if there is any day when I can spare her," she said finally. "If you will excuse me."

She lurched to her feet and waddled into the house without waiting for confirmation.

"I'm afraid she doesn't like me," Simon remarked.

"It isn't you in particular," Gina said apologetically. "She hates practically everybody, and twice as much if they're men. I sometimes think that's what keeps her alive. She's so pickled in her own venom that she's probably indestructible and will still be here in another fifty years."

"It's funny there should be such a difference between her and her brother. Al is such a big-hearted guy."

"That's true! Do you know, he takes care of the whole family and pays all the bills. He sent me to school and everything. If it hadn't been for him I don't know what would have happened to us all. When my parents were killed in a car accident they didn't have any insurance, and there was hardly any money in the bank. I was only seven at the

time, but I remember people looking at the house
and talk about selling it. Even Uncle Al was very
sick just then and everyone thought he was going
to die. But he got better and went to America, and
soon he began sending back money. He's been
looking after us ever since. And yet he hardly ever
comes near us. Aunt Maria says it may be because
he feels we'd be embarrassed by remembering how
much we owe him."

The Saint lounged in his chair with long legs out-
stretched, sipping his drink perfunctorily and listening with the appearance of only casual interest;
but under that camouflage his mind was ticking
over like a computer, registering every word, cor-
relating it with previous information, and reaching
on towards what hypotheses might be derived from
their multiple combinations. He had an extrasensory feeling that the answer to the Cartelli-
Destamio riddle was close at hand, if he could only
grasp it, or if one more link would bring it within
reach . . .

And then the fragments that were starting to fit
together were rudely pushed apart again by the
voice that spoke behind him.

"*Signore,* it is getting late for you to return to the
city." Donna Maria was returning from her errand. "It would not be well-bred to send a friend of
Alessandro's away at such an hour. You will stay
for dinner?"

Even more devastating than the astonishing reversal of her attitude was the expression that accompanied it. A ripple of life passed across her in-
flexible cheeks, and her bloodless lips curled back
to expose a fearsome row of yellow fangs. For a
moment Simon wondered if she was preparing to

leap on him and rend him like a werewolf, or whether she was merely suffering the rictus of some kind of epileptic seizure. It was a second or two before it dawned on him what was really happening.

Donna Maria was trying to smile.

3

"Thank you. You are very kind," said the Saint, making a heroic effort to overcome the shock of that horrendous sight.

Gina was more openly dumbfounded by the switch, and took a moment longer to recover.

"Well—I must get changed. Excuse me."

She ran into the house.

"And I must give some orders to the servants." Donna Maria's face was positively haggard with the strain of being gracious. "Please make yourself comfortable for a few minutes. And help yourself to another drink."

She withdrew again, leaving the Saint alone to digest the startling reversal of his reception.

And in another moment the maid reappeared, bearing a bottle of Lloyd's gin which she added to the selection on the tray.

"Donna Maria thought you might prefer this," she said, and retired again.

Simon lighted a cigarette and examined the bottle. It was new and unopened, to every appearance, and there had certainly not been time since Donna Maria's change of attitude for it to have been doped or poisoned and cunningly re-sealed; so unless bottles of pre-hoked liquor were a standard item in stock at the Destamio hacienda there could be no risk in accepting it. In moderation . . .The Saint gratefully emptied the glass he had been nursing into a flower-pot and proceeded to concoct himself a very dry martini, feeling much like a prodigal son for whom the best barrel had been rolled out.

But deep inside him he felt an intangible hollowness which came from the tightening of nerves which were not nervous but only sharpening their sensitivity and readiness to whatever call might be suddenly made on them.

He could not cherish the beautiful illusion that after a life-time of notorious malevolence Donna Maria had chosen that evening to be struck as by lightning with remorse for her churlishness, and after a brief absence to commune with her soul had returned radiant and reformed to make amends for all her past unpleasantnesses. Or that his own handsome face and charming manners had broken through an obsidian crust to the soft heart that it encased. Some very practical reason had to be responsible for the alteration, and he could not make himself generous enough to believe that it was without ulterior motive.

The question remained: what motive?

The sun had descended behind the western hills, and purple shadows reached into the courtyard, deepening the dusty gray-green of the olive trees, and the first cool breeze drifted in from the sea. With the dusk, the house was not softened, but seemed to become even more stark and sinister. Somewhere in its depths a clock chimed with deep reverberant notes that made one think of the tolling of funeral bells.

As the hour struck, a door opened under the balcony at the far end of the terrace, and a wheelchair appeared with the promptitude of a cuckoo called forth by some horlogic mechanism. Simon watched in fascination as the maid wheeled it to the table opposite him and vanished again without a word. The occupant of the chair matched the building in senescence; in fact, he looked old enough to have built it himself.

"A lovely evening," Simon ventured at last, when it became clear that any conversational initiative would have to come from him.

"Ah," said the ancient.

It extended a withered and tremulous claw, not to shake hands, but towards the glasses on the table.

"What can I get you?" Simon asked.

"Ah."

Simon made what he felt was an inspired compromise by pouring a half-and-half mixture of sweet and dry vermouths and proferring it.

"Ah," said the venerable mummy, and, after taking a small sip, carefully spilled the rest on the ground.

"What did you think of Dante's latest book?" Simon tried again.

"Ah," said the patriarch wisely, and sat back to enjoy a slow chomping of toothless gums while he examined the Saint from the blinking moist caverns of his eyes.

The possibilities of small talk seemed to have been exhausted, and Simon was wondering whether to try making faces at his *vis-a-vis* and see whether that would evoke any livelier response, when he was saved from that decision by the return of Gina, now wearing something thin and simple that clung provocatively to the curves that he could reconstruct in clinical detail from memory.

"Has Uncle been bothering you?" she asked.

"Not at all," said the Saint. "I just haven't been able to find anything to talk about that he's interested in. Or maybe my accent baffles him."

"Povero Zio," Gina said, smiling and patting the ancient's hand. "I can't even remember a time when he wasn't old, but he was nice to me when I was a little girl. He used to tell me wonderful stories about how he marched with Garibaldi in his last campaign, and I'd forget to be worried about when we were going to be kicked out of our house."

"Ah . . .ah," said the old man, straightening up a little as if the words had sparked some long-forgotten memory; but it was a transient stimulus and he slumped back down again without producing his scintillating comment.

"Uncle—you can't mean that he's Alessandro's brother?" Simon said.

"Oh, no. He's really Uncle Alessandro's uncle— and Donna Maria's."

As if answering to her name, the lady of the manse made another entrance. If she had changed her black dress for an evening model, it would have taken the eye of a *couturier's* spy to tell the difference, but she had hung a gold chain around her neck and stuck a comb set with brilliants in her hair as evidence that she was formally dressed for dinner.

"You need not trouble yourself about *Lo Zio,* Signor Templar," she said, with another labored display of her death's-head smirk. "He hears very little and understands even less, but it makes him happy to be in our company. If you have finished your drink, we can go in to dinner."

She led the way into the house, into a large dimly lighted hallway with an ornate wooden staircase that led up into a lofty void of darkness from which Simon would not have been surprised to see bats fly out. Gina pushed Lo Zio's wheel-chair, and the Saint ingratiatingly gave her a hand. The dining room was almost as spooky as the hall, illuminated only by candles which hardly revealed the dingy ancestral paintings which looked down from the walls.

"I hope you won't mind the dinner," Gina said. "We never have guests, and all the cook knows is plain country food. I'm sure it isn't the sort of thing you're used to."

"I'm sure it'll be a pleasant change," said the Saint politely.

His optimism was not misplaced. Home cooking is a much crumpled appellation in some parts of the world, too often synonymous with confections from the freezer and the can, but in Italy it still retains some of its original meaning, and occasionally in restaurants labeled *"casalinga"* one can find family-style cooking of a high order. But the literal authentic article, of course, is served only in private homes to relatives and close friends, and rarely is the foreigner allowed to penetrate this inner circle.

Nothing is purchased prefabricated by the traditional Italian housewife. If tomato sauce is needed, the tomatoes are pressed and the seeds removed by hand. The delicate doughs that enfold *cannelloni* and *cappelletti* are handrolled from a mixture of flour and egg with never a drop of water added.

Fresh herbs and spices, grown in the kitchen garden, are added with the loving care that lifts a sauce from the pedestrian to the ambrosial. It goes without saying that in the south one must expect a liberal hand in the application of garlic and olive oil; but that was no disadvantage to the Saint, who was gifted with the digestion to cope happily with such robust ingredients.

Since the evening meal is customarily a light one, it began with *olive schiacciate,* a succulent salad of olives, celery, and peppers. After this came the *Involtini alla siciliana,* a toothsome filling in envelopes of gossamer-light paste smothered in a sauce so savory that good manners could only encourage the pursuit of every last drop with mops of the crusty brown home-baked bread. A large circulating carafe of young home-made red wine provided ample and impeccable liquid accompaniment; and after observing that everyone's glass was filled from it, just as the same platters were presented to all of them to help themselves, except Lo Zio whose plate was tended by Gina sitting next to him, Simon was able to surpress all disturbing memories of the Borgias and give himself up to unstinting enjoyment of his gastronomic good fortune.

They made a strange quartet around the massive age-blackened table, and the medieval gloom around them and the echoing footsteps of the maid on the bare floor did little to encourage relaxation and conviviality, but by concentrating on Gina and the food he was able to maintain some harmless and totally unmemorable conversation, while wondering all the time why he had been invited to stay and when the reason would be revealed in some probably most unpleasant and distressing way.

"A most wonderful meal," he complimented Donna Maria at the end of it. "I feel guilty for imposing on you, but I shall always be glad that I did."

"You must not rush away. We will have coffee in the drawing room, and I will see if there is some brandy, if you would like that."

She flashed her alligator smile as she rose; and Simon, steeled now not to recoil, smiled back.

"Perhaps I should refuse," he said. "But that might suggest that you did not mean it, and I am sure you do."

As he helped Gina to push the wheel-chair again, which somehow seemed to give them a sort of secret companionship, she said: "I don't know how you've done it, but nobody ever broke her down like this before. Brandy, now!"

"Brandy, ah!" repeated Lo Zio, his head lifting like a buzzard's and swivelling around.

"You should have given me a chance in that restaurant," said the Saint. "If I could have persuaded you to stay for lunch, we might have had all the afternoon together."

The drawing room had three electric lights of thrifty wattage which made it very little brighter than the dining room. The furniture was stiff and formal, a baroque mixture of uncertain periods, upholstered with brocades as faded as the heavy drapes. Donna Maria came in with a dusty bottle, followed by the maid with a tray of coffee.

"Would you be so kind as to open it, Signor Templar? I am sure you know how to handle such an old bottle better than we women."

Simon manipulated the corkscrew with expert

gentleness, but not without the thought that he might have been given the job as yet another move to reassure him. Certainly it enabled him to verify that this bottle, with all its incrustations of age, would have been even harder to tamper with than the gin which he had drunk before dinner. He deciphered with approval the name of Jules Robin under the grime on the scarred label, and poured generous doses into the snifters which were produced from some dark recess—not omitting one for Lo Zio, who showed some of his vague signs of human animation as he fastened his rheumy eyes on the bottle.

"Salute!" Simon said, and watched them all drink before he allowed his own first swallow to actually pass his lips.

It was a magnificent cognac, which had probably been lying in the cellar since the death of Gina's father, and nothing seemed to have been done to turn it into a lethal or even stupefying nightcap.

Was all this hospitality, then, nothing but a stall to create time, during which Al Destamio might round up a few commandos and get them out to the mansion to capture the Saint or quietly mow him down?

Whatever the reason, he felt sure that Gina was not in on it. He looked again at her lovely radiant face, alight with the spontaneous pleasure of the kind of company which she could almost never have been permitted, and decided that he could lose nothing by testing just how far this astounding acceptance could be stretched.

"I am looking forward to seeing the local sights tomorrow, even though I have to do it with a commercial guide," he said, and turned to Donna

Maria. "Or now that you know me a little better, would you reconsider and let Gina accompany me?"

An observer who was unacquainted with the preceding circumstances would have assumed, at a glance, that Donna Maria was trying inconspicuously to swallow a live cockroach which she had carelessly sucked in with her brandy.

"Perhaps I was being too hasty," she said. "Since you are such a close friend of Alessandro, there is really no reason for me to object. What are you most interested in?"

The resultant discussion of Sicilian antiquities continued this time with no contribution from Gina, whose eyes had become slightly glassy and her jaw slack, either from renewed bewilderment or from trepidation lest anything she interjected would change her aunt's mind again.

Another refill of cognac was pressed on the not too resistant Saint, though curtly refused to Lo Zio, who having smacked his way through his first was plaintively extending his glass for more. But after that there was nothing left to stay for, short of asking if they had a spare room for the night.

"Tomorrow at ten, then, Gina," he said, and stood up. "And I'll tell Alessandro how nice all of you have been."

The last remark was principally intended for the reigning tyrant of the establishment, but it scored first on Lo Zio, who must have been feeling some effects from his unaccustomed libations.

"Ah, Alessandro," he said, as if some cobwebby relay had been tripped. "I told him. I warned him. Told him he should not go to Rome—"

"It is late, Lo Zio, and well past your bed time,"

Donna Maria said hastily.

She whipped the wheel-chair around with a suddenness that had the old man's head bobbing like a balloon on a string. The maid came scurrying in on a barked command, and whisked away the chair and its mumbling contents.

"Buona notte, signore," Donna Maria said, with one more spasm of her overworked facial muscles, and the impression of it seemed to remain even after she had closed the front door, like the grin of some Sicilian-Cheshire cat.

Simon made the short walk to the driveway gate with his nerves as taut as violin strings, his ears straining, and his eyes darting into every shadow. But there was no warning scuff or stir to herald an onslaught by lurking assailants, no crack of a shot to make belated announcement of a bullet. He opened the inset door, flung it open, and leapt far through it in an eruptively connected series of cat-swift movements calculated to disconcert any ambush that might be waiting outside; but no attack came. An almost-full moon that was rising above the hills showed a road deserted except for his own car where he had left it, and the only sound was the thin shrill rasping of multitudinous nocturnal insects. Feeling a trifle foolish, he turned back and shut the little door, and then walked towards the Bugatti, making a wide swing out into the road around it, just in case someone was skulking on the side from which he would not have been expected to approach. But no one was.

Then he had not been detained in order to gain time to organize a bushwacking, it seemed . . .

But the instinct of an outlaw who had carried his life in his hands so often that his reflexes had adapted to it as a natural condition was not lulled into somnolence merely because logic seemed to have suspended the immediate need for it. If anything, it was left more on edge than ever, seeking the flaw in conclusions which did not jibe with intuition.

He climbed halfway into the driver's seat and peered in search of the ignition lock. He located it and inserted the key; but as he raised his head again above the dashboard before switching on, his eye was caught by a blemish on the gleaming expanse of hood which did not belong at all on such a lovingly burnished surface.

Clearly revealed by the moonlight was the print of a greasy hand.

4

Simon very carefully withdrew the key, stepped down to the road again, and went around to examine the hood more closely. But the print seemed to have disappeared. Bending over until his face almost touched the metal, he sighted towards the radiator and found the mark again, a dull slur in the reflected moonlight.

A ghostly breath stirred the hairs on the nape of his neck as he realized how narrowly he might have missed that discovery. If he had come out a few minutes earlier or later, the moon would not have been striking the hood at the precise angle required to show it up. Or if he had not already been keyed to the finest pitch of vigilance, he might still have thought nothing of it. But now he could only remember how affectionately the garage owner had wiped the hood again after showing him the engine, and he knew with certainty that there could have been no such mark on it when he set out. He had not stopped anywhere on the way, to give anyone a chance to approach the machine before he parked it there. Therefore the mark had been made since he arrived, while he was enjoying Donna Maria's hospitality.

With the utmost delicacy he manipulated the fastenings of the hood and opened it up. The pencil flashlight that he was seldom without revealed that the mammoth engine was still there, but with a new feature added that would have puzzled Signor Bugatti.

A large wad of something that looked like putty had been draped over the rear of the engine block and pressed into shape around it. Into this substance had been pushed a thin metal cylinder, something like a mechanical pencil, from which two slender wires looped over and lost themselves in the general tangle of electrical connections.

With surgically steady fingers the Saint extracted the metal tube, then gently and separately pulled the wires free from their invisible attachments. Deprived of its detonator, the plastic bomb again became as harmless as the putty it so closely resembled.

"This one almost worked, Al," he whispered softly. "And if it had, I'd have had only myself to blame. I underestimated you. But that won't happen again . . ."

There were some excellent fingerprints in the plastic material where the demolition expert had squeezed it into place, doubtless in all confidence that there would be nothing left of them to incriminate him. Taking care not to damage them, Simon peeled the blob off the engine and put it in the trunk, wedging it securely where it could not roll around when he drove.

He cranked up the engine and drove slowly and pensively back to Palermo, the impatient motor growling a basso accompaniment to his thoughts.

It was easy enough now to understand everything that had been puzzling before. Donna Maria's first absence from the terrace had given her time to telephone Al Destamio on Capri and ask for confirmation of the alleged friendship. Al's reaction could be readily imagined. He would already have learned of the failure of the first assassination attempt; and the revelation that the Saint had had the effrontery to head straight for the Destamio mansion and blarney his way in, instead of thankfully taking the next plane for some antipodean sanctuary, must have done wondrous things to his adrenalin production. The dinner invitation must have followed on his orders, to keep the Saint there long enough for another hatchet man to be sent there to arrange a more final and effective termination of the nuisance.

And this deduction made Donna Maria's bit part somewhat more awesome. Throughout the dinner and crocodile congeniality, she had been setting him up like a clay pipe in a shooting gallery. That was why she could afford to give in so readily on the question of granting permission for Gina to go out with him the next day: she had been complacently certain that the Saint would not be around to hold her to the promise. Only one interesting speculation remained—had she known just how violently it had been intended to insure his non-appearance?

Simon tooled the big car in through the garage entrance of the hotel and slipped it into an empty stall. As the thunder of the engine died away, he was aware of an even heightened resentment.

It was bad enough to be continually sniped at himself, the perplexed target of an incomprehensible vendetta. But now these monsters had exposed the utter depths of their depravity by their willingness to destroy that historic treasure of a car merely in the process of putting a bomb under him.

It followed imperatively that no extra effort could be spared to insure that Al Destamio spent the most troubled night that could be organized for him. Even if the effort involved the prodigious hazards of trying to inaugurate a long-distance telephone communication against the obstacles of the hour and the antiquated apparatus available.

The phone in Simon's room was apparently dead, and only a great deal of bopping on the button and some hearty thumps on the bell box succeeded in restoring it to a simulacrum of life. The resultant thin buzzing was presently interrupted by the yawning voice of the desk clerk, obviously resentful at being disturbed.

"I would like to call Capri," said the Saint.

"It is not easy at night, *signore*. If you would wait until morning—"

"It would be too late. I want the call now."

"Sissignore," sibilated the clerk, in a tone of injured dignity.

There followed a series of rasping sounds, not unlike a coarse file caressing the edge of a pane of glass, followed by a voiceless silence. Far in the distance could be heard the dim rush of an electronic waterfall, and Simon shouted into it until another voice spiralled up from the depths. It was the night operator in Palermo, who was no more enthused about trying to establish a telephonic connection at that uncivilized hour than the hotel clerk had been. Too late Simon realized the magnitude of the task he had undertaken, but he was not going to back out now.

With grim politeness he acceded to obstructive demands for an infinitude of irrelevant information, of which the name and location of residence of the person he was calling and his own home address and passport number were merely a beginning, until the operator tired first and consented to essay the impossible.

The line remained open while the call progressed somewhat less precipitately than Hannibal's elephants had crossed the Alps.

A first hazard seemed to be the water surrounding the island of Sicily. It could only have been in his imagination, but Simon had a vivid sensation of listening to hissing foam and crashing waves as the connection forced its way through a waterlogged cable, struggling with blind persistence to reach the mainland. The impression was affirmed when a mainland operator was finally reached and the watery noises died away to a frustrated background susurration.

For a few minutes the Palermo operator and this new link in the chain exchanged formalities and incidental gossip, and at last reluctantly came to the subject of Simon's call. A mutual agreement was reached that, though the gamble was sure to fail,

the sporting thing would be at least to try whether
the call could be pushed any further. Both operators laughed hollowly at the thought, but switches
must have been thrown, because a hideous grumbling roar like a landslide swallowing an acre of
greenhouses rose up and drowned their voices.

Simon lighted his remaining cigarette, crumpled
the empty pack, and made himself as comfortable
as possible. The phone was beginning to numb his
ear, and he changed to the other side.

There was more of the ominous crunching, peri-
odically varying in timbre and volume, and after a
long while the second operator's voice struggled
back to the surface.

"I am sorry, I have not been able to reach
Naples. Would you like to cancel the call?"

"I would not like to cancel the call," Simon said
relentlessly. "I can think of no reason why you
should not reach Naples. It was there this morning,
and it must be there now, unless there has been
another eruption of Mount Vesuvius."

"I do not know about that. But all the lines to
Naples are engaged."

"Try again," said the Saint encouragingly.
"While we are talking someone may have hung up
or dropped dead. Persevere."

The operator mumbled something indistin-
guishable, which Simon felt he was probably better off for not hearing, and the background of
crashings and inhuman groanings returned again.
But after another interminable wait, persistence
was rewarded by a new voice saying *"Napoli."*

Reaching Capri from Naples was no worse than
anything that had gone before, and it was with a

justifiable thrill of achievement that Simon at last heard the ringing of Destamio's phone through the overtones of din. Eventually someone answered it, and Simon shouted his quarry's name at the top of his voice.

"Il Signore is busy," came the answer. "He cannot be disturbed. You must call again in the morning."

After all he had been through, the Saint was not going to be stopped there.

"I do not care how busy he is," he said coldly. "You will tell him that this call is from Sicily, and I have news that he will want to hear."

There was an explosive crackle as if the entire instrument at the other end had been shattered on a marble slab, and for a while Simon thought the servant had summarily disposed of the problem by hanging up; but he held on, and presently another voice spoke, with grating tones that even the telephone's distortions could not completely disguise.

"Parla, ascolto!"

The Saint stubbed out the remains of his last cigarette and finally relaxed.

"Alessandro, my dear old chum, I knew you'd be glad to hear from me, even at this hour."

"Who's-a dat?"

"This is Simon Templar, Al, you fat gob of overcooked macaroni. Just calling to tell you that your comic-opera assassins have flunked again—and that I don't want them trying any more. I want you to call them off, chum."

"I dunno what ya talkin' about, Saint." There was a growing note of distress in the harsh voice as it assimilated the identity of the caller. "Maybe you drink too much wine tonight. Where you calling from?"

"From my hotel in Palermo, which I'm sure you can easily find. But don't send any more of your stooges here to annoy me. The firework they planted in my car while Donna Maria was being so hospitable didn't go off. But I found out a lot of interesting things during my visit, to add on to what I knew before. And I wanted to tell you that I've just put all this information on paper and deposited it in a place from which it will be forwarded to a much less accommodating quarter than your tame *maresciallo* here, if anything happens to me. So tell your goons to lay off, Al."

"I don't understand! Are you nuts?" blustered Destamio, almost hysterically. "What you tryin' to do to me?"

"You'll find out," said the Saint helpfully. "And I hope your bank account can stand it. Meanwhile, pleasant dreams . . ."

He replaced the receiver delicately in its bracket, and then dropped the entire contraption into the wastebasket, where it whirred and buzzed furiously and finally expired.

As if on cue, there followed a light tapping on the door.

The Saint took his precautions about opening it. There was still the possibility that some of Destamio's henchmen might be working on general instructions to scrub him—it would certainly take time for countermanding orders to circulate, even if the Mafia had also penetrated the telephone service. Until the word had had time to get around, he was playing it safe.

Marco Ponti entered, and eyed with mild surprise the gun that was levelled at his abdomen. Then he calmly kicked the door shut behind him.

"That is a little inhospitable," he remarked. "And illegal too, unless you have an Italian license for that weapon."

"I was going to ask you how to get one, the next time I saw you," said the Saint innocently, and caused the weapon to vanish and be forgotten. "But I was not expecting you to call at such an hour as this, *amico.*"

"I am not being social. I wanted to hear how your visit turned out. And I have learned something that may be of value to you."

"I would like one of your cigarettes while you give me your news. It may have some bearing on what I can tell you."

"I hardly expect that," Ponti said, throwing his pack of *Nazionali* on the table. "It is only that you gave me a name, and like a good policeman I have checked the records. Though you may sneer—and I sometimes sneer myself at the middenheaps of records we keep—occasionally we find a nugget in the slag. I searched for the name you gave me, the murdered bank clerk, Dino Cartelli. I found nothing about him except the facts of his death. But I also found the record of another Cartelli, his elder brother, Ernesto, who was killed by the Fascisti."

Simon frowned.

"Now I'm out of my depth. Why should that be worth knowing?"

"In his early days, *Il Duce* had a campaign to wipe out the Mafia—perhaps on the theory that there was only room for one gang of crooks in the country, and he wanted it to be his gang. So for a while he shot some of the small fry and hung others up in cages for people to laugh at. Later on, of course, the Mafia joined forces with him, they were birds of a feather—but that is another story. At any rate, in one of the early raids, Ernesto Cartelli shot it out with the Blackshirts, who proved to be better shots."

"Do you mean," Simon ventured slowly, "that since Ernesto was a *mafioso,* his brother Dino may have been one too?"

"It is almost certain—though of course it cannot be proved. But the Mafia is a closed society, very hard to enter, and when anyone is a member it usually means that his other close male relatives are members too."

The Saint's eyes narrowed in thought as he inhaled abstractedly and deeply from the strong Italian cigarette—an indiscretion which he instantly regretted.

"So the Mafia keeps coming back into the picture," he said. "Al Destamio is in it, now it seems that Dino Cartelli was probably in it, whether or not they are the same person; and they have me at the top of their list of people to be dispensed with. I knew you would be glad to hear that they tried again tonight to put me out of the way."

"Not at the Destamio house?"

"Just outside it. If they had succeeded, it might even have broken some windows."

Simon told the story of his macabre evening, and the fortunate discovery that had not quite ended it.

"And there are some wonderful fingerprints in the plastic, which is still intact," he concluded.

"That is splendid news," Ponti said delightedly. "These Mafia scum can usually get out of anything by producing armies of false witnesses, but it is another matter to witness away fingerprints. At least this will tell us who placed the bomb, and he may lead us to someone else."

"I was sure you would be happy about my narrow escape from death," said the Saint ironically.

"My dear friend, I am overjoyed. May you have many more such close scrapes, and each time bring back evidence like that. You did bring it back, of course?"

Simon grinned, and tossed him the car keys.

"You will find it in the trunk. Leave the keys under the front seat, they will be safe enough there. I think Alessandro will take time to think out his next move."

"I hope he does not take too long," said the detective. "But whenever you want to get in touch with me again, I will give you a number to call." He scribbled on a page from his notebook, tore it out, and handed it to Simon. "This is not the *questura,* but a place which can be trusted with any messages you leave, and which can always find me very quickly." He turned and opened the door, with unconcealed impatience to get to the garage and the evidence there. "Goodnight, and good luck."

"The same to you," said the Saint.

He locked and bolted the door again, just on general principles, but he went to sleep as peacefully as a child. It had been a full and merry day, and the morrow was likely to be even livelier. Which only sustained his contented conviction that the world was a beautiful place to have fun in.

IV

How the Saint went to a Graveyard
and Don Pasquale made a Proposal

Promptly at ten the next morning Simon announced his arrival outside the walls of the Destamio estate with a brazen call on the Bugatti's horn which rebounded satisfactorily from the neighboring hills, incidentally triggering the responsive barking of dogs and a rattle of wings as a startled flock of pigeons whirled overhead, before he confirmed the announcement of his arrival more conventionally with a tug on the bell-pull at the entrance.

He did not think there was much danger that Destamio would have prepared to sacrifice his own parental portals with another charge of explosive tied to the bell, but aside from that he had no idea what he expected. Would there be another more personalized elimination squad waiting to lay on the welcome to end all welcomes, or would Destamio have refused to believe that the Saint would have the nerve to come back and claim his date with Gina? Would Donna Maria at this moment be frantically telephoning to ask what she

should do now, while Gina was being hastily in-
carcerated in whatever version of a medieval
dungeon could be found in the establishment? Or
would the house simply remain inscrutably deaf
and blind to him as to an unwelcome salesman until he gave up and went away? There had been only
one way to find out, and that was to go there and
ring the bell and see what happened.

What happened was that the gate opened and
Gina came out into the sunlight with her graceful
step that was like dancing, and Simon smiled with
sudden joy as he held the car door for her.

Whatever might be coming next, at least the adventure was not going to wallow to a soggy halt.

"This is much more than I seriously expected,"
he said, once she had settled into the leather seat
and the great car had made its thunderous take-off.

"Why?" she asked.

"I was afraid your aunt would have changed her
mind about letting you go on this expedition, or
talked you out of it."

"Why should she do that? There's nothing
wrong with my seeing you, is there?"

She forced a small smile as she said it, but a
slight halting note in her voice told him with pierc-
ing clarity not only that she was playing a part but
also that she was not relishing it. The falseness was
as transpicuous as her sincerity had been the day
before. But for the moment he was not ready to let
her know that her effort was already wasted.

"How could there be," he replied blandly, "if
neither of us has any wickedness in mind?"

He deliberately refrained from emphasizing that
studied ambiguity by glancing at her to observe its
effect, but her silence told him that she must be

thinking it over. The piquancy of waiting for her next approach added to the pleasure of what promised to be a most entertaining day.

"Sicily, fair Sicily!" he declaimed, before the pause could become uncomfortable. He waved one hand to embrace the sundrenched splendor of orchards and hills: "The crossroads of the Mediterranean, where Greek fought Phoenician, and Roman fought Greek; where the light of Christendom was shadowed by the menace of Vandal, Goth, Byzantine, and Arab ... You see, I've already boned up on the brochures."

"Is your name really Simon Templar?" she asked abruptly.

"It is. Let me guess why you ask. Head filled with history, your thoughts have leapt to the Knights Templar, a dubiously noble band not unknown in these parts. You're wondering whether I'm one of their lineal descendants. I think that depends where you draw the line. I've never looked too closely into all the birds' nests in my family tree, but—"

"Are you the Saint?"

Simon sighed.

"So you've discovered my guilty secret. I hoped to hide it from you, letting you believe that I was a simple salesman, a country-to-country drummer selling ball-point pens that only write under butter. Little did I dream that my shadier reputation would have penetrated the cloisters of your Alpine convent."

"I wasn't as cut off from the world as all that," she snapped, with a touch of exasperation. "I've always read newspapers, but I just didn't connect you at first. What are you doing here?"

"Sightseeing—wasn't that what we talked about? People always seem to disbelieve me, but I can truthfully say that I came to Italy just to look around and eat and drink like any other tourist."

"But when you're at home—you don't really go around selling pens?"

Few women could claim the distinction of having left the Saint bereft of a suitable rejoinder, and Gina may have been the first to achieve it unintentionally. But her question was perfectly serious, as he assured himself by a swift sidelong glance. Apparently her convent reading had been somewhat less catholic than she believed, and its lacunae had not been filled in by any recent briefing.

"No," he said weakly. "I don't really work at anything seriously, because I hate to take a job away from somebody who might need it."

That gave her something to think about in her turn, which occupied her until it occurred to her to ask: "Where are you going? I thought I was supposed to show you the sights, but you seem to know the way somewhere."

"I had breakfast with a map and a guide book," he said. "I thought it might help if the lamb could find its own way to the first sacrificial altar."

"I don't know of any of those near Palermo," she said seriously. "Very few of the pagan temples have survived at all, and certainly no altars."

"Well, let's give this a whirl instead," said the Saint resignedly, as he came in sight of his first destination.

He pulled into the free public parking lot, and paid the local extortioner the customary blackmail for seeing that nobody walked off with his car or any of its detachable components.

"San Giovanni degli Eremiti!" Gina cried, clapping her hands in enthusiastic recognition. "It's about the most romantic old church around here—it goes back to the Norman times. How clever of you to find it!"

"It's the natural affinity of one ancient monument for another," said the Saint, gazing up at the gray walls whose crumbling scars bore witness to the countless battles that had been fought around them. "I suppose we have to give this one the full treatment?"

He permitted himself to be led through the moldering glories of pillars and porticos, and what was unmistakably the remains of a mosque around which the thrifty Crusaders had constructed their own place of worship. When they finally arrived in a beautiful little cloistered garden, he sank down on a bower-shaded bench and drew Gina down beside him.

"It was a wonderful tour, and I can never thank you enough for showing me the antiquities of Palermo."

"But we've only just begun," she protested. "There are lots more churches—the Cathedral—the museum—"

"That's what I've been dreading. In spite of my name, I've always preferred to leave the churches and cathedrals to more deserving Saints. But we told your sweet old Aunt that we were going sightseeing, and now even you can look her in the eye and solemnly and truthfully swear that we did so. Thus having kept the letter of our word, we can turn to something more in keeping with the reality of this climate than tramping around a lot of sweltering ruins. Let's face it, if it weren't for me, would you be sightseeing today?"

"No, but—"

"But me no buts; the 'no' is quite enough. That means I'm inflicting something on you which you'd never have chosen, and I hate to be part of an infliction. Now, wouldn't you much rather be going for a swim?"

"Well yes, perhaps. But I didn't think of bringing anything with me—"

"And you can't go back home for it without probably running afoul of Auntie. Never mind. Anyone who looks as sensational as you do in a bikini should have a new one every day." Simon stood up. "Come along and prepare to revel in woman's time-honored pastime of buying clothes."

With no more delay for argument, the Bugatti was speeding on its way again in a few minutes. At the near-by seaside resort of Romagnolo they found a little beach shop which supplied the requisite minimum of water-wear; and in what seemed like little more than the span of a movie lap-dissolve he was on the beach in his trunks watching her come out of her cabana in the nearest approach to the simple costume of Eve permitted by the customs of the time.

"I didn't see you buying anything," she observed belatedly.

"I didn't have to," he said without shame. "I had these in the car, just in case we accidently decided to change our program. Now let's get in the water and cool off before you give heat-stroke to half the population of this *lido*."

They swam and splashed away the dust and stickiness of the morning, until they were completely refreshed and buttressed with a reserve of coolness to make another spell in the sun seem welcome for a while. As they came ashore, a white-coated *cameriere* greeted them at the water's edge.

"Ecco la lista delle vivande, signore," he said, extending a menu. "I am sure you have already decided to lunch at the best restaurant on the beach."

Simon had already noticed a number of attractively shaded restaurants at the edge of the strand, and realized that the more enterprising of them were not proposing to leave the selection of possible customers to chance. Such initiative would have taken a fairly dedicated curmudgeon to resist.

"Che cosa raccomandate?" he asked.

"Everything is good, but the lobster is most excellent. Do not move, and I will show you."

The waiter rushed away, to return in a few minutes with a wire basket in which a couple of lively *aragoste* squirmed and flapped in futile rebellion against their destiny.

"I suppose they could get to be a monotonous diet, if you lived here long enough," Simon said, "but I'm a long way from reaching that stage yet. How about you, Gina?"

"Donna Maria isn't an extravagant housekeeper," she said. "So they're still a treat for me."

"Then we'll make this an occasion," he said, and proceeded to round out the order.

The waiter departed again, promising to send for them when everything was ready; and they spread their rented towels on the sand and sprawled on them in sybaritic relaxation.

"At times like this," said the Saint, "I often wonder who was the fathead who first proclaimed that work was a noble and rewarding activity. Or was he a really brilliant fellow who thought of a line to kid the suckers into doing the dirty jobs and liking it?"

"But you must work at something, don't you?" she said after a pause.

"As seldom as possible."

"But you told us you had business with Uncle Alessandro."

"Do I look like a type of character who would have business with him?"

"No," she said emphatically, and then was instantly appalled and open-mouthed. "I mean—"

He grinned.

"You mean exactly what you said," he insisted gently. "I never did convince you that I was part of the ordinary commercial world, and since then you've remembered more of what you've read or heard about some of my adventures, which your educational background would have to regard as slightly nefarious. In spite of which, you apparently know that Uncle Al's private line of skulduggery is much worse than anything a comparatively respectable buccaneer like me would be mixed up in."

"I didn't say that at all!" she flared. "I know everyone says he made his money in rum-running or rackets or some of the other things you have in the United States, and I know he was in trouble with the police about taxes or something. It was in all the papers when I was at school, and the other girls teased me to death because I had the same name. I didn't dare admit he was a relation. But since then he's told me that all the best people dealt with him, only the Americans are so hypocritical, and he just happened to run up against the wrong politicians. And he's always been so good to us—"

"So when he talked to you on the phone late last night or early this morning and told you he was afraid I meant him some harm, and asked you to use our date to find out all that you could about me and what I was cooking, you felt it was your duty to take on the job."

For a moment her eyes flashed with the instinctive threat of another and even more indignant denial; and then the fire was quenched in a traitorous upwelling of moisture that she could not voluntarily control. Her lip trembled, and she dropped her face suddenly in her hands.

Simon patted her sympathetically on the shoulder.

"Don't take it so hard," he said. "You just haven't had much experience with the Mata Hari bit."

"You're a beast," she sobbed.

"No, I'm not. I'm a nice friendly bloke who hates to refuse a beautiful girl anything. To prove it, I'll answer all your questions anyhow."

The soft satin under his hand shook with another muted tremor which was somehow distractingly exciting, but he made himself go on single-mindedly:

"No, I am not a policeman. No, I am not working for the FBI, or any agency of any Government. Yes, I have the worst intentions towards your Uncle Alessandro. I think he's a very evil man and that he may be guilty of a number of murders besides lesser crimes; but there's one murder I'm morally certain he's responsible for, which I'm going to see that he pays for in one way or another. Unless he succeeds in having me murdered first, which he's already tried a couple of times."

She sat up abruptly, and he reflected that only the very very young could still look lovely with reddened eyes and tear-stained cheeks.

"That's enough," she said. "You'd better take me home now."

"Not until after lunch. Could you live with the knowledge that you'd sentenced one of those lobsters to die for nothing?"

"I expect you can eat them both."

"Why should I risk indigestion because you don't like to hear the truth?"

"I can't listen to you! It would be too disloyal. It's my family you're talking about, calling Uncle Alessandro a murderer. I want to go home."

"Then wouldn't you feel better," said the Saint deliberately, "if Al Destamio wasn't really your uncle after all?"

The shot scored, more violently even than he had hoped. Gina's reaction ran the gamut of all the conventional symptoms of shock, from staring eyes and sagging jaw to the cataleptic rigidity in which all her responses were frozen. After such a visible impact, there could be no return to pretense or hauteur.

"So—you know," she breathed finally.

"I can't go quite that far," he said candidly. "I suspect. I can't prove it—yet. But I think I shall. I need help. And I think you could give it. Now you've as good as told me, haven't you, that you've suspected the same thing."

His blue eyes held her steadily, like magic crystals defying her to try to deceive them; but this

time she made no attempt to escape their pene-
tration.

"Yes," she said. "For a long time. But I was
afraid to believe it, because I knew how much I
hoped it was true. And that seemed awful, somehow."

"But if it turned out we were right," he continued—and the subtle assimilation of their interests
into the inclusive "we" was so smooth that she
probably never even noticed it, "it'd be rather like
the start of a new life for you."

"Yes, it would."

"Then what's your problem? Al is asking you to
get involved in what you're afraid is more dirty
business. You've got suspicions which you can't
take to the police, because you're afraid of being
wrong, or of what it might mean to your family
name. I'm not the police, but I have a corny bee in
my bonnet about justice. I think I'm your obvious
answer, sent directly from heaven."

"I think you're wonderful," she said, and leaned
over and kissed him with impulsive warmth.

Simon Templar recorded a vivid impression that
her stretch in a convent had effected no irremedial
inhibitions on her Mediterranean instincts.

"La pasta è pronta," said the too-helpful waiter,
with impeccable timing.

2

The dining room was nothing more than a ver-
andah shaded with cane matting, overlooking the
beach and the sea, with the kitchen and other
working quarters in the stucco building that

backed it up. The substitute for a cellar appeared to be an immense glass-fronted refrigerator from which the wine came mountain-cold, as it should be in such a climate, especially when of the sturdy Sicilian type. The meal itself made a commendable effort to live up to its advance billing, and would have justified interrupting almost anything except what it had actually cut short. But at least it gave the Saint an opportunity to hear the rest of Gina's confession from a slightly less disturbing distance.

"It's just . . . well, a feeling that's been growing through the years. At first it seemed so fantastic that I tried to laugh it off. But the small things added up to a big thing that I couldn't put out of my mind. Now I look back, it must have all begun about the time Uncle Alessandro was so sick in Rome. I told you that I only remember that part vaguely, because I was very small. I know he had cancer, and I thought they said it was incurable; but now Donna Maria says I'm wrong, it wasn't cancer at all, and he got better. Is that possible?"

"It's not impossible. Doctors have been mistaken. And there have been what you might call spontaneous remissions, which means that the doctors don't know why the patient was cured, but he was."

"But not very often?"

"Not very often after the case has been called incurable, that have lasted as long as since you were a little girl, and with the patient looking as hearty as Al did the other day."

"Then I happened to notice that there weren't any pictures of Uncle Alessandro in any of the family albums, when he was younger. When I asked Donna Maria, she said that when he was younger he was superstitious about being photographed and would never let himself be taken."

"Perhaps he had a premonition about when he would have his picture taken with a number under it," Simon remarked.

"And then a girl whom I used to be taken out with, because her mother was an old friend of Donna Maria, who always finds the nastiest things to say about everyone and yet you usually have to admit they're true, once said that Uncle Alessandro's cure must have been more in his mind than his body, if he did so well in business in America, when all he ever did here in Italy was to throw away most of the family fortune."

"Is that what he did?"

"Oh, yes. Even Lo Zio, when it wasn't so hard for him to talk, told me how foolish he was and some of the crazy schemes he threw money away on. And I couldn't believe he had become such a different man."

Simon nodded.

"Unless he is a different man."

"But how could he be? Unless Lo Zio—"

"Who, let's face it, isn't so very bright these days—"

"And Donna Maria—"

"Yes, she would have to be in on it." The Saint held her eyes remorselessly. "And don't try to tell me you can't possibly imagine such a dear sweet old lady being involved in anything dishonest."

She made no attempt to evade the challenge; it was as if she had grown up, in one way, very suddenly. She only asked: "But why?"

"When we know that," he said, "we'll have a lot of answers."

After a while she said: "You want me to trust you, but you still haven't told me much about yourself, only the things you're not. If you aren't a detective, how did you get so interested in Uncle Alessandro?"

His hesitation was only momentary, more to marshall his recollections than to make up his mind whether or not to share them with her. After all, even if she was an extraordinarily unsuspected Delilah, capable of far more deviousness and duplicity than one could easily credit her, and this whole last performance was only another trick to gain his confidence, there was very little he could tell her that would be news to Al Destamio, or that would help the Mafia to frustrate his investigations.

Therefore he told her his whole story, from the accidental meeting with the late James Euston to the plastic bomb which he had disarmed the night before, omitting only his private luncheon conversation with Marco Ponti and his disposal of the plastic with the fingerprints on it, since even if she had come over whole-heartedly to his side those items of information might be tricked or forced out of her. At the end of the recital she was big-eyed and open-mouthed again.

"I can hardly believe it—a bomb, and right outside our house, while we were having dinner!"

"A very sensible time to do it. You should try planting a bomb in a car without being noticed, when somebody's sitting in it, driving at sixty miles an hour."

All this talk was not quite as consecutive as it reads, having been spread over several courses, with the necessary breaks for tasting, sipping, chewing, absorbing, and cogitating, and interruptions by the waiter for serving and changing plates and appealing for approbation.

It was later still, after another of those pauses divided between gastronomic appreciation and the separate pursuit of their own thoughts, that Gina said: "I did think of a way once to settle whether Uncle Alessandro really is the same man as my uncle, but of course I never had the nerve to do it."

"If that's all it takes, it's practically done. People are always complaining that I've got too much nerve. Let me offer you some of my surplus. What do we do with it?"

"It's so simple, actually. If my uncle is dead, and this man is an imposter, the real uncle will be buried in the family vault. We just have to open it and look."

The Saint frowned.

"Does that follow automatically? Wouldn't they be more likely to have buried him somewhere else, under another name?"

"Oh, no! I can't believe that they'd go as far as that. You don't know how traditional everything is in Sicily, especially with an old family like mine. Even if Donna Maria and Lo Zio allowed this Alessandro Destamio to pretend to be my uncle, for money or any other reason—and he couldn't do it without their help—nothing would make them allow my real uncle to be buried under a false name and outside the vault where all the Destamios have been buried for three hundred years. It would be almost like committing sacrilege!"

Simon pondered this, pursuing a last exquisite tidbit with delicately determined knife and fork. It was psychologically believable. And the Mafia could easily have arranged to satisfy the orthodox scruples of the close relatives concerned, with a captive doctor to juggle a death certificate and a *mafioso* priest to preside over a midnight interment.

It was a possibility. And the best prospect in sight at that moment for another break-through.

"Would you be a party to cracking the ancestral mausoleum?" he asked. "Or at least show me where it is and turn your back?"

"I'll go with you," she said.

The meal came to an end at last with fresh yellow peaches at their peak of luscious ripeness, after which Gina accepted coffee but the Saint declined it, preferring to finish with the clean taste of the fruit and a final glass of wine.

"When you're finished," he said, "I think we might throw on some clothes and run over and case the joint—if you'll excuse the expression. Anyhow we can't go swimming again right away after gorging ourselves like this."

Thus after a while they were driving back again almost into Palermo, then swinging out again under Gina's directions while the Saint registered every turning on a mental map that would retrace the route unhesitatingly whenever he called on it, by night or day. In daylight, the fine stand of cypress trees which landmark all cemeteries in Italy loomed up as an early beacon to their destination; and when they had almost reached it, a funeral cortège debouching from a dusty side road completed the identification while at the same time effectively blocking all further progress.

The hearse, unlike the dachshund-bodied

Cadillacs beloved of American morticians, was a superbly medieval juggernaut towering a good ten feet from the ground, decorated with carved flowers, fruit, and cherubs framing glass panes the size of shop windows which gave a clear view of the coffin within and its smothering mantle of flowers. It was towed by two trudging black horses in harness to match, their heads bent under the weight of huge plumes of the same stygian hue.

Behind it followed a shuffling parade of mourners. First the women, identically garbed in rusty black dresses with black scarves over their heads, bearing either long-stemmed flowers or candles; this was a big outing for them, and there was not a dry eye in the column. Then came the men—a few in their black Sunday suits, doubtless the next of kin, while the rest were more comfortable in their shirtsleeves, to which some of them added the respectful touch of black bands on the upper arm. Many dawdled along in animated conversation, as if they had attached themselves to the procession merely from a temporary lack of any other attraction, or because a social obligation required their presence but not any uncontrollable display of grief.

Simon stopped the car by the roadside and said: "We might as well walk from here, instead of dragging behind them."

He helped Gina out, and they easily overtook the phalanx of the bereaved without unseemly scurrying, and squeezed past it through the cemetery gates. He looked closely at the gates as he went through, and saw that there was no lock on them: it was unlikely that they would ever be secured in any way, though they might be kept shut at other times to keep stray dogs out.

"Our vault is over there," Gina said, pointing.

It was not so much a vault as a mausoleum, occupying a whole large corner of the graveyard, an edifice of granite and marble so imposing that at first Simon had taken it for some kind of chapel. The entrance was a door made of bronze bars that would have served very well as the gateway of a jail; beyond it, what looked at first like a narrow passageway led straight through the middle of the building to a small altar at the other end backed by a stained-glass window just big enough to admit a modicum of suitable sepulchral light. It was not until after a second or two, when his eyes adapted to the gloom, that he realized that the passageway was in fact only a constricted maneuvering space between the banks of serried individual sarcophagi stacked one upon the other like courses of great bricks which in places rose all the way to the ceiling.

"It seems to have gotten a bit crowded," he remarked. "I wouldn't say there was room for more than a couple more good generations. Do you have your nook picked out, or is it a case of first gone, first served?"

She shivered in spite of the warmth of the air.

"I don't understand jokes like that," she said stiffly; and he was reminded that in spite of everything that had drawn them together there were still distances between them that might never be bridged.

He gave his attention to the lock on the bronze gate, which had a keyhole almost big enough to receive his finger.

"Who has the key?" he asked. "Donna Maria?"

"I expect so. But I don't know where I'd look for it. I could try to find out—"

"I'm afraid that might take too long. But you needn't bother. Now that I've seen the lock, I know exactly what I need to open it. Unfortunately I don't have the tool in my pocket. And anyhow, this doesn't seem to be quite the ideal moment to start making burglarious motions." He indicated the tag-end of the funeral party, whose easily distracted concentration was now unfairly divided between the goings-on at the graveside where the hearse had halted and the contrastingly lively loveliness of Gina in her outrageously figure-moulding cotton dress. "Let's pass the time driving back to a shop where I can buy what we need."

After he had made his purchase, he suggested another swim to cool off again. Caution dictated a nocturnal return to the cemetery, when the risk of attracting unwanted attention would be practically eliminated, and meanwhile he wanted to keep Gina's mind from dwelling too much on the prospect. But the sun was still a hand's breadth from setting when she said: "If we don't go back to the vault now, you'll have to take me home."

"I don't want to go until after dark," he said. "I thought we might drift along somewhere for an apéritif and maybe an early dinner first."

"I can't have dinner with you," she said. "If I don't get home before it's dark, Donna Maria will be exploding. And she'd certainly never let me go out with you again, even if Uncle Alessandro asked her to."

Simon thought about this for a moment, and was surprisingly undepressed by the further reminder of the problems of romance in the land of

Romeo and Juliet. Much as he would have liked to spend more time with Gina, a tomb-tapping excursion would not have been his own choice of an occasion for her companionship.

"I guess you're right," he said. "And I know you weren't really looking forward to joining me in a game of ghouls. Get dressed again, and we'll make sure that Auntie has no reason to disintegrate."

She was rather silent on the drive back to the manse; but after a while she said: "What shall I tell them I found out about you?"

"Everything I told you at lunch, if you like. But of course nothing about our plan to check up on the vault."

"Then what shall I say your plans are?"

"Tell 'em you couldn't find out. Tell 'em I hinted that I'd got some sensational scheme up my sleeve, but I refused to talk about it . . . Yes, that's perfect —you can say that you think you could break me down, if you had just a little more time to work on me, and that we made a date for more sightseeing tomorrow. Then you can be sure that they won't just let you keep it, they'll beg you to."

The Bugatti stopped at the forbidding gates; and Simon came around the car and gave her a hand to dismount, and held on to it after the assistance was no longer needed.

"Till tomorrow, then," she said, with her intense dark eyes lingering on his face as if she wanted to learn it again feature by feature.

But when he bent to kiss her, she drew back with subtle skill, releasing her hand quickly and hurrying to the inset door, from which she turned to throw him another of her intoxicating smiles before she disappeared.

Verily, he thought, the conquest of Gina Destamio could be something like crossing the Alps by a goat trail on a bicycle with hexagonal wheels . . .

However, both remembrance and anticipation continued to weave her image through his thoughts during the apéritif and the dinner which he had to enjoy alone, and were only relegated to the background at the same time when he decided that the cemetery should have become as deserted and safely set up for violation as it would ever be.

Then he became purely professional. And as far as he was concerned, any similarity of his mission to the themes of gothic novels or horror movies was purely coincidental. To him, the mausoleum was just another crib to be cracked, and a much easier prospect than many that he had tackled.

He drove the Bugatti past the cemetery entrance and around the next corner before he parked it, and came silently back on foot. The moon which had been so helpful the night before was up again, giving perhaps more light than he would have ordered if the specifications had been left to him, but in compensation it made complete concealment almost as difficult for any remotely possible bushwhacker as it was for him. There was, however, most literally no other sign of life in the vicinity, and the only sound was the rustle of leaves in the hesitant breeze.

The wrought-iron gates were closed but not locked, as he had anticipated, and opened with only a slight creak. Crossing to the Destamio mausoleum, he automatically gave a wide berth to the tombs and headstones which were big enough for a man to skulk behind, and probed the shadows behind them with cat eyes as he passed; but that perfunctory precaution seemed to be in fact as unnecessary as the backward glances which he threw over alternate shoulders at brief irregular intervals while he worked on the lock which secured the bronze grille door of the vault. It succumbed to his sensitive manipulations in less than three minutes, and with a last wary look behind him he passed through into the alley between the piled-up ranks of stone caskets; and there for the first time he had to bring out his pocket flashlight to begin deciphering the inscriptions on their ends.

Then there was an instant of intense pain in the back of his head, and a coruscating blackness rose up and swallowed him.

3

A distant throbbing, as of some gargantuan tom-tom pulsating deep in the earth, thudded and swelled. An indefinite time passed before Simon became aware that the hammering drum was in his own head, and that each percussion was accompanied by a red surge of agony. He fought down the pain with his growing consciousness until after an immeasurable battle he had subjugated it enough to be able to receive other impressions.

His face was pressed against something rough and dusty that smelled of goats, and when he tried to move his head and change position he realized that his hands were bound behind his back. It took an additional effort of will to force himself to lie still while a modicum of strength flowed back into his body and the cobwebs cleared sluggishly from his brain.

It was painfully obvious that he had been hit on the head, like any numb-skulled private eye in a bosom-and-bludgeon paperback; and what made it hurt more was the proof that, for such a thing to have happened, he had to have been out-thought. He still fancied himself long past the stage where anyone could sneak up behind and cosh him if he was even minimally on his guard, as he had been at the cemetery. But now it dawned on him belatedly that he had been tricked by the simple fact of having had to pick the lock of the mausoleum grille, which had subconsciously blinded him to the possibility that someone else might have arrived before him and locked the gate again from inside. Someone who could then have crouched in the total darkness atop one of the banks of coffins and waited patiently for him to pass through the passageway below . . .

After which came the question: how could the ambush have been planned with such accurate expectation of his arrival?

A door opened near by, and heavy footsteps clacked across a tile floor and stopped beside him.

"Al," said the Saint at a venture, "if you wanted to see me again so badly, why didn't you just send me an ordinary invitation?"

A familiar rumbling grunt confirmed his guess.

It took a great effort to move, for any motion started the trip-hammers going again inside his cranium, but he forced himself to roll over so that his face was out of the filthy blanket. The scene thus revealed scarcely seemed worth the agony. He

was in a small whitewashed room lighted by a single naked bulb, with a single door and a single window covered by a soiled skimpy curtain. There was
no furniture except the cot on which he lay. A size-
able part of this dreary setting was obscured by the
form of Al Destamio looming over him like a
jellied mountain of menace.

"Don't waste your time on the jokes," growled
the mountain. "You just start tellin' me what I
wanta know, an' maybe you won't get hurt no
more than you are now."

Simon squirmed up into a sitting position with
his back to the wall, and only a faint spangling of
sweat on his forehead revealed what the exertion
cost him. Destamio saw nothing but a smile of un-
daunted mockery, and rage rose in his throat.

"You gonna talk or you gonna give trouble?"

"I love to talk, Al," said the Saint soothingly.
"Nobody ever accused me of being tongue-tied.
What would you like to chat about? Or should I
start off by congratulating you on the way you got
me here?—wherever this is. It's been quite a few
years now since I let myself get sapped like that.
But having your boy lock himself inside that crypt
and wait for me to burgle my way in was a real
sneaky switch. I must remember that one."

"You'll be lucky if you live long enough to remember anything."

"Well, I've always been rather lucky, Al. A guy
has to be, when he isn't brilliant like you—"

The words were cut off as Destamio lashed out
with his slab-sized hand and dealt the Saint a
crashing blow on the side of his head, jarring him
sideways, the heavy ring splitting the skin of his
cheek.

"No jokes, I told you, Saint. You wanna be smart, you give the right answers an' make it easy for yourself."

Simon shook his head, trying to arrest the internal pounding which the clout had started up again.

"But I meant it sincerely, Al," he said in a most reasonable tone, though the ice in his blue eyes would have chilled anyone more sensitive than the post-graduate goon confronting him. "It was really brilliant of you to figure out that my next move would be to check the names in your family bone-box. Or did Gina tell you?"

"Did she know?"

The Saint could have bitten his tongue off. Now if Gina hadn't betrayed him, he had betrayed her. It showed that the after-effects of the knock-out had left him more befuddled than he had realized.

"I didn't mean it that way," he tried to recover. "I meant, did you think of it all by yourself, or did she help you? She's smart enough to have an inspiration like that, judging by the way she was trying to pump me all day. But I didn't tell her, because I'm not such a dope that I couldn't guess what she was after."

Destamio stared at him inscrutably. For all his crudities, the racketeer was as quick as a whip; and it was no more than a toss-up, at the most optimistic, whether he would be taken in by the Saint's attempt to retrieve his slip.

"I wanta know lotsa more things you didn't tell her," Destamio said. "What was it you figured to spill to the cops, like you threatened me, if you thought I was trying to have you knocked off again? An' how you figure to do that now?"

"That's easy," Simon answered. "It's all written down and sealed in an envelope which will be delivered to the proper place whenever the person who's taking care of it doesn't hear from me at certain regular times. I know that's one of the oldest gimmicks in the business, but it's still a corker. And don't think you can force me to call this person and say I'm okay, because if I don't use the right code words he'll know that somebody's twisting my arm."

"I think you're bluffing," Destamio said coldly. "But it don't matter. Before I'm through, you'll tell me who's got this envelope, an' what the code is."

"You think so?"

Destamio met the Saint's level and unflinching gaze for several motionless seconds; and then a throaty chuckle came up from some source around his diaphragm like the grumbling sound of an earthquake, and opened the fissure of his lipless mouth as it emerged.

"You don't have to tell me you're tough. I seen plenty guys worked over in different ways, an' a few of 'em never did sing. But we don't have to work that way no more. We got scientific ways to loosen you up, an' what's more we'll know you're tellin' the truth. So since I don't have to make no promises I ain't gonna keep, like I would if I was gonna work you over in the old way, I can tell you we're just gonna give you a little shot in the arm, an' after you spill everything I'm gonna blow your brains out myself."

He went to the door and called out: *"Entra, dottore!"*

Simon Templar knew the feeling of a sinking heart, and not merely as a metaphor. Al Destamio was certainly not bluffing. In those enlightened days, there was no longer any practical need for the clumsy instruments of the medieval torture chamber, or even their more modern electrical refinements: there were drugs available which when injected into a vein would induce a state of relaxed euphoria in which the victim would happily babble his most precious secrets. Even the Saint, with all his courage and determination, could not resist that chemical coercion. Grinning idiotically, he would tell the whole truth and nothing but the truth—and once he had done that, God help him.

The man who came in was stocky and plump, although on nothing like the same scale as Destamio. He was younger, and his dewlaps were freshly shaved and powdered, his hands soft and pink; his double-breasted suit was dark blue, and his shoes, though sharply pointed, an even more conservative black. The expression on his slightly porcine features was wise and solemn, as befitted one whose trade was based upon reminders of mortality: he did not need the universal symbol of the black satchel, which he nevertheless carried with him, to identify it.

"Is this the patient?" he asked, as if he were making the most routine of house calls.

"I am if you want to prescribe something for a mild concussion, and a long cold drink to wash it down," Simon said. "If you've hired yourself out for anything else, you must have dedicated yourself to hypocrisy—not Hippocrates."

The doctor's expression did not alter as he put down his bag on the floor and opened it.

"Do you have any allergies?" he asked with stolid conscientiousness. "Sodium pentothal sometimes has side reactions, but then again so does scopolamine. It is sometimes difficult to decide which is best to use."

"My worst allergy is to medical quacks," said the Saint. "But I don't want to be unfair. Perhaps you're wonderful with horses."

"Affretate, dottore," growled Destamio impatiently.

The physician was unperturbed by either of them. Taking his own time, he brought out a vial of clear fluid and a hypodermic, filled the syringe, and went through the standard procedure of forcing a small jet of liquid through the upraised needle to remove any trapped bubbles of air—a somewhat finicky precaution, it seemed, considering that Destamio's announced program would be more positively lethal than any accidentally introduced embolism.

The Saint was turning his wrists over behind him, testing the bonds that held them. They were tied with a piece of light rope which was soft and supple with age, and there was stretch in it which could be exploited by setting his arms in certain positions known to escape artists, to gain the maximum leverage, and then applying all the power of his exceptional muscles to it. He knew that he could release himself eventually, but it would take at least several minutes. His legs, however, were not bound; and as the doctor approached Simon braced himself and measured the distance for a vicious kick which if it found its target would indubitably cause quite an interregnum in the scheduled proceedings. By fair means or foul, no matter how foul, he had to win that essential time . . .

Time was given to him, miraculously, by a man

who looked like anything but an agent of Providence, who flung open the door at that precise moment and rattled a sentence in dialect at Destamio. Simon could not understand a word of it, but it had an instantaneous effect on its recipient that would have been envied by Paul Revere. Destamio spun around with a single grating oath, and waddled to the door with grotesque celerity.

"Wait until I get back," he spat over his shoulder as he went out.

Simon watched as the doctor carefully put down the hypodermic inside his bag and strolled over to the window. He drew aside the dingy curtain and threw open the casement, giving the Saint an unimpeded view of the night sky. The lack of bars on the opening was like a symbol, and Simon felt a sudden new surge of hope. Behind his back his arms writhed and strained in desperate but disciplined hate as he did everything he could to profit by the Heaven-sent reprieve, while at the same time avoiding any struggles violent enough to attract attention.

"What is the excitement about, *dottore?*" he asked, less in expectation of an answer than to cover the small sounds of his contortions.

"It is Don Pasquale," the doctor said, his back to Simon as he continued to inhale the fresh air. "He is very old and very sick, and there are two other *medici* here besides myself to prove again that science can make old age more comfortable but never cure it."

"You must excuse my ignorance, but who is this Don Pasquale? And why does he get such a special fuss made over him?"

The doctor turned and looked at him curiously.

"Your ignorance is indeed surprising, for a man who has information that the Mafia seems to want very badly. Don Pasquale is the head of the organization, and when he dies they will have to elect a new Don. That is why the leaders are all here."

"The vultures gather . . ." Simon tried to keep any sign of effort from his face, while his sinews flexed and corded like steel wire. "And I suppose my fat friend would love to become Don Alessandro."

"I doubt if he will be chosen. He has been out of the country too long. Here in the South we tend to be rather provincial, and a little suspicious of all things foreign."

"That never seems to have stopped you exporting your *mafiosi* missionaries to less insular parts, such as the United States. I should think the organization would welcome a new top thug with international experience."

The doctor shrugged impassively. Either he was too discreet to be baited into further discussion, or he was genuinely uninterested in anything the Saint could possibly contribute. He continued to gaze at Simon as impersonally as he would have contemplated an anatomical chart, and the Saint goaded his brain frantically to think of some other gambit that might divert attention from the movements that he had to keep on making.

Then both of them turned as the door opened again. It was the messenger who had called Destamio away who reappeared.

"*Tu*," he said to the Saint, in understandable Italian. "Come with me."

"Il signor Destamio wants him here for medical treatment," the doctor interposed, without expression.

"It will have to wait," said the man curtly. "It is Don Pasquale who sends for him."

4

At this revelation the doctor pointedly lost interest again, and devoted himself to closing up his satchel as the emissary pulled Simon to his feet. The Saint for his part submitted to the new orders with the utmost docility, not only because it would have required the apathy of a turnip to resist such an intriguing summons, but also to avoid giving his escort any reason to re-check the rope on his wrists.

The tie was loosening, but it would still take him several more minutes to get free. He would have to wait for that time.

They went down a long musty whitewashed corridor with other closed doors in it, then up a flight of stone stairs which brought them into an enormous kitchen, from which another short passage and another doorway led into a vast baroque hall heavy with tapestries, paintings, suits of armor, and ponderously ornate woodwork. He realized then that the cell where he had revived was only an ignoble storage room in the basement of what could legitimately be called a *palazzo*. There was a floating population of dark men in tight suits with bulging armpits, all of them with fixed expressions of congenital unfriendliness. No further proof was needed that he had penetrated to the very heart of the enemy's camp, although not quite in the manner he would have chosen for himself.

The messenger pushed him towards the baronial stairway that came down to the center of the hall. They went up to a gallery, from which he was steered through a pair of half-open oak portals into a somber ante-room. Beyond it, an almost equally imposing inner door stood closed, and the guide tapped lightly on it. There was no reply from the interior, but he did not seem to expect one, for he turned the handle quietly and pulled the door open. Remaining outside himself, he gave the Saint a last shove which sent him in.

Simon found himself in a bedroom that was in full proportion to the other master rooms he had seen, panelled in dark red brocade and cluttered with huge and hideous pieces of age-darkened furniture. The windows were carefully sealed against the noxious vapors of the night, and effectively sealed in the half-stale half-antiseptic odors of the sickroom. Next to the high canopied bed stood an enameled metal table loaded with a pharmaceutical-looking assortment of bottles and supplies, over which hovered two men with the same unmistakably professional air as the medico who had been brought to Simon's cell, one of them gaunt and gray and the other one short and black-goateed.

The other men grouped around the bed were older, and had a subtle aura of individual authority in spite of their deference to the central figure in the tableau. There were four of them, ranging in age from the late fifties upwards. The eldest, perhaps, was Al Destamio. There was a stout smooth-faced man with glasses who could have passed for a cosmopolitan business executive, and one with

cruel eyes and the build of a wrestler whose thick
mustache gave him a pseudo-military air. The
youngest, at least from the impression of nervous
vigor which he gave, was almost as tall and trim-
waisted as the Saint, but overbalanced by a beak
which an Andean condor might justifiably have envied. Although modelled on classical Roman lines,
it expanded and enlarged the theme on a heroic
scale which would have made General De Gaulle
look almost pudding-faced. And having apparently
conceded to his shaving mirror that there was nothing he could do to minimize it, he wore it with a
defiance that would have delighted Cyrano de
Bergerac.

This was the inner circle, the peers in their own
right, assembled at the death-bed of the King to
pay him homage—and vie among themselves for
the succession.

They turned and looked at the Saint with a single
concerted motion, as if they were wired together,
leaving an open path to the bed.

At the zenith of his powers, the man who lay
there must have been a giant, judging by the breadth
of his frame. But some wasting disease had
clutched him, stripping away tissue, bringing him
down to this bed in which he must soon die. That
much was obvious; the marks of approaching dis-
solution were heavy upon him. The skin once taut
with muscle now hung in loose folds on his neck.
Black marks like smeared soot were painted under
the sunken eyes, and the gray hair lay thin and
lifeless across the mottled brow. Yet, sick as he
was, the habit of command had not left him. His
eyes burned with the intensity of a madman or a
martyr; and his voice, though weakened, had the

vibrant timbre of an operatic basso.

"Vieni qui."

It was not a request, or even an order, so much as the spoken assurance of knowledge that obedience would follow. This was the way that absolute monarchs of the past must have spoken, who had the power of life and death over their subjects, and Don Pasquale was one of the last heirs to that kind of authority.

Nevertheless, Simon reminded himself, it was no honorable kingdom of which he was supreme ruler, but a ruthless secret society for which no crime was too sordid if it showed sufficient profit. Viewed in that light, the regal-cathedral atmosphere of the gathering was too incongruous for the Saint's basic irreverence. He moved up to the foot of the bed, as he was told, but with a lazy trace of swagger that made it seem as if his hands were clasped behind his back of his own choice instead of being tied there, and a smile of brazen mockery curled his lips.

"Ciao, Pasquale," he said cheerfully, as one buddy to another.

He could feel the chieftains on either side of him wince and stiffen incredulously at this *lèse-majesté,* but the man propped up on the pillows did not even seem to notice it, perhaps because he could not fully believe that he had heard it, or because in his assured supremacy it meant no more to him than an urchin thumbing its nose.

"So you are the one they call the Saint. You have given us trouble before."

"I am pleased that it was enough for you to notice," Simon said. "But I don't remember the occasion. What were you doing at the time?"

Since Don Pasquale had addressed him with the familiar *"tu"*, which is used only to inferiors or intimates, Simon saw no reason not to respond in the same manner.

"You interfered with some plans of Unciello, who was one of us. And we had a useful man in the police in Rome, an Inspector Buono, whom we lost because of you."

"Now it comes back to me," said the Saint. "I have an unfortunate knack of crossing up crooked cops. What ever happened to the poor grafter?"

"He got in trouble in jail. A knife fight. He is dead."

Don Pasquale still had the memory of a computer. All the threads of a world-wide network of crime led back to him, and he controlled it because he knew the exact length and strength of every single one. More than ten years had passed since that incident in Rome, but he had not forgotten any of the details.

"What has the Saint done now, Alessandro?"

"He is trying to make trouble for me," Destamio said. "He has followed me, spied on me, gone to my family and questioned them, threatened to blackmail me. I have to find out what he knows, and who else knows it, and then get rid of him."

"That may be; but why bring him here?"

"I thought it was the safest place, and besides I did not want to be away myself at this time—"

"What information could the Saint have that he could possibly blackmail Alessandro with?"

It was a new voice that broke in, and Destamio started visibly at the sound of it. It came from the man with the majestic proboscis whom Simon had already intuitively assessed as the most dynamic of the council.

"Nothing, Cirano, nothing at all," Destamio replied, his voice sounding a trifle hoarser than usual. "But I want to know why he thinks he can give me trouble, who he is working with, so that I can take care of everything."

The man called Cirano—probably a nickname rather than a fortunate choice by his parents—turned his fascinating beak towards Destamio and actually sniffed, as if all his powers of perception were brought to focus in that incredible olfactory organ.

"If he cannot be dangerous, what are you afraid of, Alessandro?" he persisted mercilessly. "What is there to take care of?"

"Basta!" Don Pasquale interrupted Destamio's retort before it even came to voice. "You can wait to fight with each other after I am dead. Until then, I make the decisions."

His lips barely moved when he talked, and there was no sign of animation or emotion on the pallid face. Only the eyes were indomitably alive, and they fastened on the Saint again with a concentration which could almost be physically felt.

"I have long wanted to see you, Simon Templar," he said, still in the clear correct Italian which seemed to be used as a neutral language to bridge the differences of dialect that must have existed between some of those present, and which can make a Sicilian just as unintelligible to a Calabrian as to any foreigner. "Nobody who defies the Mafia lives so long afterwards as you have. You should have been eliminated before you left Rome, after you crossed Unciello. Yet here you are crossing us again. I should be telling Alessandro to waste no more time in putting you out of the way. But in the meantime I have heard and learned much more about you. I am not sure that you must inevitably be our enemy. With our power behind you, you could have become many times richer than you are. With your cleverness and your daring, we might have become even greater."

The room was deathly silent. Even at the end of his reign, Don Pasquale remained the unchallenged autocrat by sheer force of will-power and tradition. The satraps around him were still only his lieutenants, and would remain subservient until his extinction unleashed the new battle for supremacy.

"Do you mean," Simon asked slowly, "that after all that, you would offer me a chance to join you?"

"It is not impossible," Don Pasquale said. "Such things happen in the world. Even great nations which have been bitter enemies become allies."

The Saint hesitated for an instant, while a score of possibilities flashed back and forth across his mind like bolts of lightning, speculating on what use he could make of such a fantastic offer and how far he might play it along.

But for once the bronze mask of his face was no more defense than a shell of clear glass against the searching stare that dwelt on it.

"But no," Don Pasquale said, before he could even formulate a response. "You are thinking only of how you might turn it to your advantage, to escape from the position you are now in. That is why I had to see you, to have your answer myself. *L' udienza e finita.*"

Without affectation, he used the same words to

declare the audience finished that would have come
from a king or a pope.

Al Destamio grabbed the Saint and hustled him
to the door with what might have seemed like
almost inordinate zeal, and Don Pasquale spoke
again.

"Wait here one moment, Alessandro."

Destamio gave the Saint a push which sent him
stumbling up against the messenger who waited
outside, and snapped: "Take him back downstairs
and lock him in."

The massive door slammed shut; and the guide
grasped Simon's arm at the elbow and propelled
him forcefully across the ante-room, along the gallery, and down the magnificent stairway with such
brutal vigor that it took all the Saint's agility to
keep his footing and save himself from being
hurled down the steps on his face.

In the same bullying manner, he was marched
through the kitchen, down the back stairs, and
along the basement corridor to the room from
which he had been brought. But at that especial
moment he almost welcomed the sadistic treatment,
for under cover of a natural resistance to it he was
able to wrestle more vigorously and concentratedly
with the rope that held his wrists.

A last brutal kick with his escort's knee sent him
flying into the little cell. The door banged behind
him, and the key grated in the lock.

He was alone again, for the doctor had not
waited; but he knew it would not be for long.
Whatever business the dying Don Pasquale wanted
to conclude with Destamio could not take more
than a short while, and then Destamio would be in
even more haste to complete his own project.

But alone and unobserved, the Saint could writhe and struggle without restraint; and he already had a good start . . .

In less than three more minutes he dragged one hand free, and the cord was slack on his other wrist.

Even while it was falling to the floor, he reached the window in a soundless rush.

Until then, he had had no clue to how long he had been unconscious after he had been knocked out in the mausoleum, and with his hands tied behind him he had been unable to see the time on his wrist watch. But now, with the electric bulb behind him, he saw that the sky was no longer black but gray with the first dim promise of dawn. And that faint glimmer of illumination was enough to show him why his captors were so unconcerned about leaving him in a room with an open unbarred window.

The *palazzo* was perched on the very edge of a precipice. The window from which he leaned out was pierced in a smooth wall with no other openings for fifteen feet on either side or above. Below, the wall merged without a break into the vertical cliff which served as its foundation. And below that juncture the rock sheered away into still unfathomable blackness.

V

How Simon Templar walked in the Sun, and Drank from various Bottles

The Saint's jacket was gone, and his trouser pockets had been emptied of everything except a handful of small change which had been almost contemptuously left. He took out a five-*lire* piece and dropped it out of the window from arm's length. It vanished into the gloom below, but for as long as he strained his ears he could not hear it strike bottom. Whatever was below the window had to be a long way down.

But the door offered no alternative. It was massively constructed of thick planks bolted together and belted with iron straps; and while the lock would probably have been easy to pick if he had had any sort of tool, there was simply nothing on him or in the bare room that he could use. The window might seem like a kind of Russian roulette with five chambers loaded, but it was the only possible way out. And to remain there was certain death.

Without wasting another instant of precious time, Simon tore the blanket from the cot and began to rip it into usable strips. Knotted together, along with the cord with which he had been tied, they gave him a rope about thirty feet long and of highly speculative strength. He had often read about this standard device, like everyone else, but had had just as few occasions as anyone to try it out in practice. There was no way to test it in advance, other than by strenuous tugging, which appeared to reveal no intrinsic weakness. Less than ten minutes after he had been locked in, he had one end of the rope secured to the frame of the bed, and the bed itself propped up across the window, allowing the greatest possible length of his improvised hawser to hang down the wall.

He sat on the sill, his legs dangling over the void, and studied as much as he could of the situation. Though the details of the gorge below were still concealed by the morning mist, the sky was now rapidly lightening—enough to disclose a broadening range of topographical features.

The cliff on which the house was perched formed part of one side of a narrow valley through which straggled a small village with a fair-sized church spire reaching above the white houses. Beyond the town the hills rose again abruptly, and even higher peaks probed skyward in the distance. To the left, through the clearing haze, he could just make out a thin ribbon of road winding upwards along the opposite slope; to the right, it seemed to descend from the village. Holding on with one hand and leaning as far out as he could, he was rewarded with a glint of sunlight reflected on water, far off in the latter direction. The road to the right, then, led down towards the sea, and that would be the direction of escape. He hadn't the vaguest idea where on the map he was, but he knew that the interior of Sicily consisted almost entirely of mountain ranges, and that the main roads followed the coast line of that triangular island to connect the larger cities, all of which are on the sea.

From beyond the door behind him he heard footsteps again, and the metallic rattle of the key in the lock. If he was going to fly the coop at all, this was the positively last chance for take-off.

With a sinuous motion he twisted off the ledge until he hung supported only by his fingers. Then he shifted one hand to the blanket-rope and gradually transferred his weight, experimentally, until all of it was on the rope. The ancient fabric stretched but held; and thereafter his most urgent concern was to make the strain on it as brief as possible. He lowered himself hand under hand with a speed that came close to that of a circus acrobat, tempered only by the requirement of avoiding any abrupt jerks or jolts that might tax his makeshift life-line beyond its dubious breaking-point.

He was halfway down when a gaping face appeared from the window above him, and two yards lower before it could express its perplexity in words.

"Che cosa fai?"

Believing that anyone who asked what he was doing, in those circumstances, could not be seriously expecting an answer, Simon ignored the intrusion and concentrated even more intensely on his gymnastic performance. Therefore he was looking downwards when the man produced a gun, and the first indication he had of its presence was the crack of the shot and the dying scream of a bullet ricocheting from the wall near his head. It took an ice-nerved self-discipline to make no change in the smoothness of his descent—or perhaps he was more worried about the capacity of his rope than about the marksmanship of the man upstairs.

From above, next, he heard the voice of Al Destamio engaged in noisy altercation with the gunman. It seemed that Al didn't want him to shoot any more, for reasons which the Saint could appreciate, but which were meeting a good deal of consumer resistance from the minor *mafioso,* who had discovered a delightfully novel form of target practice and resented being deprived of it. While they wrangled, Simon descended a few more feet, and literally came to the end of his rope.

Holding on with one vise-clamped fist, he saw that his feet were still almost a metre above the bottom of the wall, which was based less than half that distance from the cliff edge. Below that lip, the rock face dropped away at a slant of about eighty degrees to an orchard that looked almost far enough to open a parachute, which he wished he had. Especially as the argument at the window overhead seemed to be compromised with a violent shaking or hauling on the flimsy filament from which he was suspended.

He had no choice but to take one more gamble.

He opened his hand and dropped . . .

He landed lightly on his toes, knees bending to cushion the steadiest possible landing. Dirt crumbled and gravel trickled down the escarpment, but the rock foundation was solid. He rested there a moment, plastered against the gripless wall of the building and envying octopods with suction cups in their tentacles.

The nearest corner of the house was at least twenty feet to his right, and he began to edge cautiously in that direction. There was a sudden silence from the window above, and it did not take much imagination to visualize Destamio and others trundling around to meet him. But there was a good chance that he could reach the side of the building before they could make their way to the same area by a more normal route through the house. Once he was off the vertiginous ledge, he would have to extemporize his next step according to what openings presented themselves. His planning had gone no farther than this, where he considered himself comparatively fortunate to be.

Which was all to the good, since he was destined never to reach the corner of the building. Another of the Mafia security corps had apparently been already outside, and upon hearing the shots had moved to investigate this unwonted matutinal activity. His head appeared like a jack-in-the-box around the angle towards which Simon was inching his precarious way.

"Buon giorno," said the Saint, with his maximum affability. "Is this the way to the bathroom?"

The reaction was fully as obvious and exaggerated as a cinematic double-take. The newcomer's sagging jaw dragged his mouth open in a befuddled O, exposing an interesting assortment of gold teeth interspersed with the blackened stumps of their less privileged fellows which had yet to benefit from auric reconstitution.

"Che cosa fai?"

The question seemed no less inanely rhetorical to

the Saint than it had on the previous occasion, but
this time he made an attempt to keep the conversation going.

"*Ebbene*, it is like this," he replied, while he sank
carefully to one knee and his other leg dropped
over the cliff edge, his toe groping for a support.
"There have been complaints about the founda-
tions of this castle. We do not want Don Pasquale's
end to be accelerated by having his sick-room fall
out from under him. So I have been called in to
examine the underpinnings. I am inclined to suspect Death Watch beetles—does that sound likely
to you?"

The opinion of his audience, which had been
half-hypnotized into watching in blank stupe-
faction while Simon meantime levered himself over
the ledge until only his chin was above its level, was
not revealed because he was suddenly yanked back
and replaced by the gunman who had taken his last
pot shot from the upper window.

"Come back!" shouted the man, with somewhat
idiotic optimism, as he tried to get into an aiming
position.

"I'm sorry," said the Saint, "but my union only
allows me to climb down. To bring me up you must
send an elevator."

The gunman's homicidal zeal was not di-
minished by this reasonable answer, but he was
severely handicapped by the mechanics of the situation. The precipice began at his feet, and the base
of the building came almost to its edge on his right.
If it had been the opposite way around, or if he had
been left-handed, it would have been simplicity
itself to poke his head and gun-hand around the

corner and bang away. But being one of the right-handed majority, there was no way he could comfortably bring his gun to bear, short of stepping out and resting at least one foot on a cloud. He tried a couple of snap shots without that levitational assistance, but with his hand bent awkwardly back from his wrist the bullets went wide and the recoils almost dislodged him from his insecure stance on the rim of the chasm.

While he struggled with this peculiar problem, his quarry was working steadily down the sheer wall with an unexpected virtuosity that would have won respect from challengers of the Eiger. And by the time he had figured out the possible solution of lying flat on his stomach and wriggling out over the void for half the length of his chest, prepared even from that extension to try a southpaw shot if necessary, he was stung to a scream of frustration by the discovery that his target had meanwhile managed to claw his way around a sufficient bulge in the illusory plane of the cliff to be completely shielded from his line of sight.

While his would-be assassin may have been mentally elaborating excuses for the one that got away, Simon was still a long drop from feeling home and safe. He had done some rock climbing, as he had tried every other hazardous sport in his time, and he had muscles and agility that many professionals might have envied, but he would never have claimed to be an expert mountaineer. High-octane adrenalin was the primitive fuel that drove him, clinging like a limpet to an almost vertical gradient, his toes scrabbling for irregularities that might lend a bare ridge of support, his fingers

hooking into grooves and crannies that only cen-
turies of weather had eaten into the unsympathetic
stone.

Having no time to be precise or technical, he
took risks that no seasoned alpinist would have
considered. He surrendered his weight to hand-
holds that had not been fully tested, and one of
them pulled away, a jagged chunk of rock that
crashed down among the trees below, leaving him
for one desperate moment without support of any
kind, except the friction of his body pressed against
the natural wall. Yet even as he slid, his hands were
racing over the fissured incline and found another
minuscule ridge, and he resumed his ingloriously
frantic descent.

At infinitely long last something brushed his
shoulder which he realized was a fruit-laden
branch. With a quick twist he grasped it, swung
down to the ground, and took off running through
the grove.

Far above him, through the clear air, he heard
the grind of a starter and the roar of a car's engine
breaking into life. Someone up there had finally realized that there might be better ways of cutting
him off towards his destination than from his starting point.

He ran.

A patch of open meadow separated the orchards, and as he crossed it there was a flurry of
echoes from high behind him, and something
whistled past his ear and thudded into the turf. He
accepted this with an equanimity which owed no
little to the cold-blooded estimate that at such a
distance a hand gun was approximately as dangerous as a well-hurled pebble. He had a more serious

threat to worry about: the howl of an over-stressed
motor came faintly down to his ears, and a large
black limousine, strangely reminiscent of movies
about Prohibition days in America, hurtled into
view on a road that came over the cliff top near the
house and zigzagged down towards the village. Its
intentions were obvious from the maniac speed
with which it attacked the descent, broadsiding on
the turns and throwing up clouds of gravel and
dust. Even though his predicament was no longer
cliff-hanging, he could still be cut off . . .

The Saint doubled his pace and fairly flew down
the more gentle slope, hurdling the tumbled-stone
fences, pitting his own speed and freedom of
choice against the more devious routes which the
faster car was obliged to follow. As soon as he
reached the shelter of the next grove, he angled off
to the right, a change of course that would be hidden from watchers at the cliff top. The limousine
was also invisible now behind the trees, but he
could trace its progress by the whine of gears and
the chatter of skidding tires. The element of desperate uncertainty was where his path and the road
would intersect.

The pain in the back of his skull where he had
been bludgeoned had long since been cured or
driven out of consciousness by the pressure of
more imperatve demands on his attention. Another
fence rose up ahead, made of the same broken
slabs of stone fitted together without mortar, and
again he took it like a steeplechaser, without breaking stride to make sure what was beyond. This was
reckless, but he had little choice: the sounds of the
car were coming much too close to permit leisured
reconnaissance. As he cleared the wall, he discov-

ered that the ground beyond had been cut away, making a drop of six feet on the other side—where the road itself was responsible for the cutting. He took the fall easily, touching his hands to the gravel with the force of the impact but instantly springing up again. But in one swift glance around he saw the top of the black sedan over the tops of some young olive trees a scant hundred yards farther up the incline. Only the configuration of the ground and an intervening hairpin bend prevented its occupants from seeing him as well.

In terms of the speed of the approaching vehicle, that advantage represented mere seconds of grace. Rebounding like a rubber ball, Simon took two more immense strides across the road and dived head first over the lower wall on the other side, landing with a paratrooper's shoulder roll and staying flat on the ground at the end of it.

A shaved moment later, the car slashed around the bend and screeched to a rubber-rending stop just beyond the place where the Saint had crossed. It was so close that spurted gravel rattled against the wall and the dust floated over his head. If he had been a fraction slower he would have been caught on the road; ten seconds slower in his breakneck run and he would have been trapped in the groves above, which the *mafiosi* were now invading.

Rising up with infinite wariness until he could look over the wall near him, he saw four of them clambering over the higher wall to spread out through the trees. The chauffeur who had navigated the projectile descent of the cliff road still sat at the wheel of the big car, and not much farther was the broad sweat-stained back of Al

Destamio himself, shouting orders to his advance pack of hoodlums. Everyone was actively oriented to the upward angles, apparently fully convinced that at that point they must have well outdistanced the Saint and need not bother to look for him below them.

The temptation to counter-attack from the rear was almost overwhelming, and if it had been only a matter of Destamio or his driver the Saint would have probably failed nobly to resist it. But the two together, spaced as far apart as they were, constituted just too much risk that any hitch in the taking out of the first might give the second a chance to raise an alarm that would reverse all the convenient preconceptions of the squad that expected the Saint to fall into their arms from above. Reluctantly, he decided that this was a case where commonsensical considerations should outweigh the superficial allures of grandstand glory.

He turned away, rather sadly remembering more juvenile days when he would have chosen otherwise, and melted silently down through the vineyard where he had landed.

2

He could count on a brief respite while the searchers above vainly combed the upper slopes where they seemed to think they had cornered him. With that preconceived idea, it would take them between half an hour and an hour to convince themselves that he had gone past them and not crawled into some undiscovered hole. Then the word would have to be passed to headquarters, and

a more widespread search would have to be organized. This would be a blanket operation that
would enlist the entire Mafia and all their sympa-
thisers, who possibly comprised most of the
island's population. Every man's hand would be
against him; but he would know where he stood
with any man.

The thought was briefly invigorating as he in-
creased his pace. Staying out of the hot clutches of
the Mafia might be the most difficult accomplish-
ment of his checkered career; but if he could survive that cliché he might be able to outlast anything.

One stairwayed vineyard led down to another as
his giant strides carried him through them towards
the valley town. The *contadini* of the outskirts were
already awake and scratching at their tiny allot-
ments with medieval mattocks. They seemed to notice Simon only disinterestedly as he passed, as if
their tenure under the very shadow of the Mafia
allowed them only to observe when specifically
called upon to do so. The sight of a hurrying man
in a torn shirt coming from the direction of the
Mafia mansion evoked no response but hastily
averted eyes: they would remember his passage if
the correct parties inquired later, but right now
they would neither hinder nor help.

Simon dismissed them as ciphers in this desperate game, and made no stop or detour on their account until he reached the first outlying buildings
of the town, where he paused briefly to do what
little he could to make himself slightly more presentable.

One shirt-sleeve was unrepairable, split up almost to the shoulder. Ripping off the cuff, he

used it as a band on which to roll up the remains of
the sleeve. When he rolled up the other sleeve to
match, the torn one was hardly noticeable. He
brushed the dirt from his hands, dusted his slacks
as best he could, and combed his hair with his fingers—wincing slightly when they touched the knot
above his occiput, and making another mental en-
try in the ledger that would have to be balanced
with Al Destamio's account when they came to a
final settlement. With that, he was as ready to go
on as he would ever be.

The nameless town which he had to enter was
already coming to life, since like any microcosm of
the south it moved more quickly in the cool of the
morning in order to doze better during the in-
cinerating afternoon. Before finally entering a narrow alley that would surely lead to the main street,
Simon checked backwards to see that his trail was
still free of pursuers, and was rewarded with an unexpected and arresting sight. His downward path
had widened his visual scope, and now he could see
not only his recently deserted prison on the over-
hanging cliff but also a more distant mountain rising beyond and dwarfing it, a summit from which
a think plume of smoke coiled lazily upwards.

Even the most superficial student of geological
grandeurs could have recognized the symptoms of
a dormant volcano; and since there is only one such
on the island of Sicily, at the same time the highest
in Europe and one of the largest in the world, Simon knew that he must be looking at Mount Etna.
And aside from any casual vulcanological interest,
it performed the important function of telling him
exactly where he was.

To visualize a map of Sicily, as the Saint did, you

might think of a piece of pie about to be kicked by
the toe of a boot, which is the shape of the Italian
peninsula. The resemblance is only in outline, and
should not lead to any symbolic inferences. The
top side of this pie-wedge is fairly straight and runs
almost due east and west. The volcano of Etna is
situated in the upper eastern corner of the triangle.
Since the Saint was looking towards it, and the sun
was rising behind it, the most rudimentary geo-
graphical acumen or even the basic training of a
boy scout would have been enough to tell him
that the road downhill from the unknown town he
was entering must run north to join the coastal
highway somewhere between Messina and
Palermo. To some exigent critics this deduction
might still have seemed to fall far short of pinpoint-
ing a position, but to Simon Templar it provided a
fix from which he would have cheerfully set a
course to Mars.

As he reached the central square of the town, he
had a clear view of the valley road that bisected it
and wandered on down to the now occulted sea.
That trail of patched macadam, he knew, was a
siren's lure that beckoned only to his death.
Though it looked open, it would be the first avenue
to be watched, closed, or booby-trapped. The
Mafia might not be overly concerned with
Destamio's personal problems, but they would be
ruthlessly jealous of their own prerogatives, which
the Saint had affronted with insulting levity. Therefore all their resources, spread like a spider cancer
through the entire community, would be devoted
to the simple objective of cutting him down. And
the main thoroughfares would be the first and most
obvious avenues for them to cover.

Across the square, in front of the town's principal and possibly only hotel, an assortment of early-rising tourists were loading their luggage and their young into various cars. Two families of beaming Bavarians, complete with *lederhosen* and beer bellies, obviously travelling together in identical beetle-nosed Volkswagens; a middle-aged Frenchman with his dependable Peugeot and a chic chick who somehow looked a most unconvincing wife; and an oversized station wagon whose superfluous fins and garbage-can-lid rear lights would have revealed its transatlantic origin long before the red and black identification of the American forces in Europe could have been deciphered on its dusty license plate. The gaudy pseudo-Hawaiian shirt worn like a pregnancy smock outside the tired slacks of its proprietor was no disguise for a certain pugnacity of jaw and steeliness of eye which stamp a professional sergeant in peace or war.

Simon's spirits rose another notch. With such a type, opportunity might not be exactly pounding at his door, but at least he could hear it tap.

He waited till the last suitcase had been jammed into the truck-sized rear deck, and the last squalling brat trapped and stowed amidships, and then he approached the near-side window just as the driver was settling in and turning on the engine.

"I hate to make like a hitch-hiker," he said, with just the right blend of fellow-American camaraderie combined with undertones of a wartime commission, "but could you drop me off a couple of miles down the valley? I had to bring my car in to be fixed at the garage here, and it won't be done till this evening."

While the sergeant hesitated momentarily, from the ingrained suspicion of all professional sergeants, his wife moved over to make room on the front seat.

"Sure," she said, making up his mind for him like any good American wife. "No trouble at all."

The Saint got in, and they pulled away. By this time, he figured that Destamio and the first pursuit squad might be debating the possibility that they had not after all headed him where they stopped on the road.

"What you doin' around here?" asked the sergeant sociably, after a time.

"Spending a vacation with some cousins," Simon answered casually, knowing that his black hair and tanned complexion would superficially support a fictional Italian ancestry. "They've got a farm down the road a piece. First time I've ever been here—my folks emigrated before I was born."

"Where you from, then?"

"New York."

A trite choice, but one where he knew he could not be caught out on any topographical details, and big enough not to lead into any aquaintance pitfalls of the "Do you know Joe Blow?" pattern.

"We're from Dallas, Texas. We don't get out much into the suburbs."

It was astonishingly easy, and might have tempted anyone to parlay his luck as far as the ride could be stretched. But the Saint had attained his present age mainly because he was not just anyone. Very shortly, his pursuers would extend their search into the town, where they would soon find some loafer in the square who had seen a man answering to Simon's description getting into an unmistakable American car. With the speed of a couple of telephone calls, the word would be flashed ahead to confreres along the littoral, and before the station wagon even reached the coast the highway in both directions would be alive with eyes that would never let it out of their sight. From that moment there would be nowhere he could leave the car without the probability of being observed and followed, while to stay in it would risk an unthinkable involvement of its innocent occupants in any splashy attempts at his own destruction.

Watching the road ahead for any side tracks that could plausibly lead to a farm, he finally spotted a suitable turning and said: "Right here—don't try to take me to the door, you'd have a job turning around to get out again. And thanks a million."

"You're welcome."

Simon got out, and the car shot off as he waved good-bye.

Now until they stopped the station wagon and questioned the driver, Destamio's cohorts would be partially baffled—unless someone realized that a man on foot could travel in any direction, if he was fool enough to climb over a sun-blasted mountain instead of skirting it. Which was precisely the Saint's intention.

But the plan was not as hare-brained to him as it might have seemed to a less original fugitive. On a previous visit to Sicily he had driven from Messina to Palermo, and had remarked on the numbers of people waiting at bus stops along the highway, who had apparently landed from boats or lived under rocks by the wayside, since they were nowhere near any visible human habitation. His companion, who knew the island, had pointed out the dusty dirt tracks that wound back between the buttresses of the hills, and explained that higher up in most of the valleys, closer to sources of precious water, there was a hidden village. Though they might be only a few miles apart on the map, the normal route from one to another was down to the sea, along the coast, and back up again—a long way around, but much more attractive in a climate that discouraged strenuous exertion. To the Saint, however, to do whatever would be most unexpected was far more important than an economy of sweat.

And sweat, in plain common language, was what his eccentricity exacted, in copious quantities. As he climbed higher, so did the sun, making it clear why Sicily had never become the Mecca of midsummer mountain-hikers. To add to its natural disadvantages for such sport, Simon Templar also had to contend not only with the after-effects of a mild concussion but also with the fact that he had had no breakfast, or any other food or drink since last night's dinner.

It was good evidence of his mental as well as his physical toughness that he set and maintained a pace which would not have disgraced a week-end hiker over some gentle undulations in an English autumn. His shirt was already sodden when the terraced groves and vineyards gave up their encroachment on a baked and crumbling mountain-side where only straggling shrubs and cacti grew; but the sun only worked harder to imitate the orifice of a blast furnace. More insidious was the temptation to let his mind dwell on thoughts of cool refreshing drinks, which only intensified the craving. The human body can go without food for a month, but dies in a few days without water. Simon was not about to die, but he had never been so thirsty as he was when he reached the summit of the range he had aimed for.

By then it was almost noon, and his brains felt as if they were being cooked inside his skull. The rocks shimmered in the blaze, heat-induced mirages plagued his vision, and the blood pounded in his temples. But if he had chosen the right ridge, he should be able to come down in a valley that would bring him to the sea from a totally different quarter and in a totally different area from where the hunters would be watching for him.

A rustling sound like wind-blown leaves came to him as he rounded a jutting promontory some way below the crest, and he found himself suddenly face to face with three startled goats. They were moth-eaten, dusty, and lean to a point of emaciation which was understandable if their only grazing was the withered herbage of that scorched hillside. Two of them were females with large but not distended udders, and the explanation of that detail dawned on him an instant too late for him to draw back behind the sheltering shoulder of magma. By that time he had seen the goatherd, and seen that the goatherd also saw him.

They stared at each other for a silent moment, the goatherd looking as surprised as his charges. He was a thin youth as dusty and tattered as the goats, in a faded shirt with the sleeves torn off at the shoulders and pants that had been mended so many times that it was difficult to tell which was the original material and which the patches. A knotted rope served him for a belt, and completed the sum of his wardrobe; the soles of his bare feet must have been calloused like hoofs to be able to ignore the abrasive and cauterizing surfaces which were all that his pastures offered them to walk on. He brushed back his uncut mop of hair to get a better view of the extraordinary apparition which had shattered all the precedents of his lonely domain.

"*Buon giorno*," said the Saint reassuringly. "A beautiful day for a walk in the hills."

"*Sissignore*," responded the young man politely, to avoid offending an obvious lunatic. He speculated: "You are English?"

Simon nodded, deciding that it was better to accept that assumption than be taken for a mad dog. He sighted a tiny patch of shade under a projecting rock and sat down to rest in it for a minute.

"It was not as hot as this when I started out," he said, in an attempt to partly explain his irrational behavior.

"You must be thirsty," the herdboy said.

Something in Simon's manner had erased his first fear and he came and squatted close by.

"My mouth is so dry that I doubt if I could lick a stamp."

"You would like a drink?"

"I would love one. I would like about six drinks," said the Saint wistfully. "Tall ones, ice-cold. I would not be fussy about what they were. Orange juice, beer, cider, wine, tomato juice, even water. Do you have a refrigerator in a cave anywhere near by?"

"You can have some of my water if you like."

The lad reached behind him and swung into sight a skin bottle that had been hanging down his back, suspended from a loop of gray string. He pulled the cork from the neck and extended the flask to the Saint, who took it in a state of numbed shock.

"And I thought you were kidding . . ."

Simon raised the bottle to his lips and let a trickle of hot, sour, but life-giving wetness moisten his tongue and flow down his throat. At any other time it would have been almost nauseating, but in his condition it was like nectar. He sipped slowly, to extract the maximum humidity from it and to give himself the impression of a prolonged draught without actually draining the container. He returned the skin still more than half full, and sighed gratefully.

"*Mille grazie*. You may have saved my life."

On the other hand, the youth might equally prove to be a contributor to the Saint's death. There was no way to make him forget the encounter, short of knocking him on the head and pitching his body into the nearest ravine, which would have been a somewhat churlish return for his good Samaritanism. But eventually the goatherd would hear about the foreigner who was being sought, and would tell about their meeting, and would be able to indicate which way the Saint had gone. With one quirk of fate, Simon had lost much of the advantage that he had toiled so painfully to gain—how much, depended on how soon the boy's story reached one of the search parties. But that was only another hazard that had to be accepted.

3

There was nothing more to be gained by perching on that ledge like a becalmed buzzard and brooding about it. Simon climbed to his feet again, counting the compensation of the brief rest and refreshment, and pointed down the steep slope.

"There is a village down that way?"

"*Sissignore*. It is where I live. Would you like me to guide you?"

"No, if I keep going downhill I must come to it."

"After you pass around that hill there with the two dead trees on the side you will see it. But I have to go back there before long in any case."

"I am in a hurry, and I have already interfered with you too much," said the Saint hastily. "Thank you again, and may your goats multiply like rabbits."

He turned and plunged on down the slope with a dynamic purposefulness designed to leave the lad too far behind for further argument before any such argument could suggest itself.

He only slackened his pace when he felt sure, without turning to look back, that the goatherd had been left shrugging helplessly at the incontestable arbitrariness of Anglo-Saxons, and when the precipitousness of the path reminded him that a twisted ankle could eventually prove just as fatal as a broken neck. He had to work his way across a perilous field of broken scree on the direct course he had set for the two dead trees which had been pointed out as his next landmark, but soon after he passed them he scrambled over another barren hump to be greeted by a vista that justified all the toil and sweat of its attainment.

In the brown hollow of the hills far below clustered the white-washed buildings of another village, with a road leading away from them down the widening canyon that could ultimately meander nowhere but to the coast. His venture seemed to have paid off.

His descent from the heights seemed like a sleigh ride only by comparison with the preceding climb. A steep downhill trail, pedestrians whose walking is confined to city pavements might be surprised to learn, is almost as tiring as an uphill: the body's weight does not have to be lifted, but its gravitational pull has to be cushioned instead, and the shocks come on the unsprung heels which make the muscles of the thighs work harder to soften the jolts. It was true that he had had a cupful of water to drink, but to boil it off there was an afternoon heat more intense if possible than the morning. Having breakfasted on nothing but thin air, he was now sampling more of the same menu for lunch. If he had been inclined to self-pity, he could have summarized that he was parched with thirst, faint with hunger, stumbling with fatigue, and baked to the verge of heat prostration; but he never permitted himself such an indulgence. On the contrary, renewed hope winged his steps and helped him to forget exhaustion.

Nevertheless, a more coldly impersonal faculty warned him that he couldn't continue drawing indefinitely on nothing but will-power and his stored-up reserves of strength. He would have to find liquid and solid sustenance in the village. If he by-passed it, he might be able to reach the coast on foot, but he would be in no shape to cope with any minions of the Mafia that he might meet there or run into on the road. The risk of attracting attention in town had to be balanced against the physical and mental improvement that its resources of food and drink could give him.

As he worked his way closer to it, suffering all the added disadvantages of pathfinding as the price of refusing the young goatherd's offer of guidance, the echoing clangor of the inevitable church bell reached him, striking the half-hour which his wrist watch confirmed to be one-thirty. Ten minutes later he slithered by accident across a well-worn path which would probably have brought him as far with half the effort if he could have been shown it, but which at least eased the last quarter-hour's slog to the most outlying cottages.

But the delay had not necessarily penalized him. In fact, it might have improved the conditions for his arrival. The reassembly of the inhabitants under their own roofs, and the serious business of the *colazione*, the midday and most important meal of the southern peasant, would have run their ritual courses, and a contentedly inflated populace should still be pampering the work of their digestive juices in the no less hallowed formality of the siesta. Even if any of them had already been alerted, which in itself seemed moderately unlikely, for a while there would be the fewest eyes open to notice him.

The pitifully stony terraces through which he made the last lap of his approach, the dessicated crops and scattering of stunted trees, prepared him in advance for the poverty-stricken aspect of the town. Indeed, it was hard to imagine how even such a modest community could wrest a subsistence from such starved surroundings—unless one had had previous immunization to such miracles of meridional ecology. But the Saint knew that within that abject microcosm could be found all the essentials that the fundaments of civilization would demand.

Like all the Sicilian villages of which it was prototypical, it had no streets more than a few feet wide. The problems of motorized traffic were still in its fortunate future. Its twisted alleys writhed between those houses which were not prohibitively Siamesed to their neighbors, only to converge unanimously on what had to be deferentially called the town square. Having accepted the inevitability of ploughing that obvious route, Simon strode boldly and as if he knew exactly where he was heading through a débris-cluttered alley which squeezed him between two high walls overhung with wilted flowers into the central *piazza*. The overlooking windows were tightly shuttered, lending an atmosphere of timeless somnolence to the scene.

The Saint's pace slowed into a pace compatible with his surroundings, trying to tone down obtrusive brashness, for the benefit of any wakeful observer, without inversely suggesting nefarious stealth. But there was no sign of any interest in his deportment, or even that his entrance or his mere existence had been discerned at all. The pervading heat dwelt there like a living presence in the absence of any other life. Nothing whatever moved except the flies circling a mangy dog that lay in a dead sleep in one shaded doorway.

There was no central fountain in the square; but somewhere near, he was sure, there had to be a town tap, or pump, or at least a horse-trough. He walked around the western and southern sides of the perimeter, keeping close to the buildings in order to benefit by their shade, and wondering how long it would be before the first food shop would re-open.

"Hi, Mac! You like a nice clean shave an' freshen up?"

The voice almost made him jump, coming in heavily accented but fluent English from the open doorway he was passing. Overhead there was a crudely painted sign that said PARRUCCHERIA. A curtain of strings of beads, southern Europe's primitive but effective form of fly barrier, screened the interior from sight, and he had assumed that a more solid portal had been left open merely to aid the circulation of air while the barber snored somewhere in the back of the shop; but apparently that artist was already awake and watching from his lair for any potential customer to pass within hooking range.

Simon, having been halted in his tracks, grated a hand across his thirty-six-hour beard and pretended to weigh the merits of the invitation. In reality he was weighing the few coins in his pocket and considering whether he could afford it. A delay of a quarter-hour or so should make little difference, and might be more than made up by the new vigor he could generate in such an interlude of complete repose. A clean-up would not only make him look less like a desperate fugitive, but would give him a psychological boost to match its outward effect. There would certainly be water—that thought alone almost jet-propelled him into the shop—and during, the ministrations he might elicit much information ... or even something more mundane to chew on.

The arguments whirled through his head in a microfraction of the time it takes to set them down, and his choice was made well within the limits of any ordinary decision.

"You sold me, bub," he said, and went in.

Dim coolness wrapped him around, the perpetually surprising phenomenon of thick-walled architecture that had evolved its own system of air-conditioning before Carrier tried to duplicate it mechanically. In the temporary partial blindness of the interior, he allowed himself to be guided into a barber chair that felt positively voluptuous, and to be swathed to the neck in a clean sheet. Then, as his eyes grew more accustomed to the half-light, he perceived something which he thought at first must be a hallucination conjured up by his thirst-tortured senses. A white foam-plastic box stood against the wall, filled with chunks of ice from which projected the serrated caps of four bottles.

"What's that you've got in the ice?" he asked in an awed voice.

"Some beer, Mac. I keep a few bottles around in case anyone wants it."

"For sale?"

"You bet."

"I'll buy."

It took the barber four steps to the cooler, where the ice rattled crisply and stimulatingly as a bottle was withdrawn, and four steps back; each step seemed to take an eternity as the Saint counted the footfalls. It took another age before the top popped off and he was allowed to grasp the cold wet shape which seemed more exquisitely conceived than the most priceless Ming vase.

"*Salute,*" he said, and emptied half of it in one long delicious swallow.

"Good 'ealth," said the barber.

Simon delayed the second installment while he luxuriated in the first impact of cool and tasty liquid on his system.

"I suppose you wouldn't have anything around

that I could nibble?" he said. "I always think beer tastes better with a bite of something in between."

"I got-a some good salami, if you like that."

"I'm crazy about good salami."

The barber disappeared through another bead curtain at the back of the room, and returned after a few minutes with several generous slices on a chipped plate. By that time Simon had finished his bottle and could indicate with an expressive gesture that another would be needed to wash down the sausage.

"What made you speak to me in English?" he asked curiously, while it was being opened.

"The way you was lookin' aroun', I can see you never been in dis town before," said the barber complacently. "So I start-a thinkin', how you got your last hair-cut an' how you dress an' carry yourself. People from different countries all got their own face expressions an' way of walkin'. You put a German in an Italian suit an' he still don't look Italian. I work-a sixteen years in Chicago an' I seen all kinds."

He was trending into his sixties, and with his smoothly shaven and powdered blue jowls and balding head with a few carefully nurtured strands of hair stretched across it he was himself a sort of out-dated but cosmopolitan barber-image. How and why he had gone to America and returned to this Sicilian dead-end was a story that Simon had no particular desire to know, but which he was sure he would be hearing soon, if there was any truth in the traditional loquacity of tonsorial craftsmen.

While he could still do some talking himself, however, before being partly gagged by lather and the need to maintain facial immobility, the Saint thought it worth trying to implant some protective fiction about himself.

"And only an English-speaking tourist would be nutty enough to hike all the way up here from the coast in the middle of a day like this," he said.

If that version took hold, it might briefly dissociate him from someone else who was believed to have come over the crest from the other direction. Perhaps very briefly indeed, but nothing could be despised that might help to confuse the trail.

The barber deftly washed the dust of the hills from the Saint's face and replaced it with a soothing balm of suds. His inscrutably lugubrious air might have seemed to mask the thought anyone who was not condemned to permanent residence in that backwater of civilization should not complain about the purely transitory discomfort of a mere day's visit, no matter how arduous.

"You like-a ver' much walking, I guess?"

"Somebody sold me on getting off into the back country and finding the real Sicily that the ordinary tourists miss," Simon answered between swigs at his second bottle. "Unfortunately I didn't ask all the details I should have about the gradients and the climate. I'm glad I saw this town, but I can't say I'm looking forward to walking back down that road I came up. Does there happen to be a taxi in town, or anyone who drives a car for hire?"

"No, nothing like-a that, Mac." The barber was stropping his formidable straight-edge razor. "There's a bus twice a day, mornin' an' evenin'."

"What time?"

"Six o'clock, both times. Whichever you choose, you can't-a go wrong."

Far from feeling that he had made a joke, the barber seemed to sink into deeper gloom before this illustration of the abysmal rusticity of the campagna where ill fortune had stranded him. He placed his thumb on the Saint's jawbone and pulled to tighten the skin, and scraped down despondently with his ancient blade.

"You're a big-a fool to get in trouble wit' da Mafia," he said without a change of intonation.

It was an immortal tribute to the Saint's power of self-control that he didn't move a fraction of a millimeter in response to that sneak punch-line. The razor continued its downward track, skimming off a broad band of soap and stubble, but the epidermis behind it was left smooth and bloodless where the slightest twitch on his part would have registered a nick as surely as a seismograph. The cutting edge rested like a feather on the base of his throat for a moment that seemed endless, while the barber looked down glumly into his eyes and Simon stared back in unflinching immobility.

Then the barber shrugged and turned away to wipe the lather from his lethal weapon on the edge of the scarred rubber dish kept for that purpose.

"I don't understand you," said the Saint, to keep the conversation going.

"You bet you do, Mac. I been sitting 'ere lookin' out, you can see down da road to da first turn, an' that ain't where you come from. No, sir. You come over da mountain from Mistretta, an' you sure got 'em stirred up over there."

He took aim with the razor again, at the Saint's other cheek, but this time it was easier for Simon to wait passively for the contact. If the man had any serious butchering intentions, he would scarcely have passed up his first and best opportunity.

"What happened in Mistretta?" Simon asked, studiously speaking like a ventriloquist without using any external muscles.

"I don' know an' I don' wanna. I don' want-a no beef wit' da Mafia. But dey been onna phone, I got one-a da t'ree phones in dis crummy dump, an' I gotta pass on da word. I hear how you look, how you speak English, how everyone should watch for you."

There was no point in any more pretense.

"Do they know I came over here?"

"Naw. It's-a kinda general warning. They don' know where you are, an' everybody calls up everybody else to keep-a da eye open."

"So you weren't being such a Sherlock Holmes after all when you spotted me."

"Don' ride me, mister. I wanted to 'ear you talk, find out what kinda feller you are."

"Why didn't you cut my throat just now when you had the chance, and maybe earn yourself a reward?"

"Listen, I don't 'ave to kill you myself. I coulda just let you walk by, then talked on da phone. Let da Mafia do the job. I woulda been sittin' pretty, an' mos' likely pick up a piece o' change too. So don' ride me."

"Sorry," said the Saint. "But you must admit it's a bit surprising for anyone to find such a pal in these parts."

The barber wiped his razor and stropped it again with slow slapping strokes, and examined the gleaming edge against the light from the doorway.

"I ain't your pal, but I ain't-a no pal o' da Mafia neither. They done nothin' for me I couldn't 'a done better for myself. Kick in, protection, just like-a da rackets in Chicago. Only in Chicago I make-a more money, I can afford it better. I know da score. I shoulda stayed where I was well off; but I thought I could take it easy here on my Social Security an' what I'd-a saved up, an' just work enough to pay da rent. I should-a 'ad my 'ead examined."

"That still doesn't explain why you didn't turn me in."

"Listen, when I get dis call, dey gimme your name. Simon Templar. Probably don' mean nothin' to dese peasants; but I been around. I know who you are. I know you made trouble for lotsa racketeers. Dat's okay with me. I'd-a turn you in in a second, if it was my neck or yours. But I don' mind if I can get you outa dis town—"

Suddenly there was the snarl of a motor-scooter's exhaust coming up from the valley and roaring into the square like a magnified hornet with hiccups. The barber stopped all movement to listen, and Simon could see the blood drain out of his face. The scooter's tempestuous arrival at this torpid hour of the day obviously meant trouble, and trouble could only mean the Mafia. While the barber stood paralyzed, the mobile ear-splitter added a screech of brakes to its gamut of sound effects, and crescendoed to a stop outside the shop with a climactic clatter that presaged imminent disintegration.

"Quick!" Simon whispered. "A wet towel!"

Galvanized at last into action by a command that connected helpfully with established reflexes of professional habit, the barber stumbled over to the dual-purpose cooler and dredged up a sodden serviette from under the ice and remaining bottles. He scuttled back and draped it skilfully around and over the Saint's face as ominous footsteps clomped on the cobbles, and the beaded door-curtain rattled as someone parted it and pushed through.

It was an interesting situation, perhaps more appealing to an audience than to a participant. The barber was in a blue funk and might say anything; in fact, to betray the Saint, he didn't even need to say anything, he only had to point to the customer in the chair. He owed Simon nothing, and had frankly admitted that he would not hesitate over a choice between sympathy and his own skin. The Saint could only wait, blind and defenseless, but knowing that any motion might precipitate a fatal crisis. Which was not merely nerve-racking, but diluted his capacity to enjoy the exhilarating chill of the refrigerated wetness on his face.

Out of necessity, he lay there in a supine immobility that called for reserves of self-dominance that should have been drained by the razor-edge ordeal of a few minutes ago, while the rider rattled questions and commands in incomprehensible answers, but at last the curtain rattled again and the footsteps stomped away outside and faded along the sidewalk.

The towel was snatched from Simon's face and the chair tilted up with precipitate abruptness.

"Get out," rasped the barber, from a throat tight with panic.

"What was he saying?" Simon asked, stepping quietly down.

"Get-a goin'!" The man pointed at the door with a shaking forefinger. "He's a messenger from the

Mafia, come-a to call out all da *mafiosi* in dis village. They found out you didn't go down to da coast from Mistretta, so now they gonna search all-a da hills. They don' know you been here yet, but in a coupla minutes they'll be out lookin' everywhere an' you ain't-a got a chance. They kill you, an' if they find out you been 'ere dey kill-a me too! So get out!"

The Saint was already at the door, peering cautiously through the curtain.

"What was that way you were going to tell me to get out of town?"

"Fuori!"

Only the fear of being heard outside muted what would have been a scream into a squeak, but Simon knew that he had used up the last iota of hospitality that was going to be extended to him. If he strained it another fraction, the trembling barber was almost certain to try to whitewash himself by raising the alarm.

The one consolation was that in his frantic eagerness to be rid of his visitor the barber had no time to discuss payment for the beer and salami or even for the shave, and the Saint was grateful to be able to save the few coins in his pocket for another emergency.

"Thanks for everything, anyway, pal," he said, and stepped out into the square.

4

Propped upright in the gutter outside, the unguarded scooter was a temptation; but Simon Templar had graduated to automobiles long before vehicles of that type were introduced, and it would have taken him a perilous interval of fumbling to find out how to start it. Even then, it would have provided anything but unobtrusive transportation; indeed, the noise he had heard it make under full steam would be more help to any posse in pursuit of him than a pack of winged bloodhounds. Regretfully he decided that its locomotive advantages were not for him.

He strolled across the square to the corner from which the main road ran downhill, schooling himself to avoid any undue semblance of haste, but feeling as ridiculous as an elephant trying to pass unnoticed through an Eskimo settlement. The first few shutters were opening, the first few citizens emerging torpidly from their doors, and he was acutely aware that in any such isolated community any stranger was a phenomenon to be observed and analyzed and speculated upon. The best that he could hope for was to be taken for an adventurous tourist who had strayed off the beaten track, or somebody's visiting cousin from another province who had not yet been introduced around. When there was no outcry after the first few precarious seconds, it suggested that the barber had ultimately decided to keep quiet: if he shouted as late as this, the messenger might remember the towel-draped anonymity in the chair and wonder . . . Therefore the Saint could still hope to slip through the trap before the jaws closed.

And as each stride took him farther from the town center and the risk of total encirclement, his spirits rose to overtake the physical resurgence that the interlude of refreshment and recuperation in the barber shop had quickened—so much that

when he saw a hulking and beady-eyed ruffian staring fixedly at him through every step that led
through one of the last blocks of the village buildings, it was only a challenge to the oldest recourse
of Saintly impudence, and he walked deliberately
and unswervingly into the focus of the stare until it
wavered uncertainly before the arrogant confidence of his approach.

"*Ciao,*" said the Saint condescendingly, with a
superior Neapolitan accent. "He will be coming in
a few minutes. But do not glare at him like that, or
he will turn back and run."

"What am I to do, then?" mumbled the bully.

"Pretend to be busy with something else. After he
passes, whistle *Arrivederci, Roma,* very loudly. We
shall hear it, and be waiting for him."

He strode on, disdaining even to pause for ac-
knowledgement of the order, though the back of
his neck prickled.

But it worked. He had broken another cordon,
and the way he had done it proved how much he
had recuperated. He felt his morale beginning to
soar again. More nets would be cast, but his inex-
haustible flair for the unexpected would take him
through them.

In a few more moments he had left the last cottages behind, and then a curve in the road took him
altogether out of sight of the village and the
watcher on the outskirts who should now be watching the opposite way anyhow.

He quickened his step to a gait which from any
distance would still have looked like a walk, attracting less attention than a run, but whose deceptive-
ly lengthened stride covered the ground at a speed
which most men would have had to run to keep up

with. At the same time his eyes ceaselessly scanned the barren ridges on either side, alert for any other sentinels who might be watching the road from the heights. The road wound steadily downhill, making his breakneck pace possible in spite of the stifling heat, and he kept it up without sparing himself, knowing that the canyon he followed could be either his salvation or a death trap.

If he had not met the goatherd on the summit, and then had to stop in the last village, he might have had more latitude of choice, perhaps spending a night in the trackless hills and continuing across country until he could drop down into Cefalù, which he should have been able to locate from some peak if he was in the approximate area which he had deduced from his glimpse of Etna. But that was impossible now after where he had been seen. So far he was ahead of the chase, and had succeeded in out-thinking it as well, but that advantage would be lost as soon as the reports filtered in and were coordinated. His only hope now was to reach the coast before he was completely cut off, and lose himself in the crowds which could still be treacherous but could give better cover than any scrawny growth on the stark uplands.

From somewhere ahead came a plaintive squealing sound that slowed his headlong course as he tried to identify it. It repeated itself regularly, but grew no louder; if anything, it seemed to grow fainter as he went slower. He resumed his pace with redoubled alertness, and the intermittent squealing became gradually louder, showing that it must come from something that he was overtaking on the road.

Prudence should have dictated holding back for

a safe distance, but curiosity was equally cogent, and besides he could not afford to be slowed down indefinitely by some nameless obstruction. Instead, he accelerated again until he won a glimpse of it.

Soon the road made two consecutive horseshoe bends, bringing him to a clear view of the next level down the rutted track, where he saw that he was being preceded by a *carretta siciliana,* the picturesque Sicilian mule cart made famous by fifty million picture postcards. The rhythmic creaking which he had heard came from its inadequately lubricated hubs. It carried no load, and—except for its nodding driver—no passengers; but a bacchanalian scene of country maidens dancing with flower-wreathed satyrs graced its sides, while intricate patterns of fruit and foliage revolved on the fellies of its high wheels in an explosion of primary colors that pained the eyes.

Without hesitation Simon turned off the road, avalanched through the intervening gully, and raced into the wake of the trundling cart.

As he caught up with it, he saw that the driver, a gray-whiskered rustic, appeared to be asleep, the reins draped limply from one hand and his hat tilted over his eyes, but he raised his head and scowled down as the Saint came level with him.

"Buon giorno," Simon said in the standard greeting, falling back to a walk without a hint of short-windedness to betray that he had been hurrying.

"You would not say it was a good day if you had listen to my wife's tongue cracking like a whip all morning," said the driver crossly.

"Cattiva giornata," amended the Saint, ever flexible in such situations.

"Hai ragione. It is the worst kind of day. Have a drink."

The man produced a damp bottle from a mound of rags between his feet and proffered it. Unlike the goatherd's wineskin, this flagon contained its proper beverage, and was even moderately cool from the evaporation of the wet cloths in which it had been nested.

Simon enjoyed a second long pull and handed it back. The driver seized the excuse to have one himself, and it was obvious from the way he weaved the bottle up and down that it was not his first drink of the day. The Saint could not be discourteous, and when the bottle was handed him again he forced himself to accept another pleasant swallow of the thin slightly acid wine, walking with one hand on the cart to balance himself while the patient power plant trudged phlegmatically along.

"Where are you going?" asked the driver.

"To Palermo," Simon replied.

It was in his mind that if that statement were ever relayed to Al Destamio, the hoodlum's devious psychology would automatically assume that he was heading the opposite way, towards Messina; whereas he really did hope to get back to Palermo. He had left too many loose and unfinished ends there, of which Gina was not the least troubling.

From far behind the valley, at the very limit of audibility, came something like the buzzing of a distant hornet, which swelled rapidly to the proportions of an airplane's drone and then to a rattle like a pneumatic drill gone beserk. It was no feat of memory for Simon to recognize the sound: he had heard it all too recently—unless there were two internal combustion engines in the area with identically obnoxious exhausts.

The envoy was coming back down from the village. And on the way he had probably spoken with the picket on the outskirts . . .

"Let us keep each other company," said the Saint, and with a nimble leap he swung himself up to the seat beside the outraged driver.

"Who asked you?" demanded the latter in befuddled resentment. "What are you doing?"

"Joining you so that we can hurry to the nearest *vinaio* and buy some more of that excellent beverage which you have been sharing so generously with me. And here is the price of the next round."

Simon slapped the remaining change from his pocket on to the wooden seat. Small as the sum was, it was sufficient to buy two or three liters of wine at the depressed local prices. The peasant looked at it with heavy-lidded eyes, and picked it up without further protest. He even let Simon take another drag from the bottle before he reclaimed it.

The Saint relinquished his grip and listened calculatingly to the thrumming roar that was now reverberating from the valley walls.

"Drink up," he said encouragingly, "and let me do your work for you."

As he spoke, he gently detached the reins from the other's limp hold. The erstwhile driver turned and opened his mouth for another outburst of indignation, to be greeted with a smile of such seraphic innocence and friendliness that he forgot what he was going to complain about and wisely settled for another swig at the flagon. As his head went all the way back to drain the last gulp from it, the cart lurched over a well-chosen rut and his hat fell off. Simon caught it neatly and put it on his own head, tilted down over his eyes. In an instant his shoulders slumped with the defeat of the over-worked and underfed, and the reins drooped as list-lessly from his fingers as they had from those of the previous holder.

The timing and the performance were perfect. As the motor-scooter blatted deafeningly up behind and hurtled past, the rider should have seen only a pair of local peasants, the younger one dozing over the reins, the older one groping foggily for some-thing he seemed to have lost in the back of the cart.

Nevertheless the courier jammed on his brakes and skidded to a halt in a billowing cloud of dust, squarely across the road in front of them. From the fact that he did not threaten them with a weapon, Simon could still hope that it was only a routine check, a matter of asking the cartmen if they had seen anything of the quarry. His crude disguise might still be effective, enhanced as it was by his authentically local companion and the wagon they were riding in.

"Alt!" shouted the messenger. "I want to talk to you!"

In spite of the torrid temperature, he wore the short black leather blouse required by the protocol of his fraternity, inside which he must have enjoyed all the amenities of a portable Turkish bath; but as he pushed back his goggles Simon realized that he had seen him before, even though they had been hidden from each other in the barber's shop. It was one of the stone-faced security guards who had lurked sleeplessly around the marble columns of

Don Pasquale's *palazzo* above Mistretta.

With every faculty pitilessly aware of its thin margin for survival, the Saint lazily flicked the reins to urge the jenny as close as possible to the gunman—just in case . . .

"What kind of way is that to talk to anyone?" grumbled the chariot's owner, blinking perplexedly at the interception.

Then, as he turned to his passenger for confirmation, he saw for the first time something that drove the more complex affront completely out of his fumbling mind.

"You stole my hat, *ladrone!*" he squawked.

He reached to retrieve the disputed headgear, but his alcoholic aim combined with Simon's instinctive divergence only succeeded in knocking it off the Saint's head. It fell almost at the feet of the startled scooterist, who had moved around to the side of the cart for less stentorian conversation, and whose reciprocal recognition was a coruscating gem of over-statement.

Then the *mafioso's* right hand darted inside his jacket for the hardware that he should have displayed from the beginning.

Simon Templar moved even faster. He shifted sideways and swung his outside leg faster than the gunman could disengage his gun, and there was a distinct and satisfying crunch as the toe of his shoe caught the thug accurately in the side of the temple.

The man folded quietly to the ground and lay face down in the dirt.

Simon was leaping down for the clincher even while his opponent was falling, but no further effort was necessary. The scooter jockey had lost all interest in his mission, and would not be likely to regain it for a long time.

The Saint swiftly took possession of the half-drawn automatic, and tucked it inside his shirt under the waistband of his trousers where his belt would hold it in place. Then he ran through the man's other pockets, and came up with a switch-blade knife and a well-stuffed wallet. He looked up from it to find that his travelling companion had clambered down from the cart and was staring with mounting bewilderment at the sundry components of the scene.

"What is this all about?" pleaded the cart-driver distractedly.

Simon faced his next problem. The old man would inevitably be grilled by the Mafia before long, and he was likely to have an uncomfortably hard time absolving himself of complicity in the Saint's escape. Unless he was provided with evidence that would convince even the hard-boiled *mafiosi* that he was only another hapless fellow-victim of the Saint's lengthening list of atrocities.

There was an inordinate number of five-thousand-*lire* notes in the wallet, besides other denominations, and Simon extracted four of them and tucked them away under a sack of melons in the cart, while the driver gaped at him.

"If I gave those to you now, they might search you and find them," he said. "Say nothing about them, and leave them there until you get home. Also, when you are questioned, remember how I jumped on your cart and forced you to let me stay there. Now, I am sorry to repay you so unkindly, but it will hurt you less than if the Mafia thought you had helped me."

"What is this talk of the *Mafia?*" muttered the

other blearily, swaying a little.

"Look at those birds in the sky," said the Saint, steadying him; and as the man raised his chin he hit him under it as crisply and scientifically as he knew how.

The driver crumpled without a sound into another peaceful siesta.

For a second time Simon was tempted by the scooter, purely for its ground-covering potential; and now he might be able to afford a little time to unravel its mechanical secrets. But nothing less than a major operation would silence it, and he was still in a situation where stealth seemed to offer more advantages than speed.

He fired a single shot into its gas tank to eliminate it from further participation in the pursuit, and set off again at a mile-eating trot that tried to ignore the heat.

The mountain road twisted and doubled back upon itself like a tortured serpent. At some of the turns, when no unscaleable cliff or other geological barrier intervened, a rough footpath short-circuited the loop for the benefit of pedestrians. The Saint took advantage of all of them without slackening speed, although some of them dropped at forty-five degree angles and any slip might have meant violent injury.

The slopes were broken and rough, with little but cactus and thorny bushes holding their superficial shale together, and twice he picked his own route across the pebble-strewn beds of gullies gouged by torrents of some mythical rainy season rather than following even the slightly more cautious trail worn by previous short-cutters.

He was in the middle of one of these when he

heard the anguished whine of an automobile's straining gear-box coming up the valley from below, and he did not need to call on his clairvoyant gifts to divine that no innocent tourist conveyance would be in such a screaming rush to get to the drab *cittadina* at the head of that forsaken gorge.

There was no cover in the flat stream bed, and he would be instantly noticeable from anything crossing the stone bridge forty yards away. The bridge itself offered the only possible concealment, but that meant running towards the approaching car with the certainty of being still more conspicuous if he failed to win the race. Simon sprinted with grim determination, the loose rocks spurting from under his feet and the shrill grind of the car coming closer with terrifying rapidity. He dived under the shadow of the bridge's single arch only a heart-beat before the car rumbled over it and yowled on up the grade.

The Saint allowed himself half a minute to be sure it was out of sight, and to let the heaving of his lungs subside. Then he climbed the bank to the road above.

His decision not to try to help himself to the scooter had vindicated itself even more promptly than he had anticipated.

But now, through a gap in the hills ahead, he could see the benign blue Mediterranean less than a mile away.

It was only a question of whether he could reach it before the hunters turned around and overtook him again.

VI

How the Saint enjoyed another Reunion and Marco Ponti introduced Reinforcements

Simon knew how far he had come from where he had abandoned the cart, and could figure how long it would take the second automobile to climb to that spot. In his mind's eye, as he ran, he saw the car braking, the examination of the sleeping scooterist, the reviving and questioning of the peasant. In that way he kept a sort of theoretical clock on the progress of developments behind him against which he could continuously measure his chances of reaching the coast before the pursuit turned their car around—in itself a substantially time-consuming maneuver on that narrow road—and set off to overtake him. And his spirits rose with every stride as his glimpses of the sea came closer and the picture in his mind was still not frantically ominous.

Even in his athletic prime he would have had to leave the four-minute mile to the specialists, but on a downhill course and under the spur of life preservation he thought he could come close. And on the highway there would be buses and trucks, and beside it the coastal railway as well . . .

Every run of bad cards must have a break, however brief, as every gambler knows; and as the Saint reached the main road at last, and his visualization of the most imminent menace still had the warriors up the hill only now looking for a place to turn their oversize chariot, it seemed to him that his turn was veritably setting in. For less than a hundred yards away on his right, a heavily laden *autobus* was grinding noisily towards him, with the inspiring name PALERMO on the front to indicate its destination.

There were no other vehicles in sight at this moment, and no surly characters with artillery in their pockets to bar his way. The next steps towards escape only had to be taken across the highway, and called for no additional effort beyond flagging down the driver.

Brakes protested, and the bus lurched to a stop. Simon climbed in, the door slammed behind him, and he was on his way again.

But as he paid his fare, he felt that his arrival was causing a minor stir among the passengers. It was a local bus, and the riders seemed to consist mostly of regional habitants and their produce, progeny, and purchases. Perhaps that was the cause of their interest: the Saint was a stranger and obviously a different type, and for lack of anything better to do they would study and speculate about him. Yet there seemed to be an undercurrent of tension running counter to this simple bucolic curiosity. Unless he was excessively self-conscious, he felt as if the other passengers were allowing him far more room than they gave each other. In fact, he had a distinct impression that they were moving as far away from him as the packed conditions would allow.

Considering the aromas of garlic and honest sweat which pervaded the interior in multiple combinations with other less readily recognizable perfumes, it was somewhat disturbing to speculate on what exotic odor he might be diffusing about which even the best Sicilian wouldn't tell him. Perhaps he was being unduly sensitive; but the events of that day and the previous night would have undermined anyone's confidence in his popularity or social magnetism.

He tried his most innocent and endearing smile on one of the women nearest to him, who was staring into his face with a fixed intensity which suggested either extreme myopia or partial hypnosis, and she crossed herself hurriedly and squirmed back into the engulfing crowd with a look of startled panic.

He hadn't been imagining things. Someone had already identified him, and the whispered word had been passed around.

The fact could be read now in the tense lines of their bodies, their petrified immobility or nervous fidgeting, and the way their eyes fastened on him and then slid away when he looked in their direction. The Saint's description had clearly been circulated throughout the entire district, with promises of reward for finding and/or threats of punishment for hiding him, and in every crowd there was likely to be one who had heard it.

There didn't seem to be any Mafia hirelings on the bus itself, or they would already have gone into action; but he could expect no allies either. None of these people might actively try to attack him, nor would they give him any aid or comfort. Even if they were not sympathizers with the Mafia, they had been terrorized for so long that they would do exactly what the organization had ordered.

The bus ground protestingly up the grades and clattered recklessly down the alternating slopes that made up for them, obedient to the latent death-wish of the normal Italian driver; and with each kilometer the suspense drew tauter, but not from the inherent uncertainties of Sicilian public transportation.

Sometimes the conveyance stopped to pick up new travellers or to let others off; and Simon did not need extrasensory perception to know that as soon as telephones could be reached the wires would be humming with reports of his sighting.

And at each stop there was a rearrangement of seating and standing room, until there were only men around him, uneasy but grim. He wondered how much longer it would be before one of them might be tempted to try for a medal, and he moved his hand to rest it near the butt of the gun under his shirt.

If the pressure seemed to be creeping too close to an explosion point he would have to get off before Palermo. It might be a wise precaution in any case. He had no idea how long the full trip would take, but it would certainly be long enough for a welcoming delegation to muster at the terminus. The equation of survival that had to be solved required a blind guess at the unknown length of time he could stay with the bus to gain the maximum escape mileage, before warnings telephoned ahead would have a reception committee assembled and waiting for him at the next stop.

He had been keeping most of his attention on the other riders, who had packed themselves closer to suffocation in their desire to keep beyond contamination range of him, but he had been careful to reserve some portion of his awareness for the outside world through which they travelled. He was not concerned with noting all the spots of scenic interest, but with observing any other vehicles whose occupants might evince unusual interest in the one he rode in. And now his circumspection suddenly paid off. A large American sedan pulled around from behind the bus with a screaming horn, as if to pass it, and then simply stayed level with it, while swarthy faces carefully scanned the interior.

Trying not to make any sharp conspicuous movement, Simon edged farther towards the opposite side, bending his knees and slumping his spine to diminish his height, and trying to keep the heads of other passengers between the parallel car and the smallest segment of his face which would let him keep an eye on it and its occupants.

It was a good try, but there was a typically neutralist consensus against it. As his fellow travellers also became aware of the car keeping alongside, they separated and shrank away, either as a pharisaic way of pointing him out without pointing, or to remove themselves from the line of fire if there was to be any shooting. Either way, the result was disastrously the same. A lane opened up across the bus, with passengers trampling each other's corns on both sides but leaving a clear space between Simon and the windows. Even the seated riders found themselves suddenly irked by the burden on their buttocks, and got up to join the sardine pack of standees.

Simon Templar, willy-nilly, was given as un-obstructed a view of the men in the car as they were given of him.

But after the first glance there was only one face that held his attention: the face of the man in front, beside the driver. A fat, reddened, unshaven face that cracked in a lipless grin like a triumphant lizard as the recognition became mutual.

The face of Al Destamio.

Simon wished he had been wearing a hat, so that he could have raised it in a mocking salute that seemed to be the only possible gesture at the moment. Instead, he had to be content with giving his pursuer a radiant smile and a friendly wave which was not returned.

Destamio's exultant travesty of a grin was replaced by a vindictive snarl. The barrel of an automatic appeared over the sill of his open window, and he steadied it with both hands to aim.

The Saint's smile also faded as he snatched the pistol from his belt and ducked to shelter as much of himself as possible below the dubious steel of the bus's coachwork. He had no misgivings as to who would be the victor in a straight shoot-out under those conditions; but when Destamio's henchmen chimed in, as they would without caring how many bystanders were killed or injured in the exchange, a lot of non-combatants were likely to become monuments to another of the perils of neutralism. And pusillanimous as they might have shown themselves, and perhaps undeserving of too much consideration, Simon had to think of the consequences to himself of a lucky score on the bus driver at that speed.

The problem was providentially resolved when Destamio suddenly disappeared. His startled face slid backwards with comical abruptness, taking the car with it, as if it had been snagged by some giant hook in the pavement; it took Simon an instant to realize that it was because the driver had been forced to jam on his brakes and drop back to avoid a head-on collision with oncoming traffic. No sooner had the sedan swung in behind the bus than an immense double-trailered truck roared by in the opposite direction, followed by a long straggle of weaving honking cars that had accumulated behind it.

The Saint didn't wait to see any more. His guardian angel was apparently trying to outdo himself, but there was no guarantee of how long that inordinate effort would continue. He had to make the most of it while it lasted—and before a break in the eastbound lane gave the Mafia chauffeur a chance to draw level again.

Through the broad windshield could be seen the outskirts of a city, and a cog-wheeled sign whipped by with its international invitation to visiting Rotarians, followed by the name CEFALÙ. Now he knew where he was, and it would do for another stage.

As he pushed towards the front again, and the door, one of the men in a seat behind the driver was leaning forward to mutter something in his ear, and the bus was slowing.

"There is no need to stop," Simon said clearly. "No one wants to get off yet."

He was in the right-hand front corner by then, one shoulder towards the windshield and the other towards the door, and the gun in his hand was for everyone to see but especially favored the driver.

"I am supposed to stop here," the man mumbled, his foot wavering between the accelerator and the brake.

"That stop has just been discontinued," said the Saint, and his forefinger moved ever so slightly on the trigger. "Keep going."

The bus rumbled on, and its other passengers glowered at the Saint sullenly, no longer trying to avoid his gaze, plainly resenting the danger that he had brought to them more violently and immediately than if he had been the carrier of a plague, but not knowing what to do about it. Simon remained impersonally alert and let his gun do all the threatening. Everyone received the message and declined to argue with it; the driver stared fixedly ahead and gripped the wheel as if it had been a wriggling snake.

From behind came repeated blares from the horn of the following sedan, and fresh sweat beaded the driver's already moist forehead. Through the length of the bus and over the heads of the other riders, Simon could catch glimpses of the sedan hanging on their tail and fretting for a chance to draw alongside again, but the increasing traffic of the town gave it no opening. And in the longitudinal direction, the passengers who were now crowded into the rear two-thirds of the bus could not open up a channel through which the Saint could be fired at from astern. Yet with all its advantages, it was a situation which could only be temporary: very soon, a traffic light or a traffic cop or some other hazard must intervene to change it, or the pursuing *mafiosi* would become more desperate and start shooting at the tires.

Simon decided that it was better to keep the initiative while he had it. He threw a long glance at the road ahead, then turned to wave the passengers back into submission before any of them could capitalize on his momentary inattention.

"Put your foot over the brake," he told the driver, "but do not touch it until I tell you to. Then give it all your weight—which can be alive or dead, as you prefer."

He had photographed the next quarter-mile of road on his memory, and now he waited for the first landmark he had picked to go by.

"Hold on tight, *amici*," he warned the passengers. "We are going to make a sudden stop, and I do not want you to fall on your noses—or on this very hard piece of metal."

Again, through a momentary opening in the crowd, he glimpsed the trailing sedan edging out behind the left rear corner. And the wine-shop sign he had chosen for a marker was just ahead of the driver. The timing was perfect.

"*Ora!*" he yelled, and braced himself.

The brakes bit, and the bus slowed shudderingly. The standing passengers stumbled and collided and cursed, but miraculously held on to various props and managed to avoid being hurled down upon him in a human avalanche. And from the rear came a muted crash and crumpling sound, accompanied by a slight secondary jolt, which was the best of all he had hoped for.

The bus had scarcely even come to a complete standstill when he reached across the driver and in a swift motion turned off the ignition and removed the key.

"Anyone who gets out in less than two minutes will probably be shot," he announced, and pulled the lever that controlled the door next to him.

Then he was out, and one glance towards the rear confirmed that the Mafia sedan was now most satisfactorily welded to the back of the bus which it had been over-ambitiously trying to pass. Its doors were still shut, and the men in it, even if not seriously injured, were apparently still trying to pick themselves off the floor or otherwise pull themselves together. The car itself might or might not be out of the chase for a considerable time, but the bus solidly blocked any vehicular access to the alley across the entrance of which it had parked itself with a symmetry which the Saint could not have improved on if he had been driving it himself.

He had put the pistol back in his waistband under his shirt during the last second before he stepped out of the bus, so that there was nothing to make him noticeable except the fact that he was walking briskly away from the scene of an interesting accident instead of hurrying towards it like any normal native. But even so, those who passed him were probably too busy hustling to secure a front-row position in the gathering throng to pay any attention to his eccentric behavior.

He strode down the alley to where it crossed another even narrower passage, flipped a mental coin, and turned left. Half a block down on the right, a youth in a filthy apron was emptying a heaped pail of garbage into one of a group of overflowing cans, and went back through the battered door beside them, which emitted an almost

palpable cloud of food and seasoning effluvia
before it closed again. The Saint's nostrils twitched
as he reached it: scent confirmed sight to justify the
deduction that it was the back door of a restaurant,
which had to have another more prepossessing entrance on the other side. Without hesitation he
opened the door and found himself in a bustling
steaming kitchen, and still without a pause he
walked on through it, as if he owned the place or
owned the proprietor, with a jaunty wave and an
affable *"Ciao!"* to a slightly perplexed cook who
was hooking yards of spaghetti from an enormous
pot, heading for the next door through which he
had seen a waiter pass. It took him straight into the
restaurant, where other waiters and customers disinterestedly assumed that he must have had business in the kitchen or perhaps the men's room and
hardly spared him a second look as he ambled pur-
posefully but without unseemly haste through to
the front entrance and the street beyond.

Three or four zigzagging blocks later he knew
that Al Destamio and his personal goon squad
would only pick up his trail again by accident. But
that didn't mean he was home safe by any means.
Unless they had all been knocked cold in the collision, which was unlikely, the Mafia knew now
that he was in Cefalù, and the size of the town
would not make it any less of a death trap than the
last mountain village.

The only remedy was to leave it again as soon as
possible.

He noted the names of the cross streets at the
next intersection, then bought a guide book with
a map of the town at a convenient newsstand. He
quickly oriented himself and headed for the rail-

road station, hoping that he might catch a train there before the Ungodly reorganized and bethought them of the same move.

The station was swarming with a colorful and international jumble of tourists, besides the normal complement of more stolid population statistics going about their mundane business, and Simon merged himself with a boisterous group of French students who were heading for the platform entrance gates and a train that was just loading. He did not know its destination, but that was of secondary importance. It could only be Messina or Palermo, and either would do as long as he boarded unobserved. Fortune still seemed to be smoothing his way: the students were dressed very much like he was, and if necessary he could pass for French himself. Anyone who was not too suspicious could pass him over as their tutor or guide. Only a handful of *mafiosi* actually knew him by sight, and a mere verbal description would hardly be enough to single him out of the group he had joined. And the odds were encouragingly reasonable against the station being staked out by one of Destamio's hoods who had personally seen him before.

He had figured all that out to his own satisfaction just before he saw Lily standing by the barrier, at the same moment as she saw him.

2

In the fragment of a second between one step and the next, he marshalled and evaluated every possibility that could tie into her presence there, and

went on to adumbrate what could follow or be
filched from it. Coincidence he ruled out. Everything in her stance and positioning marked her as
watching for somebody, and it was too great a
stretch to imagine that that could be someone else.
Although the Saint had been thinking automatically in terms of masculine malevolence, she
was one of the very few in Destamio's immediate
entourage who had been qualified to pick him out
of any mob. But the sketchiest calculation showed
that she could not possibly have been sent there
since he abandoned the bus. She could only be part
of the general net that had been spread around the
area; but because she could positively identify him,
she had been given one of the most strategic spots.

Simon Templar put down his other foot with a
chilling respect for the murderous efficiency re-
demonstrated by the opposition, but knowing precisely how the score totalled at the instant that was
tearing towards him, and what alternatives he
could try to throw at it.

He continued to walk steadily towards her, as if
they had even had a rendezvous, with a smile that
not only did not falter but broadened as he came
nearer.

"Well, well, well," he murmured, with the lilt in
his voice which was always gayest when everything
around was most grim. "How long can it be since
we met? It seems like a million years!"

He took her firmly by both hands and gazed
fondly into the gigantic opaque sunglasses trimmed
with plastic flowers. He wondered what her eyes
would be like when and if he ever saw them. Maybe she didn't have any. But at least the full red
mouth was concealed only by lipstick. He kissed it

for the second time, and it still tasted like warm paint.

"Don't scream, or try to pretend I'm insulting you," he said, without a change in his affectionate smile, "because if I had to I could break your nose and knock all your front teeth out before anyone could possibly come to your rescue. And it'd be a shame for a pretty face like yours to be bashed in like the wings of an old jalopy."

He kept hold of her hands, just in case, but the resistance he felt was light and only momentary.

"Why?" she asked, in that voice that throbbed monosyllables like organ notes, and with as little individual expression.

"You mean you weren't waiting for me here?"

"Why should I?"

"Because Al sent you."

"Why?"

It was a perfect defense—in terms of the Maginot Line. He laughed.

"Don't tell me you've forgotten the last message I asked you to give him. You did deliver it, didn't you?"

"Yes."

"Well, you know how Al is about these things. He's been trying to get even ever since. Didn't he tell you why he wanted you to put the finger on me?"

"No."

"You tripped, Lily," said the Saint quietly. "So you *are* here to point me out to the mob, and not just to see who else you could pick up in your new clothes."

In deference to the conventions of an ordinary Italian town, she was wearing a full wraparound skirt that hid half the length of her sensational legs, but her upper structure was clearly limned by a sleeveless sweater that would have been barred at the doors of the Vatican.

"Where are the boys?" he asked, with an insistence that was outwardly emphasized only in the invisible tightening of his grip.

Her head moved a little as if she glanced around, but it was only an impression which could not be verified through those ornately floriferous blinders.

"I don't know what you mean," she said.

Without letting go of her, as if it were only an unconscious waltz step in a lovers' tryst, he had edged around to reverse their positions, so that his back was to the railings; but he saw no indication of any *mafiosi* closing in or watching for a cue to do so. And he was becoming increasingly fascinated by the fact that she still made no attempt to scream for help, legitimate or illegitimate. His threat might have checked her in the beginning— long enough to let him improve his strategic position and maneuver her obstructively into the line of fire—but by now she should have been thinking of some counter to that. Unless her mind was as completely barren as her dialog . . .

If there were any guns around, they must have been of very low caliber. But the wild idea grew stronger that there might not even be any. The railroad station at Cefalù was a way-out shot, a vague chance, the kind of improbable possibility that a doll might have been sent to cover, just for luck, but without giving her any heavy backing. It would be figured that if by some remote fluke he did show up there, she would be capable of latching on to him, overtly or covertly, until—

"We mustn't be seen here together," she said. "Can we go somewhere and talk?"

His hunch anchored itself solidly enough at that to provide a springboard for tentative exultation.

"Why not?" he said.

He turned her around and changed his grip more swiftly than she could have taken advantage of the instant's liberty. Now locking the fingers of her right hand in his left, with his arm inside hers holding it tight against his side, he steered her briskly towards the station exit, as firmly attached to him as if they had been Siamese twins. But she went along as obediently as a puppet; and if any of Destamio's men were waiting for a sign from her, they did not seem to get it.

He opened the door of the first cab on the rank outside, and followed her in without letting go her hand.

"I suppose you know this town," he said. "Where would be a safe place to go, where we won't be likely to run into Al or any of his pals?"

"The Hotel Baronale," she said at once, and Simon repeated it to the driver.

Obviously the Hotel Baronale was a prime place to avoid, but Simon waited till they had whipped around the next corner before he leaned forward and pushed a bill from his stolen roll over the driver's shoulder.

"I think my wife is having me followed," he said hoarsely. "Try to shake off anyone behind us. And instead of the Baronale, I think it would be safer to drop us at the Cathedral, if you understand."

"Do I understand?" said the chauffeur enthusiastically. "I have so much sympathy for you that it shames me to take your money."

Nevertheless, he succeeded in stifling his shame sufficiently to make the currency vanish as if it had been sucked up by a starving vacuum cleaner. But he also made a conscientious effort to earn it, with an inspired disregard for the recriminations of a few deluded souls who thought that even in Sicily there were some traffic courtesies to be observed.

Looking back through the rear window, Simon became fairly satisfied that even if any second-team goons had been backing up Lily at the station, which seemed more unlikely every minute, they were now floundering in a subsiding wake.

"What are you so afraid of?" Lily asked, ingenuously.

"Mainly of being killed before I'm ready," said the Saint. "I suppose I'm a bit fussy; but since it's something you can only do once, I feel it should be done well. I've been working up to it for years, but I still think I need a few more rehearsals."

His flippancy bounced off her like a sandbag off a pillow.

"It can only be Fate, meeting you again like this," she said solemnly. "I never thought it would happen. I thought of you, but I didn't know where to find you."

It was a long speech for her, and he regarded her admiringly for having worked it out.

"Why were you thinking of me?" he inquired, resigning himself to playing it straight.

"I've left Al. When I found out how much he was mixed up in, I got scared."

"You didn't know this when you took up with him?"

"I haven't been with him as long as that. I'm a

dancer. I was with a troupe doing a tour. I met him at a club in Naples, and he talked me into quitting. I liked him at first, and I wasn't getting on with the producer who booked the tour. Al took care of everything. But I didn't know what I was getting into."

In uttering so many sentences she was forced to give away clues to her mysterious accent; and with mild surprise he finally placed it as London-suburban cramped with some elocution-school affectations, and overlaid with a faint indefinable "foreign" intonation which she must have adopted for additional glamor.

"But if you've left Al, how did you get here to Cefalù?"

"I was afraid he'd catch me if I tried to get out of Italy by any of the ways he'd expect. You see, I took some money—I had to. I took the plane to Palermo and I thought I could take the next plane to London, but it was full up. There's only one a day. I was afraid to wait in Palermo, because Al has friends there, so I came here to wait till tomorrow."

The Saint had no way to know whether she was adlibbing or if her lines had been carefully taught her, but he nodded with the respectful gravity to which a good try was entitled.

"It's lucky that I ran into you," he said. "Luckier than you know, maybe. These men are dangerous!"

The cab shook as the driver spun it around another corner and braked it to a squealing halt in front of the Cathedral. Simon tossed another bonus into his lap, with the generosity which is best indulged from some other rogue's misappropriated roll, and dragged Lily quickly out and across the fronting pavement.

"Why do you come here?" she protested, tottering to keep up with him on her high stiletto heels.

"Because all cathedrals have side doors. If cab-driver got inquisitive, he couldn't cover all of them; and if anyone asks him questions, he won't know which way we went after he dropped us."

Inside, he slowed to a more moderate pace, and he noticed that he no longer seemed to have any resistance to overcome. He surmised that now she was temporarily parted from any protective hoodlums who may have been posted in the vicinity of the station—or the Hotel Baronale—she must feel that her most vital interest was to stay close to him rather than escape from him, for if she lost track of him now she might be in the kind of trouble that it was painful even to imagine. He felt free enough to take out his guide book and turn the pages, making like any swivel-eyed tourist.

"The columns," he said, cribbing brazenly from the book; "take particular note of the columns, because they're the handsomest you are going to see in a long while. And those capitals! Byzantine, by golly, intermixed with Roman, and all of them standing foursquare holding up those stilted Gothic arches. Don't they *do* something to you? Or anything?"

"We can't stay here," Lily said, with a suppressed seethe. "If you're in trouble with Al, you must get out of town too."

"What do you suggest?"

"If you're afraid of the railway, there is a bus station—"

"I came here on a bus," he said, "and something

happened that makes me feel that I'm probably *passeggero non grato* with the bus company."

"What, then?"

"I must think of you, Lily. I suppose you made a reservation on the plane to London tomorrow?"

"Yes."

"Then you daren't go back to Palermo. By this time, Al could have checked with the airlines and found out about it. So we can fool him by going the opposite way, to Catania. We can get a plane from there to Malta—and that's British territory."

"How do we get there?"

"You don't feel like walking?"

She gazed at him in silent disgust.

"Maybe it is a bit far," he admitted. "But if we try to rent a car, that's the next thing the Ungodly will have thought of, too. There must be something left that they won't think of—if I can only think of it . . ."

He riffled the pages of the guide book, fumbling for an inspiration somewhere in its recital of the antique grandeurs and modern comforts of the city. To lose themselves in a population of less than 12,000 was a very different problem from doing the same thing in New York or even Naples. But there had to be a solution, there always was.

And suddenly it was staring him in the face.

"I know," he said. "We'll go to the beach and cool off."

Lily's mouth opened in an expression not unlike that of a beached fish—an expression which the Saint had a fatal gift of provoking, and which always gave him a malicious satisfaction. With no intention of prematurely alleviating her bewilderment, he captured her hand again and led her down an aisle and out into a tree-shaded cloister. From there, a small gate let them out into what his map showed to be the Via Mandralisca, where he turned back in the direction of the sea.

Towing the baffled but obedient Lily beside him, he stopped at the first clothing store they came to and bought a knitted T-shirt in horizontal blue and white stripes and a pair of cheap sandals. He changed into them quickly in the next convenient alley, discarding his former soiled shirt and scuffed shoes in the nearest trash barrel. A little farther on, at a cubicle of tourist superfluities overflowing on to the sidewalk, he acquired a pair of sunglasses and a huge garish straw bag which he gave Lily to carry.

Only a block from the approaching vista of blue Mediterranean, he made a last stop at a well-stocked *salumeria,* where an apparently unsuspicious proprietor was delighted to wrap bountiful packages of cheese, ham, sausage, artichoke hearts and ripe olives, together with a loaf of crusty bread and a flagon of the sturdy purple Corvo that would agreeably moisten their passage. These were all stowed in the capacious sack with which he had thoughtfully provided Lily.

"What is all this for?" she queried plaintively.

"For either of us who gets hungry. It might be late before we get a proper dinner."

None of the shopkeepers he had patronized seemed to have been alerted; or perhaps Destamio's grapevine had been too busy trying to block the more obvious exits, so far, to diffuse itself over the general prospect. At any rate, they reached the beach without any alarming signals registering on Simon Templar's ultrasensitive antennae, looking like any other tourist couple

among the clutter of humanity that was reclining
or romping according to age and temperament.

Once among them, he made himself even more
typical and less memorable by peeling off his T-
shirt, putting it with the sandals in the catchall bag,
and rolling his trousers up to the knee. His bronzed
torso matched the most common tint of the other
vacationers; and even if his musculature was considerably more striking than the average, it was not
outstandingly different from that of any weight-lif-
ting beach boy. There was nothing much else about
him for anyone to notice or describe.

Lily was a little more difficult to camouflage, but
he made her roll her sweater up above her midriff
until it was almost a brassiere, and unbutton her
skirt to bare the maximum length of thigh as she
walked barefoot like himself, with her shoes joining the other discards in the big bag. She had already tied up her dazzlingly bleached hair in a scarf,
at his suggestion, while he was changing his shirt.

So they completed their crossing of the beach as
reasonable facsimiles of any two commonplace
holiday-makers, hand in hand, to the water's edge
where there were drawn up some of the Mediterranean's most popular pleasure craft, those
companionable catamarans made just for a couple
to sit in side by side and pedal themselves lazily
around with the aid of the paddle-wheel housed between the pontoons. Practically, however, they can
be propelled faster and much more effortlessly
than the ordinary rowboat, and are far more sea-
worthy and comfortable in moderately messy
weather; and in fact it was the guide book's mention of this littoral attraction which had led him
there.

The concessionaire came to meet them as they

arrived, beaming with mercenary optimism.

"*Che bellissimo giorno, signore!* And a beautiful afternoon for a ride in a *moscone*. This is the best time of day!"

"It is late," Simon said dubiously. Any appearance of urgency or eagerness might kindle suspicion if there were already a spark for it to fan, and in any case would be sharply remembered later. "There will not be much more sun."

"It is only the middle of the afternoon!" protested the operator, waving his arms to the heavens for witness. "And when the sun is going down, it is nice and cool. Besides, I will make you a special price."

"How much?"

There followed the inevitable formality of bargaining, and a price was finally agreed on to cover the remaining duration of daylight. Simon paid it in advance.

"In case we are a little late," he said with an elaborate wink, "you will not have to wait for us."

The man grinned in broad fraternity.

"*Capito! Grazie! E buona sorte!*"

Simon handed Lily into her seat, and helped the proprietor push the paddle-cat into the water before he hopped nimbly aboard and took the tiller, turning their twin prows westward as he began to pedal in unison with her.

It was all he could do to refrain from laughing out loud. Behind him, the town would be swarming with Destamio's minions: he formed a whimsical picture of them pouring in from all directions until they outnumbered both natives and tourists. The railroad station was probably infested with them by now, and likewise the bus depot; unless

Destamio's car had hit the bus harder than it sounded, he could have organized coverage of every outlying road and even footpath, and even the little port might not have been overlooked; but Simon was joyfully prepared to bet his life that he had hit on the one possible exit that a serious-minded creep like the former Dino Cartelli would never think of until it was too late. It had become a truly Saintly escape, outrageous in its originality—and now spiked with a bonus that he would not have tried to incorporate in his dizziest dream.

"Isn't Catania the other way?" she said after a while.

"You're brilliant," he assured her reverently. "This is the way to Palermo. The *moscone* merchant has to see us going this way. All the clues should keep pointing to Palermo. Only you and I know where we're really going."

When they were far enough out for their features not to be recognizable to the naked eye, but not so far that it would look as if they were setting out on a major voyage, he held a course parallel with the coast, searching the shore line for a special kind of topography that would lend itself to what he had in mind. It was not too long before he found it: a tiny cove floored with a half-moon of sand, not much wider than the length of a *moscone,* walled around with sheer cliffs rising twenty feet or more, and flanked by massive falls of rock so as to be almost inaccessible except from the sea. It was at least a mile from the nearest public beach.

Simon steered towards it, appreciating its advantages more and more as it came closer, and kept on pedalling until the pontoons grounded gently on the sand. He jumped off and held Lily's hand to balance her as she walked along a pontoon to step off daintily without wetting her feet; then he hauled the boat higher to secure it from being dislodged by the gently lapping wavelets, off-loaded the bulging bag, and sat down with it above the high-water mark.

Lily stared down at him in blank befuddlement. "You're not going to stay here?"

"Only until after sunset. Then we can double back past Cefalú again and keep heading towards Catania. We'll pedal far enough to get well outside any cordon that Al may have thrown around here, and slip ashore somewhere in the dark." He patted the sand beside him invitingly. "Meanwhile, it's nice and shady here, and we've got everything we need to ward off death by thirst or starvation. Why not enjoy it?"

She sat down, slowly, while the Saint uncorked the wine, which he had kept well wrapped in the bottom of the bag for insulation from the sun and warmth, and poured some into the small plastic tumblers which the *negoziante* had efficiently added to his bill.

"I guess we're in this together now, Lily," said the Saint. "I'll get us out of it, though. Just stick with me. I can't help feeling responsible, in a way, for the trouble between you and Al, but I'll try to make up for it."

She gave him a long impenetrable scrutiny in which he could feel wheels revolving as in a primitive adding machine. There was only one arithmetical conclusion that they could reach, but the fringe benefits could transcend the limitations of mechanical bookkeeping.

He waited patiently.

"To hell with Al," she said finally. "I like you much better, anyway."

After the warm paint was washed off with enough food and wine, there was nothing wrong with her lips at all.

3

When the brief twilight had turned to dark, the Saint stood up and dusted off his pants.

"All good things come to an end," he said sadly. "It's been wonderful, but I've got to be moving on."

It had become cool enough, when he was away from her, for him to be glad to put on his T-shirt again, while she rearranged the scarf over her hair. He also took his sandals out of the bag and carried them to the *moscone,* where he put them on the bench between the seats. Then he lifted the forward end of the nearest pontoon and pushed until the craft was well afloat again.

Lily came down to the edge of the water, carrying the bag.

"Just a minute," he said smoothly.

She stood still, while he climbed aboard and settled in the starboard seat. He put his feet on the pedals and took a tentative turn backwards, making sure that his weight hadn't taken the shallow draft down to the sand again.

"I hate to do this, Lily," he said, "but I'm not taking you any farther. If you get chilly, pile some sand on yourself—it'll keep you warm. There'll be plenty of boats around in the morning that you can hail. I wouldn't try to scramble out over the rocks tonight—you don't have the right shoes for it, and in the dark you'd be likely to break a leg."

"You're crazy," she gasped.

"That has been suggested before," he admitted. "And some people have thought I'd fall for the goofiest stories. But your yarn about how you got to Cefalù and just happened to be loafing around the station was stretching the long arm of coincidence right out of its socket, even for me. I only went along with the gag because I didn't have any choice. But I still say thanks, because it helped me out of a tough spot."

If he needed any confirmation of his analysis, he had it in the name she called him, which cannot be quoted here, in deference to the more elderly readers of these chronicles.

"You're a naughty girl, Lily," he said reproachfully. "You didn't see anything wrong with trying to finger me for the Mafia, and you'd have been just as ready to do it in Catania, and turn your back while they mowed me down. If you want to play Mata Hari, you should be a good sport about losing your bait."

Sometime about sunset he had taken off her glasses, and verified that she actually had eyes—smoky gray ones, which by then were deliciously sleepy. Now he could no longer distinguish them in the gloom; which made liars of a whole school of authors, who he was certain would have described them as spattering sparks and flame.

She kept coming forward, regardless now of splashing into the sea over her ankles and then to the depth of her streamlined calves; and he prudently back-pedalled enough to keep the *moscone* always retreating beyond her reach.

"It's an awful long swim back," he cautioned her, "unless you're in the Channel-crossing class. And nasty things come out in these waters at night, like slimy eels with sharp teeth. It's not worth it, honestly. I'm sure Al will understand."

She stopped with the water up to her knees, screaming abuse with an imaginative fluency that was in startling contrast to her usual inarticulateness, while he backed up with increasing acceleration until he had put enough distance between them to be able to come forward again in a long turn past the cove and outwards.

"Don't spoil the memory, Lily," he pleaded as he went by. "I said thank you, didn't I?"

It was a wasted effort. Her invective followed him as far as her voice would carry, and made him wonder how a nice girl could have picked up that vocabulary.

He kept pointing towards the Pole Star until the shrieks faded astern, and then made a slow turn to the left.

Westwards. Towards Palermo. Not Catania.

It was an especially snide trick to add to the wrongs he had done Lily, after she had given so much to the Mafia cause, but he couldn't afford to be sentimental. Whenever she was rescued or made her own way to a telephone, she would swear that the Saint was making for Catania. And that could make all the difference to his first hours in Palermo.

His legs pumped steadily, at a rate which he could keep up for hours and yet which pushed the *moscone* along at its maximum hull speed, beyond which any extra effort would have achieved nothing but churning water. Nevertheless this terminal velocity was not inconsiderable, so far as he could judge from his impression of the inky water slipping past, for a vessel that wasn't designed for racing and relied only on muscular propulsion.

The slight evening breeze had dropped and the sea was practically dead calm. It was easy to navigate basically by keeping Polaris over his right shoulder. The twinkling illumination of small settlements on the coast, and occasional flashes of headlights on the highway, located the shore line; and he kept far enough from it to feel secure from accidental discovery by any headlights that might be turned capriciously out to sea.

Eventually, of course, when he figured that he had put enough miles behind him, he had to edge shorewards again. He had heard one train rumbling along the coastal track, and thought he had identified its cyclopean headlamp flashing between cuttings and embankments; he had to hope that the next one would not pass too soon, or be too far behind. He would be afraid to risk another bus, because the driver by that time might have heard of the adventure of another bus driver and be abnormally observant of all passengers; but a long wait at a train stop also had its hazards.

He made his final approach along a fair stretch of dark coast preceding the lights of another town, nursing the little waterbug in until the dim starlight found him a sheltered beach to run up on. He hauled the boat well up above the tide line, where it would be safe until the indignant owner could locate it, and stumbled over some rocks and through a stony patch of some unrecognizable cultivation to a road which led into the hardly less murky outskirts of the community.

The sign on the railroad station, which he located simply by turning inland until the tracks stopped him, and then following them, read CAMPOFELICE DI ROCCELLA; and the waiting room was deserted. Simon strolled in, studied the timetable on the wall, and purchased a ticket to Palermo. The next train was due in only ten minutes; and precisely on schedule it pulled in, hissed its brakes, discharged a handful of passengers, and clankingly pulled out again—a performance for which a certain Benito Mussolini once claimed all the credit.

There were only a few drowsy *contadini* and a couple of chattering families of sun-drenched sightseers aboard, and none of them paid any attention to the Saint during the hour's ride into Palermo.

Disembarking there was a fairly tense moment. He was not seriously expecting a *mafiosa* delegation of welcome, but the penalties of excessive optimism could be too drastic to be taken lightly. He stayed close to the tourist families, using the same technique that he had tried with the students at Cefalú, and hoping that anyone who had only a description to go by would dismiss him as one of their party. But his far-ranging gaze picked out no greeters or loiterers with the malevolent aspect of Destamio's goondoliers. The hue and cry was still far behind, apparently—and hopefully pointing in other directions.

Outside the station, he let himself be guided by the brighter lights and the busier flow of people, in order to melt as far as possible into the anonymous multitude, until the current drifted him by the kind of nook that he wanted to be washed into.

This was a small but cheerfully sparkling trat-
toria which provided him with a half-litre of wine
and the small change for a phone call. He rang the
number that Marco Ponti had given him, and knew
that the cards were still running for him when the
detective's own crisp voice answered the buzz, even
though it sounded tense and edgy.

"Pronto! Con chi parlo?"

"An old friend," said the Saint, in Italian, "who
has some interesting news about some older friends
of yours."

The phone booth is a refinement which has made
little progress in Sicily, and he was well aware of
the automatic neighborly interest of the *padrone*
and any unoccupied customer within earshot. Even
to have spoken a word of English would have
aroused a curiosity which could ultimately have
been fatal.

"Saint!" the earpiece rasped loudly. "What happened to you? Where are you! I was afraid you
were dead. An impossibly large Bugatti was reported abandoned in the country, and was towed
in here to the police garage. By a lucky accident I
took the job of tracing the owner—who told me
that *you* had hired it, and . . . Wait, what did you
say about friends of ours? Do you mean—"

"I do. The ones we are both so fond of. But tell
me first, where is the car now?"

"The owner came to the *questura* with an extra
set of keys and wanted to take it away with him,
but I did not want to release it until I found out
what had happened to you, in case it should be examined again for clues, so I had it impounded."

"Good! I was going to tell you to grab a taxi and
join me, but the Bugatti might be more useful. I

have a lot of news about our friends which would take too long to give you over the phone. So why not un-impound the Bug and drive it here? I am in a restaurant named *Da Gemma,* somewhere near the station—you probably know it. The food smells are making my mouth water, so I shall order something while I wait. But hurry, because I think we have a busy night coming up."

The only answer was an energized click at the other end of the line; and the Saint grinned and returned to his table and an assay of the menu for some sustaining snack. Enough time and exercise had intervened since his picnic with Lily to create a fresh appetite; and fortunately, late as it was getting by northern standards, it was not at all an exceptional hour for supper in the meridional tradition.

He was chasing the last juicy morsels of a tasty *lepre in salmi* around his plate with a crust of bread when he heard the reverberant gurgle of an unmistakable exhaust outside, and Ponti burst through the pendant strips of plastic that curtained the door. Simon waved him to the place on the other side of the table, where a clean glass and a fresh carafe of wine had already been set up.

"I did not come here to get drunk with you," the detective said, pouring himself a glass and draining half of it. "Be quick and tell me what has happened."

"Among other things, I have been conked on the head, kidnaped, shot at, and chased all over by an assortment of bandits who must have a real grudge against your Chamber of Commerce. But I suppose it would bore you to hear all my private misadventures. The part that I know will interest you involves the location of a *castello* where you can find, if you move quickly enough, a beautiful sampling of the directors of that Company in full session, along with the chairman of the board himself, whose name seems to be Pasquale.''

Although they were talking in low voices that could hardly have carried to the nearest occupied table, it still seemed circumspect to make certain references only obliquely.

"I know all about that meeting," Ponti said. "Everything, that is, except the location. Where is it?"

"I wouldn't know how to give you the address, but I could take you there." Simon refilled their glasses. "But you surprise me—you seem to know a lot more about this organization than you did the last time we talked."

"I should claim to have done some extraordinary secret research, but I am too modest. I owe it all to the sample of one of their products that was left in your car, the one that was designed to make the loud noise. You remember, there was a certain kind of signature on the plastic. I photographed it myself, and checked it against the identification files while the clerk was at lunch. The Fates smiled, for a change, and I discovered that the marks were made by a local dealer named Niccolo who has been accused of handling similar goods before, but of course was absolved for lack of evidence. I brought him in to the office myself and managed to question him privately."

"But I thought those people would never tell anything. The *omerta,* and all that. You yourself told me they would die before they talked."

"That is the rule. But it has been broken, usually

by women. In 1955, one Francesca Serio denounced four of these salesmen for putting her son out of business—permanently. They were sent to prison for life. In 1962 another, Rose Riccobono, who lost her husband and three sons to a vendetta with the same Company, gave us a list of more than 29 who were charged with controlling the business in her village. These women defied the penalty because of love, or grief. With Niccolo, I used another argument. An inspiration."

"Worse than death?"

"For him. And more permanent that torture."

"Do tell."

"I put a white coat on the old man who sweeps the building—a very distinguished old fellow, but weak in the head—and laid out a row of butcher knives, and one of the masks that are kept for tear gas. I told Niccolo that we were going to anesthetize him, very humanely, but unless he talked"—Ponti leaned forward and dropped his voice even lower, almost to a sepulchral depth— "he would wake up and find he had been castrated."

Simon regarded him with unstinted admiration.

"I felt there was a spark of genius in you, from our first meeting," he said sincerely. "So Niccolo talked."

"It is apparently common gossip throughout the organization that Don Pasquale's health will soon force him to retire. And when the chairman is on his way out, the other Directors gather to compete for the succession. In such a crisis, an organization becomes a little disorganized, and the opposition has a chance to compete against weakness. All I needed was to know the meeting place. If you know it, we can proceed. Shall we go?"

The detective's quietly controlled voice was a contrast to the creased urgency of his earnest old-young face. The Saint started to raise a quizzical eyebrow, and left it only half lifted.

"Whatever you say, Marco," he acquiesced, and looked around for a waiter and a bill.

In a few minutes they were outside, where the gleaming masterpiece of Ettore waited at the curb; but as Simon instinctively aimed himself towards the driver's seat, Ponti contrived to interpose himself quite inoffensively.

"You will allow me? It will be easier, since I know the way."

"To where?"

"What I learned from Niccolo was interesting enough for me to send a prepared message to Rome, which has resulted in a picked company of *bersaglieri* being flown into Sicily. I wanted to have some reliable help on hand whenever I completed the information I needed to use them. You are about to do that."

"Then I'm the one who knows the way."

"Not to where the troops are."

Simon nodded and went around the front of the car to crank it. It started as it had before, at the first turn of the handle, with an instancy which made electric starters seem like effete fripperies; and the Saint got in to the passenger seat.

"Do you intend to leave the police out of this altogether?" he asked, as they thundered away.

"I am the police," Ponti said. "But I do not know which others I can trust. If I tried to work through them there would be delays, confusions, and slow mobilization. By the time we got to this *castello* it would be empty. I knew this before I ever came to Sicily, and arrangements were made in Rome to have these soldiers prepared for an 'emergency maneuver' whenever I might need them."

"And you know that they are reliable?"

"Completely. Only their commander knows their mission here, but his men are absolutely loyal to him and would follow him into hell on skis if he ordered it. As far as we can tell they have not been penetrated by the Mafia, so they should look forward to the fun of roughing up these *canaglie*. Now tell me everything you have been doing."

4

Ponti himself was no slow-poke at the wheel, it turned out, and he spurred the giant Bugatti along at a gait which would have had many passengers straining on imaginary brakes and muttering silent prayers; but the Saint was fatalistic or iron-nerved enough to tell his story without faltering or losing the thread of it. The only things that he left out were certain personal details which he did not think should concern Ponti or affect his official actions.

"So," he concluded, "they should still think they have me cordoned in at Cefalú, and even when they hear from Lily they should believe I'm making for Catania. Anyhow they ought not to have felt that they have to vacate their headquarters in a hurry. They think I'm on the run and busy trying to save my own skin. And Al would never expect me to be talking to you like this."

"I have tried not to allow that impression," Ponti said, "by putting out an order that I want you for personal questioning about a political conspiracy. I did that partly to try to find some trace of you, of course, and to make sure that if you were picked up you would not be beaten up by some stupid cop who would take you for a common criminal. I have found that when any political implications are mentioned, the police are inclined to proceed with caution."

"When I think of some of my celebrated rude remarks about policemen," said the Saint, "your thoughtfulness brings a lump to my throat. And no one would dream you had an ulterior motive."

"I have only one motive—to show these *fan- nulloni* that they are not bigger than the law. And here we have the means to do it."

The treacherous mountain road over which they had last been bouncing ended at a gap in a wire fence guarded by a sentry with rifle and bayonet. As he barred the way, a young officer appeared out of the darkness and saluted when Ponti gave his name.

"Il maggiore L'aspetta," he said. "Leave your car over here."

There was no illumination other than the lamp over the gate and their own headlights, and when the latter were switched off they stumbled through rutted dirt until a vague hut shape loomed up before them. A door opened and a white wedge of light poured out; then they were inside the bare wooden building.

"Ponti," said an older officer in an unbuttoned field tunic, grasping the detective's hand, "it is good to know we shall have some action. Everything is ready. When shall we move?"

"At once. This is Signor Templar, who knows the location of our objective. Major Olivetti."

The commandant turned to Simon and acknowl-
edged the introduction with a crunching grip. The
top of his bald head hardly came to the Saint's
chin; but there was nothing small about him. He
had a chest like a barrel and arms like tree-trunks.
The right side of his face was a webwork of scars
that stood out clearly on his swarthy skin, and a
black patch covered that eye, which would have
given him a highly sinister appearance but for the
merry twinkle in the other.

"*Piacere!* I have heard of you, Signor Templar,
and I am glad to have you on our side. Over here
I have maps of all Sicily, on the largest scale. Can
you show me on them where we have to go?"

"I think so," said the Saint, and bent over the
table.

The lieutenant who had brought them from the
gate, together with another lieutenant and a sergeant who were already in the hut, joined Olivetti
and Ponti around the map and watched intently
while Simon traced his way over the contours from
the junction on the coast where he had caught the
bus to Cefalú, back up the dry river bed to the village and up over the mountain ridge to the other
valley and the combination of remembered land-
marks which enabled him to pinpoint the site of the
eyrie from which he had escaped.

"This road is unpaved," he said, running a fin-
gernail along the route down from the house. "I
haven't been on this upper stretch, but their car
came down it at speed with no trouble. I don't
know anything about this other road marked along
the top of the cliff."

Olivetti studied the terrain with professional
minuteness.

"On either road, there is a risk that they may

have outposts who would give warning of the approach of a force like ours. You mentioned descending this cliff in the dark. Could we send men up that way?"

"Even Alpine troopes, I think, would need to use pitons, and the hammering would make too much noise. I came down that way because I had to, and some of it was just dropping and sliding and hoping for the best."

"I could deploy my men from these points and let them make it on foot, but then I could not guarantee they would be ready to close in before dawn."

"I know there is no logical reason why this convocation should panic and pack up in the middle of the night," Ponti said, "but I must admit that each hour that we leave the trap open will make me more afraid of finding it empty when we close it."

"May I make a suggestion?" asked the Saint.

"Of course. You are the only one of us who has already seen this area in daylight."

"And I think it would be a commando's nightmare. On the other hand, if you got there and found that the birds had flown, I should feel sillier than anyone. So I think we should try for speed rather than stealth. Of course, I would try to cut all the telephone lines in the area—and apologize to the telephone company afterwards, otherwise some Mafia sympathizer among the operators would certainly send out a warning. But after that, I would move in as fast as possible, and hang the uproar. I take it your company is mechanized, *maggiore?*"

"*Si*. That is, we have no tanks, but we have trucks and troop carriers."

Simon pointed to the two roads to the Mafia hideout.

"Then if you split them into two units, and send one up by this road and one by this, timed to meet at the top—once they start, they themselves will be blocking the only roads that the mobsters could escape by, if they still *are* up there. However, if they find themselves cornered like that, the jokers might decide to fight rather than surrender. Are you prepared to go as far as a shooting war?"

"I should welcome it!" Olivetti bellowed, and struck the flimsy trestle table a great blow with his fist that threatened the support of its legs. "If Ponti has the authority—"

"That is quite a point," Simon admitted, turning to the detective. "Can you justify launching an offensive like this?"

Ponti showed his teeth in a vulpine grin.

"I can if you are not deceiving me, and unless you let me down. In which case I would do worse to you than I promised Niccolo. But on your testimony I have plenty to charge them with—assault, kidnaping, attempted murder. Then there is a very legalistic charge involving criminal intentions, which an assembly of persons of bad repute can be assumed to be plotting, in certain circumstances. But best of all would be if one of them does fire a shot at us—then we need no more excuses."

"So, it is decided," Olivetti said, with ebullient enthusiasm. "The *tecnici* will go out first, in pairs, on motorcycles. Then, look, the first and second *plotoni*—"

His subalterns and the sergeant crowded up to follow his pointings on the map as he developed the plan in greater detail; and Ponti caught Simon's eye and beckoned him away from the briefing.

"I imagine you would like to go back to your hotel and get some sleep, but that might be dangerous. Let me give you the key to my apartment. The Mafia will never look for you there. I will see you there after all this is over. You will have to identify the ones that we capture, and make a deposition to support the charges. The address is—"

Simon had already begun to shake his head, before he interrupted.

"There you go again, Marco, trying to kill me with kindness," he murmured. "It makes me feel an ungrateful bum to turn you down, but I have sat through too many acts of this opera to be eased out before the grand finale. I shall come along and be ready with more of my brilliant advice in case the military needs it."

"But you are a civilian. You do not have to expose yourself—"

"Someone should have told me that a few days ago. But now I still have those personal problems of my own which you know something about, and I want a chance to straighten them out before some trigger-happy *bersagliere* blasts away any hope of getting the answers. If you refuse me that little bit of fun, I might be so upset as to get an attack of amnesia, and be completely unable to identify any of your prisoners. Such things can happen to hysterical types like me."

"Your blackmail is shameful. But I am forced to bow to it. However, I take no responsibility for your safety, or for any legal trouble you may get into."

"You never did, did you?" said the Saint innocently.

The map-table conference broke up, and the lieutenants and the sergeant hurried out.

"Well, the operation will be rolling in eight minutes," Olivetti said. "The Company was put on full alert as soon as you telephoned, Ponti—and since then there has been no telephoning."

With a broad smile, he held up his huge hand and clicked a pantomime wire-cutter.

"I, too, take no chances," he said, and looked at the Saint. "I am glad you are going with us. It will help to have someone who knows the layout of this *castello*."

"He insists," Ponti said wryly. "He is afraid that he may become hysterical if he is left alone. He has been through a lot, you know."

"Now you try to explain that, Marco," Simon grinned, and went out.

He was checking the gas and oil in the Bugatti when the advance scouts set out, the wasp-whine of their Guzzi motorcycles splitting the still night. They were followed by the snore of truck engines grumbling into life.

Satisfied that his borrowed behemoth was still fuelled for any kilometrage that it was likely to be called on to cover, he was buckling down the hood when a Fiat scout car skidded to a stop beside him with all four wheels locked. Major Olivetti was at the wheel. In the rear seat, a lieutenant and the radio-man braced themselves stoically, being no doubt inured to their commander's mercurial pilotage; but in the other front bucket Ponti had his hands clamped to the dashboard with a pained expression which hinted that he might have preferred the vehicle which brought him to the camp.

"Follow my column," Olivetti bawled, "and join me when we stop. Do you want a gun?"

He proferred his own automatic.

"Thank you; but it must be illegal for foreign civilians in this country to possess military fire-arms. And in any case I already have an illegal weapon obtained from the Mafia. But don't tell your *poliziotti* friends."

Ponti opened his mouth, but whatever contribution he may have had in mind was not forthcoming, at least in Simon's hearing. For at that moment the grinning major snapped in the clutch, and the scout car vanished into the night with a jolt that could have whiplashed the necks of its occupants.

A column of trucks growled after it while Simon was winding up the Bugatti and turning it around. He fell in after the scout car that brought up the rear.

Strangely or naturally, according to which school of psychology you favor, he was not wondering how Lily was making out, but what had happened to Gina. Gina with the dark virginal eyes and the wickedly nymphic body and the young eagerness and unsureness, who was another part of the intricate house of Destamio, and who could be destroyed with it—if it had not already destroyed her first . . .

VII

How the Fireworks went Off
and Cirano turned up his Nose

It was a slow drive. Olivetti was obviously holding
their speed down in order to give the engineers the
half-hour's lead he had allowed for them. If his
timing was right, they should meet the motorcycle
advance guard at the exact moment scheduled for
the assault.

They saw nothing of the coast or the sea, since
the Major had wisely chosen to use only the interior roads that wound their way through the
mountains. For the most part these roads were
bad, and frequently they were terrible. Sometimes
when they branched off on to an unpaved track to
avoid a town, clouds of dust billowed up and swept
suffocatingly over the Bugatti. Simon stopped
more than once to let the worst of the dust settle,
and then caught up with the column again, having
no fear of losing it while there was still a trail of
powdery fog to trace it by.

This dilatory progress continued until after midnight, when Simon felt they could not be much
farther from the Mafia headquarters. They ground

through a darkened village, then up a precipitous track that appeared to have been scratched out of the face of a cliff.

Lights flashed in the Saint's eyes from his rear-view mirror as a car came up behind and blinked its headlights to pass. He pulled courteously over to the side, and at the same instant was possessed by a prickling presentiment of danger.

What possible reason could an ordinary car have for being on such a road at this time of night—and in enough of a desperate hurry to risk trying to pass a convoy of trucks on such a dangerous cornice? Only an errand of more than ordinarily reckless urgency. This did not ineluctably mean that the car was driven by Mafia sympathizers. But with the telephone wires cut, anyone who wanted to warn the Mafia headquarters of the approaching column would have to go by road. This road.

This reasoning went through the Saint's head in the brief moment during which the car was overtaking him, and as soon as it was past he swung out behind it and kicked on his high beams. They blazed out like twin searchlights and impaled a long open Alfa-Romeo, not new but obviously still capable of a good turn of speed. The driver kept his eyes on the road, but the man beside him turned, shading his eyes from the glare with the turned-down brim of a black hat.

Simon sounded a warning series of blasts on his horn to attract attention, and the officer in the scout car ahead was not stupid. He waved the Alfa-Romeo back as it started to pass him, and held up a gun to show that he meant business.

The reply from the Alfa-Romeo was in-stantaneous. The driver accelerated, and his companion produced a pistol and began firing at the scout car. The officer ducked down, and the Alfa-Romeo went safely by, staying in the scanty lane between the trucks and the sheer drop into the valley.

It was a long chance, but it looked as if they might get away with it. The trucks trundled stolidly along on the right-hand side of the trail, while the Mafia car tore up on their left, its wheels within inches of the unfenced verge. The scout car swung out of line behind it and raced in pursuit, the occupants of both cars exchanging shots, though neither seemed to be having any effect.

The end came with shocking suddenness as one of the truck drivers farther up the column became aware of what was occurring. He must have seen the flash of gunfire or heard the shots above the grinding of engines, and reacted with commendable intelligence and initiative. As the Alfa-Romeo came up to pass his truck, he edged out of line and narrowed the space between the flank of his vehicle and the edge of nothingness. The Mafia driver, crowded by the scout car immediately behind him, held down blaringly on his klaxon and made a frantic bid to squeeze through. The truck remorselessly held its course and hogged a little more. Finally the sides of the two vehicles touched, with much the same effect as a ping-pong ball grazing a locomotive. The Alfa-Romeo was simply flipped sideways off the road, and was gone. There was a delayed crash and a flash of fire from the ravine below, but the convoy had rolled on well beyond that point before the final reverberations could rumble up to its level.

This was the only crisis that disturbed the purely

figurative smoothness of the trip. Within minutes the road levelled out, and brake-lights glowed as the column ground to a halt. Major Olivetti's car roared back down the line and stopped beside Simon.

"The engineers are there, and report all the wires cut as ordered," he said. "We're ready to go in. According to the map, the house is only about a kilometer ahead. The scouts will go first and I will follow, and it would be best if you kept close to me. I must have positive identification of the house before there is any shooting."

He was away again before the Saint could do more than half-salute in answer. Simon gunned the Bugatti after the Fiat scout car and followed it down the road, until a motorcyclist waved them to a stop. They pulled off into an open orchard, and with instinctive prospicience Simon backed his car into a position from which it would be free to take off again in any direction. After this they continued on foot through the orchard, until the trees thinned out to disclose a house looming ahead across a clearing, blacked out and silent.

"Is that the place?" Major Olivetti asked.

"It could be," Simon answered. "I can't be absolutely certain, because I never saw it from this side. It looks something like the right shape. Does the location fit the description I gave you, on the edge of a cliff?"

"Perfectly. And the scouts report no other house near here that fits it. You can see the beginning of the road there that leads down to the village, gravel surfaced as you described it. Another column is down there, blocking any escape that way. We can go into action as soon as you are absolutely certain that this is the right place."

"Are all your men in position?"

"On all sides. The mortars should be down and sighted by now, the machine guns set up as well."

"Shall I go and ring their front door bell?" Simon asked, straightening up and taking a few steps into the moonlit clearing.

"Don't be a fool—get down! They can see you from the house!"

"That is precisely the idea," Simon said. "The people inside must have heard your trucks, and if they have guilty consciences they should now be keeping a rather jittery lookout."

He stood gazing intently at the building for several seconds, and then stepped back with exaggerated furtiveness behind a thick-trunked tree.

He had gauged the impression he would give, and its timing, with impudent accuracy. There was a rattle of gunfire from the house, and a covey of bullets passed near, some of them thunking into the tree.

"That seems to settle it," Simon remarked coolly. "And now that they've started the shooting, you have all the justification you need for shooting back."

With or without the reassurance of such legalistic argument, some of the deployed soldiers were already returning the fire. The house promptly sparkled with more flashes as its occupants accepted the challenge. Bullets whipped leaves from the trees and keened away in plaintive ricochets. Someone turned a spotlight on the building, and before it was shot out they could see that most of the heavy shutters on the windows were open for an inch or two to provide gun slits, and most of them seemed to be in use.

"Very nice," Olivetti said, crouching beside Simon and Ponti, "You ask me to help you make a raid on some criminals, but you did not tell me we should be fighting a minor battle."

"Mi despiace, Commandante," Ponti said. "I did not plan it this way."

"You are sorry? This is the best thing that could have happened! In the summer no skiing, and all they do is chase girls and drink. We shall sweat some of the wine out of them tonight! All I want to know is in what condition you want those men inside the house. If it is dead, it will be easy. Only there will be a certain amount of mortar fire necessary, and before entering rooms we would roll in a grenade or two. That way, there may be very few prisoners."

"There are some that I want alive," Ponti said. "The leaders only. The rest, your soldiers can practise their training upon, and save the courts much useless expense. But I want the men at the top, to identify them and bring them to a public trial which will focus the attention of the whole country. If they are only killed here they will become martyrs: the lesser leaders will take over, and the whole organization will soon be flourishing again."

Simon thought of reminding them that Gina Destamio might also be in the house, for all he knew. But if she were, the *mafiosi* themselves would protect her as much as they could, if only until they could use her as a hostage. And as a mere possibility it was too speculative to justify holding up the assault.

"That is more difficult, but we can try," Olivetti was saying. "I will blow open the front door and the ground floor windows, and we will rush them from three directions. We shall have some casualties, but—"

Suddenly headlights blazed on the far side of the house, and a car roared around the driveway and careened into the road. It was closely followed by another. Both were large sedans and apparently well manned, for their windows blazed with a crackle of small arms.

"Aim for the drivers!" bellowed the Major, in a voice that could be heard easily above the rising crescendo of gunfire. "Then we can take the others alive!"

The leading car drove straight at the front of the army truck which had been strategically parked across the road, without slackening speed, smashed into it, and burst into flame. Frantic men tumbled out and stumbled away from the flickering light. The second car braked violently, but not enough to lose all momentum as it crashed into the rear of the first. It then became clear that the whole sequence was deliberate: the first impact had slewed the truck around enough to leave a car's width between its bumper and the bordering stone wall, and the second car was now ramming the burning wreck of its companion through the gap.

Soldiers were running in from all sides now, firing as they came. It seemed impossible that the second car could still move: two of its tires were flat, and gasoline was pouring from its tank. Yet its rear wheels spun and gripped and it managed somehow to plough on, pushing the first car through with a horrible groaning and clanking of metal and making an open path for itself.

"Give me that!" roared the Major, and snatched

an automatic rifle from a trooper.

He scarcely seemed to aim, but the gun barked five times and glass flew from the driver's window. The man slumped over the wheel, and the car careered wildly down the road and smashed into a tree. Two passengers scrambled out and fled into the darkness.

"I want every one of those thugs," Olivetti shouted. "But only wounded. They can recuperate in a prison hospital."

"I don't think any of the leaders were in those cars," Simon said, coming up beside him. "They were only creating a diversion or clearing a way. We must look out for another break."

The accuracy of his hunch was proven at that instant by the black bulk of a third automobile that surged out of the driveway. It had obviously been parked around the same angle of the building as the first two cars, in a courtyard probably flanked by former stables, and its occupants had been able to embark with impunity during the distraction caused by the first sortie. In the light of the burning wrecks Simon recognized the car that had tried to chase him down the road after his escape: it had reminded him then of a bootlegger's limousine from the brawling days of Prohibition, and this resemblance turned out to be more than superficial. As it plunged forward the soldiers had a perfect target, and streams of automatic fire converged on it; but the windows were all shut and there were no answering shots.

"It's bullet-proof!" the Major howled in frustrated rage. "The tires—shoot off the tires!"

But even there the bullets had no effect: the tires must have been solid rubber. Not designed to give a featherbed ride, perhaps, but an excellent insurance against inopportune deflation. The car aimed at full speed for the space between the wall and the interlocked truck and trail-blasting sedan, and hurtled through with only a scraping of fenders. A storm of bullets dimpled its high square stern but did not penetrate. It rocketed away down the road.

"Tenente Fusco, take my scout car and get after that thing!" yelled the Major, jumping up and down with wrath. "Stop it with grenades if you can, but at least stay with it and keep in touch with me by radio. You others—how much longer must I wait for you to clean out that rats' nest?"

Men with trained reflexes leapt obediently to their assignments. A mortar, already ranged in, exploded a shell against the front of the building, and a yawning hole appeared where one of the shuttered windows had been. The scout car was already bouncing on to the road when Simon grabbed hold of Ponti, who seemed momentarily petrified with indecision as to which unit he should be joining.

"Come with me!" snapped the Saint. "The soldiers will take care of the house—but I bet nobody is left there who would interest you much." He hustled the dazed detective into a run as he talked. "The big shots are in the car that got away—and the Bugatti has more chance of catching it than a Fiat."

The Bugatti growled with delight as he aroused it to life again, and as soon as Ponti was beside him he slammed it forward in a bank-robber's take-off, using the violent acceleration to swing the doors shut. He went on to justify his boast of its speed by thundering past Lieutenant Fusco's command car while still in third gear, turning to wave mockingly as he went by.

The escaping limousine, for all its armored weight and overworked springing, was harder to catch, thereby vindicating at least a part of the Saint's prognosis, but after several minutes he caught it in his headlights as he came around a corner. As he started to overhaul it he saw something else, and switched his foot abruptly to the brake as little tongues of flame spat towards him and were followed by the whip-crack reports of cordite.

"Very neat," Simon said. "Real gang-war stuff. There is a firing port just under the rear window, I saw the gun muzzle when it poked out. Luckily the road is too bumpy for them to have much chance of scoring at this range, but they could do better if we came much closer. Now we shall just have to keep them in sight from a safe distance while you think of some plan to stop them."

2

Ponti muttered curses under his breath, but not far enough under to deprive Simon of some of the more picturesque imprecations. He looked back for the scout car, but they had already left it far behind and were almost certainly increasing their lead.

"We need grenades, at least. On one of these hairpin bends, we might lob one ahead of them. Perhaps we should slow down and wait for Lieutenant Fusco."

"And maybe never see our quarry again," retorted the Saint. "Have you noticed that the speedometer is reading around a hundred and fifty kilometers most of the time? At that speed, they only have to be out of sight for a couple of minutes at any crossroads, and we should be flipping coins to help us guess which way they went. That car may look as if it belongs in a museum, but so does this one, and you can see how un-decrepit we are. We simply can't afford to fall any farther behind than we have to to avoid stopping a bullet."

Ponti answered with a short pungent phrase which summed up the situation more succinctly than anything printable.

"I thoroughly agree," said the Saint sympathetically. "But it still leaves us nothing to do except follow them. So you might as well relax on this luxurious upholstery until your fine mind comes up with something more constructive."

There was obviously no simple solution. They were in something like the classic predicament of the man who had the tiger by the tail. There seemed to be no way to improve the hold; and although letting go might be less disastrous, it was an alternative which neither of them would consider for a moment.

"Eventually they must run out of gas," Ponti said, not too optimistically, as he watched the tail light weaving down the road ahead of them.

"And so must we. Of course, if it happens to them first, you and I can surround them."

Simon Templar was in much better spirits, perhaps because he had had more opportunities in his life to become acclimated to tiger-tail-holding. From his point of view, the night so far had been a howling success. The Ungoldly were on the run,

and he was right behind them, goosing them along.
The next move might be a problem; but so long as
nothing as yet had positively gone wrong, everything should be considered to be going well. The
dying autocrat whom he had seen was probably
dead by now: even if nature had not taken its
course, he would have been in no condition to be
moved, and could likely have been helped over the
last step out of this vale of tears rather than left to
be captured. Certainly the men in the scudding carriage ahead could only be the most vigorous and
determined aspirants to the throne. And among
them was surely Al Destamio—or Dino Cartelli—
the man who was the main reason for Simon's involvement in the affair.

He refused to believe that Fate would cheat him
of a show-down now . . .

There was a faint smile on the Saint's lips, and a
song in his throat that only he could hear above the
drone of the motor.

Crossroads flashed by, and occasional tricky
forks, but Simon followed the limousine through
them all. It could not outdistance him or shake him
off. Most of the time he stayed maddeningly just
out of hand-gun range, but he always managed to
creep up when it counted most and when the
rough-riding swings of the pursued car made it
least risky. What he feared most was a lucky hit on
a tire or the Bugatti's radiator, but none of the
fugitive's erratic shots found such a mark. It did
not seem to occur to the Saint that he could be hit
himself, though one bullet did nick the metal frame
of the windshield and whine away like a startled
mosquito with hi-fi amplification.

Another village loomed up, lining a straight

stretch of road that the limousine's headlights showed clear for a quarter of a mile ahead. The limousine seemed to slacken speed instead of accelerating, and Simon eased up on the throttle and fell even farther behind.

"What's the matter?" Ponti fumed. "This is your chance to pass them!"

"And have them nudge us into the side of a building?" Simon said. "Either that, or have a nice steady shot at us as we catch up. No, thank you. I think that's just what they want to tempt us to do."

But for the first time his intuition seemed to have lost its edge.

The car in front braked suddenly, and swung into a turning in the middle of the village which made a right-angle junction with the main road—if such a term could be applied to the one they were on.

Simon raced the Bugatti towards the corner, but slowed up again well before he reached it and made the turn wide and gently, for it was an ideal spot for an ambush. The side road was empty, but in a hundred yards it made another blind curve to the left, and again Simon negotiated the turning with extreme caution. Again there was no ambush, but the black limousine was less than fifty yards ahead and putting on speed up a grade that started to wind up into the mountains. Simon could judge its acceleration by his own, as he revved up in pursuit and yet at first failed to narrow the gap between them.

Then as he whipped the Bugatti around another bend, and began to gain a yard or two, something clicked in his mind, and he laughed aloud with exultation.

Ponti stared at him in amazement.

"May I ask what is so funny?"

"The weird whims of Providence, and the philosophical principle of the Futility of Effort," said the Saint. "Here we are racking our brains to find a way to end the stalemate, and forgetting that the Ungodly must have been doing the very same thing. Now they have made their move, and I think I know what it was. Let us catch up and make sure."

"You are crazy! Just now you would not catch up because they would fill us with bullets!"

"But now I don't think they will. However, the only way to be sure is to try it—as the actress said to the bishop."

"I was a fool to ever have anything to do with you," Ponti said, taking out his gun and preparing to die with honor.

In a minute they screamed out of another turn only a couple of lengths behind the limousine, but there were no shots and the firing port remained closed. The full beam of the Bugatti's headlights blazed into the rear window of the car ahead as the road straightened.

"They are gone!" Ponti shouted incredulously. "It is empty except for the driver! Unless they are crouching down—"

Taking advantage of the straight stretch, Simon poured on the gas, and the Bugatti surged forward as if a giant hand had slapped it from behind.

"No, there is only the driver," he said calmly, as they thundered alongside. "And I think he is making the fatal mistake of lowering his window so he can shoot at us."

Ponti was prepared. He sat sideways, his left

hand cupped under his right elbow to steady it, and took careful aim. When the bullet-proof glass had dropped far enough, while the driver was still raising his own gun, Ponti's pistol barked once. The driver's head was slammed sideways and he flopped over the wheel. Simon braked quickly as the limousine veered wildly across the road, rolled over, and somersaulted crazily out of sight.

Still braking, Simon spotted a cart track on his right, spun into it, and backed out to face the way they had come. He stopped again, and got out.

"You can send for the body later," he said. "But now slide over and take the wheel. You are getting a second chance to enjoy driving this marvelous car."

"Why?" Ponti asked blankly, as Simon got in on the other side.

"Because two can play the trick that they thought of. Did you notice that it took them entirely too long to make that double jog out of the village, and how close we were behind them even though I deliberately slowed up? That was because they stopped for a moment while they were out of sight, and the passengers piled out, counting on the driver to lead us on a wild-goose chase through the hills."

Ponti had the Bugatti in gear and moving again by that time.

"Then they are probably still hiding in the village! We only have to locate the house—"

"And get mowed down when we do it. At one time I saw at least four passengers in that car, and wherever they went to earth is bound to be a nest of more *mafiosi*. No, you will have to go back and meet Fusco's scout car, and radio for reinforcements."

"And give those *fannulloni* time to slip away!"

"That is why I made you take the wheel. You will go through the village in low gear, making a terrific noise, and skidding your tires around the corners, so that they will hear everything and have no doubt that you went through without stopping. But actually as you come into the main street you will only be doing about fifteen kilometers an hour, and that is when I shall leave you. If they do try to slip away, I shall either follow them or try to detain them."

"It is an insane plan. What chance would you have?"

"What better chance do *we* have? Try to apply the power of positive thinking, Marco *mio*. Look on the bright side. This may be where the Ungodly are delivered right into our hands. And I feel lucky tonight!"

Running downhill, the dark outskirts of the village were before them surprisingly quickly, and the curve into the side street that would intersect the main road.

"Down into second gear," snapped the Saint. "Give them the full sound effects. With enough tire-squealing, exhaust-roaring, and gear-grinding, they should be convinced that you went through here like a maniac, and it will never occur to them that we are plagiarizing their brainstorm."

"I only hope," Ponti said gloomily, "That you know some rich industrialist who will give a job to an ignominiously discharged police officer, if there is not a happy ending to this night's work."

But he obeyed his instructions, taking the bend on two protesting wheels and slipping the clutch to get an extra howl out of the engine. Simon unlatched the door on his side and braced himself, holding it ready to let it fly open at the right moment as they blatted down the narrow street. With the main street junction rushing towards them, Ponti added the extra touch of a blast on the horn which raised stentorian echoes from the sleepy walls, and which Simon could only hope would give pause to any other vehicle which might happen to be on a collision course on the main road. Then came another screech of rubber, and the Bugatti broadsided around the corner.

Ponti took the clutch out again as soon as he had steadied the car, but kept the throttle open to maintain the level of exhaust noise, and during that instant of minimum speed Simon threw the door open and jumped. He had not touched the ground when Ponti let the clutch in again and set the red monster racing away.

The Saint landed running, the slap of his feet drowned in the departing reverberations of the motor, and in five long strides he was sheltered in the darkness of a doorway. The Bugatti vanished down the road, its uproar died away, and stillness descended again like a palpable blanket.

3

He was alone once more, in a citadel of potential enemies.

For five minutes he stood in the doorway, unmoving and silent as the ancient walls. He saw no

lights and heard no sounds, and the windows of the
buildings opposite from which he might have been
observed remained shuttered and dark. A scrawny
cat stalked down the sidewalk, paused to gaze at
him speculatively, and hurried on. Other than that
there was no sign of life. It was impossible that the
tumultuous passage of automobiles had not disturbed anyone, but either the inhabitants had
learned that discretion was the better part of
curiosity in those Mafia-dominated hills or they
were more bucolically interested in getting back to
sleep for the last hour or two of rest before another
morning's toil.

With the luminous dial of his watch turned to
the inside of his wrist so that its glow would not
betray him to any hidden watcher, if there were
one, he verified that it was twenty minutes past
three. So much had happened that night that it
seemed as if it should already have been completely
spent, yet he estimated that there must still be
about an hour of darkness left. An hour which
would give him the most concealment, before the
early risers began to stir and the gray pre-dawn exposed him to their view.

Which was either plenty of time, or nothing like
enough . . .

At first impression, it might have seemed an impossible task, to locate the hideout of Al Destamio
and his buddies among all those barred and silent
buildings. But actually it was by no means a search
without clues. In the first place, by far the greater
part of the village, through which Simon had had
the limousine in sight, could be ruled out. Second-
ly, his quarry's choice of that particular town had
not been dictated by its cultural amenities or pic-

turesque charm, nor would it have been picked on
the spur of the moment: the Ungodly must have
known exactly what refuge they were going to dive
into when they hopped out of their car, without
trusting that blind luck would let them blunder
into something suitable. Nor would this merely be
the home of some known sympathizer, since this
would have involved an impossible delay for bang-
ing on the door to rouse him and waiting for him to
open up. It had to be a place that they could get
into at once; and since the telephone lines to the
château had been cut long before their flight, they
could not have called ahead to announce their arrival and prepare anyone to receive them. Therefore it would have to be a place to which they had
a key, or where they knew that some door was
always unlocked. Therefore it was most probably
the home of one of them. And to qualify as the
domicile of such an exalted member of the Mafia,
it would have to be perceptibly more pretentious
than the average of its neighbors. So that again a
greater part of the remaining theoretical possibilities could be eliminated.

Satisfied now that he was not being observed,
Simon Templar eased himself out of the doorway
and made his way back up the side street as soundlessly as the cat.

The hideout was almost certainly beyond the
second turning at the end of the block, since that
would have given the fugitives more time to disap-
pear before the Bugatti could come in sight of them
again, and somewhere within the fifty-yard stretch
that had separated him from the limousine when he
saw it again. The Saint moved more slowly from the
corner, staying in the deepest shadows and

assessing the buildings on each side, his eyes and
ears straining to pick up any glimmer of light or
whisper of sound that would betray a suspiciously
early wakefulness within.

The houses were ranged shoulder to shoulder,
but not in an even line, some having chosen to set
farther back from the road than others. Simon
prowled past two, then three, a small shop with
living quarters above, another tall narrow building,
none of them giving any sign of life. Then there was
something only about two meters high which
pushed out closer to the road than any of its neighbors, and in a moment Simon realized that it was
not the projection of a ground floor but simply of
a wall enclosing the front garden of a building
which was itself set back quite a distance from the
street.

And as he drifted wraith-like towards the angle,
he heard from beyond it a soft scuff of footsteps,
and his pulse beat a fraction faster at the virtual
certainty that this must be the place where
Destamio & Co had holed up.

As he flattened himself against the side wall,
with his head turned to allow only one eye to peep
around the corner, a black shape took one step out
from a gateway in the front and stood to glance up
and down the road. The firefly glow of a cigarette-
end brightened to reveal the coarse cruel face of a
typical subordinate goon, and to glint on the barrel
of what looked like a shotgun tucked under his
arm.

That was the obliging clincher. A large house,
behind a walled garden—and an armed guard at
the gate. Any skeptic who insisted on more proof
would probably have refused to believe that an H-

bomb had hit him until his dust had been tested with a Geiger counter.

So now all that Simon had to do was to withdraw as softly as he had come, meet Ponti and the soldiers outside the town, and lead them to the spot.

Except that such relatively passive participation had never been the Saint's favorite rôle. And it would certainly have been an anticlimactic dénouement to the enterprise which had brought him that far. Besides which, he had already been pushed around too much by the Mafia to complacently leave others to administer their comeuppance. Major Olivetti and his *bersaglieri* had been fine for a frontal attack on the castle fortress, the boom of mortar shells and the flicker of tracer bullets had made it a stirring production number worthy of wide-screen photography; but Simon felt that something more intimate was called for in his personal settlement with Al Destamio.

He waited motionless, with infinite patience, until finally the bored sentinel turned and went back into the garden.

With the fluid silence of a stalking tiger the Saint followed behind him, and sprang.

The first intimation of disaster that the sentry had was when an arm snaked over his shoulder and the braced thumb-joint of its circling fist thumped into his larynx. Paralyzed, he could neither breathe nor yell, and he never noticed the second blow on the side of his neck that rendered him mercifully unconscious.

The Saint caught the shotgun as it dropped, and with his other hand clutched the man's clothing and eased his fall to the ground into a mere rustling collapse. Then he picked the limp form off the driveway and carried it to the shadow of a clump of bushes and rolled it under.

The driveway led straight to the doors of a garage, a status symbol which had obviously been cut into one corner of the ground floor of an edifice much older than the horseless carriage, and a flagged path branched from it to three steps which mounted to the front door. Simon tiptoed up the steps, and the door yielded to his touch—which was no more than he expected, for the Ungodly would harldly have been old-maidishly apprehensive enough to have locked the guard outside. The hallway inside was dark; but light came from a crack under a door at the back, and a deep murmur of male voices. With the shotgun in one hand, Simon inched towards the light with hypersensory alertness for any invisible obstacle that might catastrophically trip him.

The voices came through the door distinctively enough for him to recognize the hoarse rasp of Destamio's; but the conversation was mostly in Sicilian dialect, mangled and machine-gun fast, which made it almost impossible for him to follow. Occasionally someone would slip into ordinary Italian, which was more tantalizing than helpful, since the responses instantly became as unintelligible as the context. There seemed to be a debate as to whether they should lie low there, or leave together in a car which appeared to be available, or disperse; the argument seemed to hinge on whether their assembly should be considered to have completed its business for the present, or to have only been adjourned. The controversy flowed back and forth, with Destamio's voice becoming increasingly louder and more forceful: he seemed to be well on the way to dominating the opposition. But the next most persistent if quieter voice cut in with some proposal which seemed to find unanimous acceptance: the general mutter of approval merged into a scraping of chairs and a scuffle of feet, the inchoate clatter of men rising from a council table and preparing to fly the coop.

Which was precisely the move that Simon Templar had undertaken to deter.

He had no time to make any plan, he would have to play it entirely by ear, but at least he could give himself the priceless advantage of the initiative, of throwing them off balance and forcing them to react, while giving them the impression that he knew exactly where he was going.

Before anyone else could do it, he flung open the door and stood squarely in the opening, the shotgun levelled from his hip.

"Were you looking for me?" he inquired mildly.

Pure shock froze them in odd attitudes like a frame from a movie film stopped in mid-action, a ludicrous tableau of gaping mouths and bulging eyes. The apparition on the very threshold of their secret conclave of the man they had been trying to dispose of in one way or another for a day and two nights, who must have been responsible for their recent rout before the armed forces of justice, and who they had every right to believe had at least temporarily been shaken off, would have been enough to immobilize them for a while even without the menace of his weapon.

There were four of them: nearest the Saint, a stocky man with a porcine face and a scar, and a taller cadaverous one with thick lips which made him look like a rather negroid death's-head, both of whom Simon had seen at the bedside of Don Pasquale, and behind them Al Destamio and the man called Cirano with the nose to match it. They had been sitting around a circular dining table on which were glasses and a bottle of *grappa,* under a single light bulb with a wide conical brass shade over it. Cigarette and cigar ashes and butts soiled a gilt-edged plate that had been used as an ashtray.

Destamio was the first to recover his wits.

"It's a bluff," he croaked. "He only has two shots with that thing. He dare not use it because he knows that even if he gets two of us the other two will get him."

He said this in plain Italian, for the Saint's benefit.

Simon smiled.

"So which two of you would like to be the heroes, and sacrifice yourselves for the other two?"

There was no immediate rush of volunteers.

"Then move back a bit," ordered the Saint, swinging the shotgun. "You're not going anywhere."

Scarface and Skullface gave ground, not unwillingly; but Destamio kept behind Skullface, whose bulk was not quite sufficient to mask the protrusion of Destamio's elbow as his right hand crept up his side. Simon's restless eyes caught the movement, and his voice sliced through the smoky air like a sword.

"Stop him, Cirano! Or you may never find out why he is a bad security risk."

"I would like to know about that," Cirano said, and widened his mouth in a tight grin that made double pothooks on each side of his majestic nose.

He did more than talk; he caught hold of Destamio's right wrist, arresting its stealthy crawl towards the hip. Their muscles conflicted for a second before Destamio must have realized that even the slightest struggle would nullify any advantage he might have sneaked, and hatred replaced movement as an almost equally palpable link between them.

"You would listen to anyone if he was against me, *non è vero?*" Destamio snarled. "Even to this—"

"A good leader listens to everything before he makes up his mind, Alessandro," Cirano said equably. "You can be the first to sacrifice yourself when he has spoken, if you like, but there can be no harm in hearing what he has to say. You have nothing to cover up, have you?"

Destamio growled deep in his throat, but made no articulate answer. He abandoned his effort reluctantly, with a disgusted shrug that tried to convey that anyone stupid enough to accept such reasoning deserved all the nonsense that it would get him. But his beady eyes were tense and vicious.

"That's better," drawled the Saint. "Now we can have a civilized chat."

He advanced to within reach of the bottle on the table, picked it up, and took a sampling swig from it, without shifting his gaze from his captive audience. He lowered the bottle again promptly, with a grimace and a shudder, but did not put it down.

"Ugh," he said politely. "I don't wonder that people who drink this stuff start vendettas. I should start my first one with the distiller."

"How did you get here?" Cirano asked abruptly.

"A stork brought me," said the Saint. "How-

ever, if you were wondering whether I had some
connivance from your guard at the gate outside,
forget it. He never drew a disloyal breath, poor fellow. But he had an acute attack of laryngitis. If he
is still breathing when you find him, which is somewhat doubtful, I hope you will not add insult to his
injuries."

"At the least, he will have to answer for negli-
gence," Cirano said. "But since you are here, what
do you want?"

"Some information about Alessandro here—for
which I may be able to give you some in return."

"He is playing for time," Destamio rasped
shrewdly. "What could he possibly tell any of you
about me?"

"That is what I should like to know," Cirano
said, with his great nose questing like a bird-dog.

He was nobody's fool. He knew that the Saint
would not be standing there to talk without a reason, but he was not ready to jump to Destamio's
conclusion as to what the reason was. Even the remote possibility that there might be more to it than
a play for time forced him to satisfy his curiosity,
because he could not afford to brush off anything
that might weight the scales between them. And
being already aware of this bitter rivalry, Simon
gambled his life on playing them and their parti-
sans against each other, keeping them too preoc-
cupied to revert to the inexorable arithmetic which
added and subtracted to the cold fact that they
could overwhelm him whenever they screwed up
their resolve to pay the price.

"Of course you know all about his riper or even
rottener years," said the Saint agreeably. "But I
was talking about the early days, when the Al we

know was just a punk, if you will excuse the expression. Don Pasquale may have known—but doubtless he knew secrets about all of you which he took with him. But Al is older than the rest of you, and there may not be anyone left in the mob who could say they grew up with him. Not many of you can look forward to reaching his venerable old age: there are too many occupational hazards. So there can't be many people around unlucky enough to be able to recognize him under the name he had before he went to America."

"He is crazy!" Destamio choked. "You all know my family—"

"You all know the Destamios," Simon corrected. "And a good sturdy Mafia name it is, no doubt. And a safe background for your new chief. On the other hand, in these troubled times, could you afford to elect a chief with an air-tight charge of bank robbery and murder against him on which he could not fail to be convicted tomorrow—or with which he might be black-mailed into betraying you instead?"

4

Simon Templar knew that at least he had made some impression. He could tell it from the way Skullface and Scarface looked at Destamio, inscrutably waiting for his response. In such a hierarchy, no such accusation, however preposterous it might seem, could be dismissed without an answer.

"Lies! Nothing but lies!" blustered Destamio, as if he would blast them away by sheer vocal volume. "He will say anything that comes into his head—"

"Then why are you raising your voice?" Simon taunted him. "Is it a guilty conscience?"

"What is this other name?" Cirano asked.

"It might be Dino Cartelli," said the Saint.

Destamio looked at the faces of his cronies, and seemed to draw strength from the fact that the name obviously had no impact on them.

"Who is this Cartelli?" he jeered. "I told you, this Saint is only trying to make trouble for me. I think he is working for the American government."

"It should be easy enough to prove," Simon said calmly, speaking to Cirano as if this were a private matter between them. "All you have to do is take Al's fingerprints and ask the Palermo police to check them against the record of Dino Cartelli. No doubt you have a contact who could do that—perhaps the *maresciallo* himself? Cartelli, of course, is supposed to be dead, and they would be fascinated to hear of someone walking around alive with his identical prints. It would call for an urgent investigation, with the whole world looking on, or it might pop the entire fingerprint system like a pin in a balloon. But I'd suggest keeping Al locked up somewhere while you do it, or a man at his time of life might be tempted to squeal in exchange for a chance to spend his declining years in freedom."

Destamio's face turned a deeper shade of purple, but he had more control of himself now. He had to, if he was going to overcome suspicion and maintain his contested margin of leadership. And he had not climbed as high as he stood now through nothing but loudness and bluster.

"I will gladly arrange the fingerprint test myself," he said. "And anyone who has doubted me will apologize on his knees."

It was the technique of the monumental bluff, so audacious that it might never be called—or if it was, he could hope by then to have devised a way to juggle the result. It was enough to tighten the lips of Cirano, as he felt the mantle of Don Pasquale about to be twitched again from hovering over his shoulders.

"But that will not be done in these two minutes," Destamio went on, pressing his counter-attack. "And I tell you, he is only trying to distract you for some minutes, perhaps until more soldiers or police arrive—"

His black button-eyes switched to a point over the Saint's shoulder and above his head, widening by a microscopic fraction. If he had said anything like "Look behind you!" Simon would have simply hooted at the time-worn wheeze, but the involuntary reaction was a giveaway which scarcely needed the stealthy creak of a board from the same focal direction to authenticate it.

The Saint half turned to glance up and backwards, knowing exactly the risk he had to take, like a lion-tamer forced to take his eyes off one set of beasts to locate another creeping behind him, and glimpsed on the dimness of a staircase disclosed by the light that spilled from the room a fat gargoyle of a woman in a high-necked black dressing-gown trying to take two-handed aim at him with a shaky blunderbuss of a revolver—the wife or housekeeper of Cirano or Skullface or Scarface, whoever was the host, who must have been listening to everything since the dining-room door opened, and who had gallantly responded to the call of domestic duty.

In a flash Simon turned back to the room, as the hands of the men in it clawed frantically for the guns at their hips and armpits, and flung the *grappa* bottle which he still held up at the naked light bulb. It clanged on the brass shade like a gong, and he leapt sideways as the light went out.

The antique revolver on the stairs boomed like a cannon, and sharper retorts spat from the pitch blackness which had descended on the dining room, but the Saint was out in the hall then and untouched. He fired one barrel of the shotgun in the direction of the dining-room door, aimed low, and was rewarded by howls of rage and pain. The pellets would not be likely to do mortal damage at that elevation, but they could reduce by one or two the number of those in condition to take up the chase. He deliberately held back on the second trigger, figuring that the knowledge that he still had another barrel to fire would slightly dampen the eagerness of the pursuit.

Another couple of shots, perhaps loosed from around the shelter of the dining-room door frame, zipped past him as he sprinted to the front door and cleared the front steps in one bound, but respect for his reserve fire-power permitted him to make a diagonal run across the garden to the gate without any additional fusillade.

Outside the gate he stopped again, listening for following footsteps, but he did not hear any. He could have profited by his lead to run on down the road in either direction, leaving the Ungodly to guess which way he had chosen; but that would also have left them one avenue of escape where he could not hinder them or see them go. Now if two of them came on foot, he worked it out, he would have to slug the nearest one with his gun barrel and hope he would still have time to fire it at the second; if there were three or more, the subsequent developments would be very dicey indeed. On the other hand, if they came by car, he would have to shoot at the driver and hope that the glass was not tough enough to resist buckshot.

He waited tensely, but it seemed as if the pursuers had paused to lick their wounds, or were maneuvering for something more stealthy.

Then he heard something quite different: a distant sound of machinery rumbling rapidly closer. It was keyed by the throaty voice of the Bugatti, but filled out by an accompaniment of something more high-pitched and fussy. Lights silhouetted the bend from the village and then swept around it. The Bugatti, with Ponti at the wheel and Lieutenant Fusco beside him, was plainly illuminated for a moment by the lights of the following scout car, before its own headlights swung around and blinded him. Simon ran towards them, holding both hands high with the shotgun in one of them, hoping that it would stop any trigger-happy warrior mistaking him for an attacking enemy.

The Bugatti burnt rubber as it slowed, and Simon side-stepped to let it bring Ponti up to him.

"You took long enough," he said rudely. "Did I forget to show you how to get into top gear?"

"Lieutenant Fusco would not abandon his scout car, and I had to hold back for them to keep up with us," said the detective. "Did you have any luck?"

"Quite a lot—and in more ways than one." Simon thought the details could wait. "There are at least six of them in that house behind the wall: four live ones, big shots, a guard whom I may have killed, and a woman who would make a good mother to an ogre."

Fusco jumped out and shouted back to his detachment: "Report to the Major where we are and that we are going in after them, then follow me."

"A good thing we're not trying to surprise them," Simon remarked. "But they already know they're in trouble. The only question is whether they will surrender or fight."

They went through the gate and up the short driveway together. The three soldiers from Fusco's scout car followed, their boots making the noise of a respectable force before they fanned out across the lawn.

Ponti produced a flashlight and shone it at the front door which Simon had left half open.

"Come out with your hands up," he shouted from the foot of the steps, "or we shall come in and take you."

There was no answer, and the beam showed no one in what could be seen of the hall.

"This is my job," Ponti said, and shoved Simon aside as he ran up the steps.

Fusco ran after him, and Simon had to recover his balance before he could get on the Lieutenant's heels. But no shots greeted them, and the hall and staircase showed empty to the sweep of Ponti's flashlight. A flickering yellow luminance came from the door of the dining room, however, and when they reached it they saw Skullface and Scarface lying on the floor groaning, while the woman of the house tried to minister to their bloodstained legs by the light of a candle.

Cirano also lay on the floor, but he was not

groaning. There was a single red stain on his shirt, and his eyes were open and sightless. His magnificent nose stood up between them like a tombstone.

Ponti bent over him briefly, and looked up at the Saint.

"Did you do this?"

Simon shook his head.

"No. The others, yes—with this." He broke the shotgun, extracting one spent and one unused shell. "I didn't have a pistol. But Destamio did, and so did these two, and so did Florence Nightingale. I broke the light"—he pointed to it—"and they were all blazing away in the dark. It *could* have been an accident. You will have to try matching bullets to guns. But there is one gun missing." He turned to the woman. *"Dov'è Destamio?"*

She glared at him without answering.

"There must be a back way out," Simon said. "Or else—"

He turned and pushed two of the *bersaglieri* who were crowding at the door.

"Go and watch the garage," he snapped. "And one of you block the driveway with you car."

He went on across the hall and opened the door on the opposite side. It led to the kitchen, which was lit by a weak electric bulb over the sink. He strode across it to another door, which was ajar. Ponti was following him. They stepped out into darkness and fresh air.

"Your back way," Ponti said. "We should have looked for it before we came in at the front."

"If Al used it, he was probably gone before you got here," said the Saint. "Now, is he holed up somewhere else in the village, or would he try to make it out of here on foot? If Olivetti and his troops catch up soon enough, you might still be able to cordon off the area."

The detective was shining his flashlight this way and that. They were in a small walled courtyard with an old well in one corner, garbage cans in another, and an opening to a narrow alley in a third. The light swung to the fourth corner, and a brief pungent malediction dropped from Ponti's lips.

"I think we are already much too late," he said.

In the fourth corner, a short passage led back to a pair of large wide-open doors, beyond which was a bare-walled emptiness, and at the back of that the inside of another pair of doors, which were closed.

"God damn and blast it, the garage!" Simon gritted. "With doors at both ends, and a back alley to drive out. What every Mafia boss's home should have. And if there was a boss-grade car in it, he could be twenty kilometers away already."

They returned through the house, and Simon went on out of the front door and across to the gate. Ponti stayed with him.

"The guard I incapacitated is under those bushes," Simon said, pointing as he passed them.

"Where are you going?" Ponti asked.

Simon squeezed past the scout car which had been moved into the opening.

"I'm taking back my car and going home, thanking you for a delightful evening," said the Saint. "There's nothing more I can do here. But if I happen to run into Al again I will let you know."

"I think you have an idea where to look for him, and I ought to forbid you to try anything more on your own," Ponti grumbled. "But since you would only deny it, I can only ask you to let me see him alive if possible. The two whose legs you peppered, I know them, and they will be good to see in the dock, but Destamio would make it still better."

"I'll try to remember that," said the Saint ambiguously. He cranked up the Bugatti and climbed in. "Which is the way to the coast road?"

"Turn to the right on the main street, and take the next fork on the left. It is not very far. *Arriverderci.*"

"*Ciao,*" said the Saint, and backed the great car around and gunned it away.

It was in fact less than ten minutes to the coast highway, and it was with a heartfelt sigh of relief that he greeted its firm paving and comparatively easy curves. In spite of his steel-wire stamina, the accumulated exertions and shortage of sleep of the last few days had taken their inevitable toll, and he was beginning to fight a conscious battle with fatigue. Now it was less of a strain to make speed, and in the next miles he broke all the speed limits and most of the traffic laws; but fortunately it was still too early for any police cars or motorcycles to be abroad.

The sky was paling when he roared into the outskirts of Palermo and slowed up to thread through back roads that were already becoming familiar. There was just one piece of evidence that he had been cheated of, which he still needed before this adventure could be wound up; and when he finally brought the Bugatti to a stop, the gates of the cemetery which he had visited the night before had just slid past the edge of its headlights before he switched them off.

The gates were not locked, but the padlock on the Destamio mausoleum had been fastened again.

He had no key this time, but he had brought a jack handle from the car which would do just as well if more crudely. He inserted it and twisted mightily. Metal grated and snapped, and the broken hasp fell to the ground.

He knew that there was no fallacy like the cliche that lightning never strikes in the same place twice, but for someone else to be lurking there to attack him again, as he had been waylaid on his previous visit, would have been stretching the plausibilities much farther than that. Secure in the confidence that no biographer could inflict such a dull repetition on him, he walked inside without hesitation or trepidation, aiming for the tomb that he had so narrowly missed seeing before.

His pocket flashlight had long since vanished, but he had found a book of matches in the glove compartment of the Bugatti. He struck one that flared high in the windowless vault. There was a bronze casket almost at his eye level which looked newer than the others, though it was itself well aged and coated with dust. He bent close, and brought the match near the tarnished bronze plate on the side.

It read:

ALESSANDRO LEONARDO DESTAMIO

1898—1931

VIII

How Dino Cartelli Dug It,
and the Saint made a Deal

The main portals of the Destamio manse stood
wide open when the Saint saw them again. It was
the first time he had seen them that way, and his
pulse accelerated by an optimistic beat at the
thought of what this difference could portend. As
his angle of vision improved, he discerned on the
driveway inside the shape of a small but very
modern car limned by the dim light of a bulb over
the front door. It had been backed around so that
it faced the gateway, as if in readiness for the speed-
iest possible departure; and it did not seem too
great a concession to wishful thinking to visualize
it as the vehicle in which the man known as
Alessandro Destamio had made his getaway from
the village hideout, and its position as indicating
that this was not for a moment intended to be the
end of the flight.

But, now, it seemed that it could be the end of
the story . . .

Simon came on foot, after coasting the Bugatti
to a stop a good two hundred yards away, since its

stentorian voice was impossible to mute to any
level consistent with a stealthy approach towards
apprehensive ears. But as he cat-footed up the
drive, he began to hear from inside the villa a
steady thumping and hammering which might well
have drowned out any exterior noise except during
its own occasional pauses. Yet, far from being
puzzled by the clangor within, the Saint had an in-
stantaneous uncanny intuition of the cause of it,
and a smile of beatific anticipation slowly widened
his eyes and his mouth.

Even while he was enjoying a moment of his
mental vision, however, his active gaze was already
scanning the windows of the upper floor. All of
them were dark, but one pair of shutters was open
a few inches, enough to show that they were not
bolted on the inside, and those gave on to the
balcony formed by the portico over the front door.
For a graduate second-story man, it was no more
than an extension of walking up the front steps to
climb one of the supporting columns and enter the
room above.

There was a sound of heavy breathing and a
movement in the room as he crossed it, and a light
clicked on over the bed. It revealed the almost
mummified features of Lo Zio, sitting up, the ruf-
fled collar of a nightshirt buttoned under his chin
and a genuine tasselled nightcap perched on his
head.

The Saint smiled at him reassuringly.

"Buon giorno," he said. "We only wanted to be
sure you were all right. Now lie down again until
we bring your breakfast."

The ancient grinned a toothless grin of senile recognition, and lay down again obediently.

Simon went out quickly into the corridor, where

a faint yellow light came from the stairway. The hammering noises continued to reverberate from below, louder now that he was inside the building, but before he investigated them or took any more chances he had to find out whether Gina was in the house. It was unlikely that she would be on that floor, from which escape would have been too easy, but the stairs continued up to another smaller landing on which there were only four doors. Simon struck a match to observe them more clearly, and his glance settled on one which had a key on the outside. He tested the handle delicately, and confirmed that it was locked, but with his ear to the panel he heard someone stir inside. There could be only one explanation for that anomaly, and without another instant's hesitation he turned the key and went in.

In a bare attic room with no other outlet than a skylight now pale with dawn, Gina gasped as she saw him and then flung herself into his arms.

"So you're all right," he said. "That's good."

"They accused me of showing you the vault where they caught you. Of course I denied it, but it was no use," she said. "Uncle Alessandro told Donna Maria to keep me locked up until he found out what else you knew and saw to it that you wouldn't make any more trouble. I thought they were taking you for a ride like they do in the gangster movies."

"I suppose that was the general idea, eventually," he said. But people have had plans like that before, and I always seem to keep disappointing them."

"But how did you get away? And what has been happening?"

"I'll have to tell you most of that later. But you'll

hear the important answers in a minute, when Al and I have a last reunion." Reluctantly he put away for the time the temptations of her soft vibrant body. "Come along."

He led her by the hand out on to the landing. The thudding and pounding still came from below.

"What is it?" she whispered.

"I think it's Uncle Al opening another grave," he replied in the same undertone. "We'll see."

As they reached the entrance hall, Simon took the gun from his pocket for the first time since he had been in the house.

The door of the once somberly formal reception room was ajar, and through the opening they could see the chaos that had been wrought in it. The furniture in one far corner had been carelessly pushed aside, a rug thrown back, and the tiles assaulted and smashed with a heavy sledge-hammer. Then a hole had been hacked and gouged in the layer of concrete under the tiles with the aid of a pickaxe added to the sledge, which had afterwards been discarded. The hole disclosed a rusty iron plate which Destamio was now using the pickaxe to pry out. He was in his shirt-sleeves, dusty, dishevelled, and sweat-soaked, panting from the fury of his unaccustomed exertion.

Donna Maria leaned on the back of a chair with one hand, using the other to clutch the front of a flannel dressing-gown that covered her from neck to ankle, watching the vandalism with a kind of helpless fascination.

"You promised me that nothing would go wrong," she was moaning in Italian. "You promised first that you would leave the country and never return, and there would be enough money for the family—"

"I did not come back because I wanted to," Destamio snarled. "What else could I do when the Americans threw me out?"

"Then you promised that everything would still be all right, that you would keep away from us with your affairs. Yet for these last three days everything has involved us."

"It is not my fault that that goat Templar came to stick his horns into everything, old woman. But that is all finished now. Everything is finished."

Grunting and cursing, he finally broke the sheet of metal loose, and flung it clanking across the room. He went down on his knees and reached into the cavity which it exposed, and lugged out a cheap fiber valise covered with dust and dirt. He lifted it heavily, getting to his feet again, and dumped it recklessly on the polished top of a side table.

"I take what is mine, and this time you will never see me again," he said.

It seemed to the Saint that it would have been sheer preciosity to wait any longer for some possibly more dramatic juncture at which to make his entrance. It was not that he had lost any of his zest for festooning superlatives on a situation, but that in maturity he had recognized that there was always the austerely apt moment which would never improve itself.

He pushed the door wider, and stepped quietly in.

"Famosè ultime parole," he remarked.

The heads of Alessandro Destamio and Donna Maria performed simultaneous semicircular spins as if they had been snapped around by strings attached to their ears, with a violence that must have come close to dislocating their necks. Discovering the source of the interruption, they seemed at first to be trying to extrude their eyes on stalks, like lobsters.

Destamio had one additional reflex: his hand started a snatching movement towards his hip pocket.

"I wouldn't," advised the Saint gently, and gave a slight lift to the gun which he already held, to draw attention to it.

Destamio let his hand drop, and straightened up slowly. His eyes sank back into their sockets, and from the shift of them Simon knew that Gina had now followed him into the room.

Without turning his head, the Saint gave a panoramic wave of his free left hand which invited her to connect the wreckage of the room and the hole in the corner with the dusty bag on the table.

He explained: "The game is Treasure Hunt. But I'm afraid Al is cheating. He knew where it was all the time, because he buried it himself—after he stole it from a bank in Palermo where he worked long ago under another name."

"Is that true, Uncle Alessandro?" Gina asked in a small voice.

"I'm not your uncle," was the impatient rasping answer. "I never was your uncle or anybody's uncle, and you might as well forget that nonsense."

"His real name," Simon said, "is Dino Cartelli."

Cartelli-Destamio glowered at him with unwavering venom.

"Okay, wise guy," he growled in English. "Make like a private eye on television. Tell'em my life story like you figure it all out in your head."

"All right, since you ask for it," said the Saint agreeably. "I've always rather liked those scenes myself, and wondered if anyone could really be so brilliant at reconstructing everything from all the way back, without a lot of help from the author who dreamed it up. But let's see what I can do."

Gina had moved in to where he could include her in his view without shifting his gaze too much from its primary objective. It made it easier for him than addressing an audience behind his back.

"Dino—and let's scrub that Alessandro Destamio nonsense, as he suggests," he said, "is a man of various talents and very lofty ambitions. He started out as a two-bit punk right here in Palermo, and although he is still a punk he is now in the sixty-four thousand dollar class, or better. He once had an honest job in the local branch of a British bank, but its prospects looked a bit slow and stodgy for a lad who was in a hurry to get ahead. So he joined the Mafia, or perhaps he was already a member—my crystal ball is a little unclear on this point, but it isn't important. What matters is that somebody thought of a bigger and faster way to get money out of the bank than working for it."

Cartelli's eyes were small and crafty again now, and Simon knew that behind them a brain that was far from moronic was flogging itself to find a way out of its present corner, and would take advantage of all the time it could gain by letting someone else do the talking.

"That's a good start," Cartelli croaked. "What's next?"

"Whether it was Dino's own idea, because he'd al-

ready been tapping the till in a small way and an
audit by the bank examiners was coming up, or
whether he was recruited for the job from higher
up, is something else I can't tell you which doesn't
matter either. The milestone is that the bank was
robbed, apparently by some characters who broke
in while he was working late one night. He seems to
have put up a heroic fight before he was killed by
a shotgun blast in the face and hands which
mutilated him beyond recognition or even routine
identification. But have you read enough detective
stories to guess what really happened?"

"Go on," Cartelli said. "You're the guy who was
gonna dope it out."

"For a first caper, it was quite a classic," Simon
went on imperturbably. "In fact, it was a variation
on the gimmick in quite a few classic stories. Of
course, the robbers were Dino's pals and he let
them in. He helped them to bust the safe and
shovel out the loot, and then changed clothes with
another bloke who'd been brought along to take
the fall. He was the one who was killed with the
shotgun—but who would ever doubt that it was the
loyal Dino Cartelli? Dino got a nice big cut off the
cake in return for disappearing, a lot of which I
think is still in that valise; the Mafia got the rest,
and everyone was happy except the insurance company that had to make good the loss. And maybe
the man with no face. Who was he, Dino?"

"Nobody, nobody," Cartelli said hoarsely. "A
traitor to the Mafia, why not? A nobody. Don't tell
me you care about some sonovabitch like that!"

"Maybe not," said the Saint. "If the Mafia confined themselves to knocking off their own erring
brothers, I might even give them a donation. But

then, many years after, in fact just the other day, something went wrong with the perfect crime that Dino thought had been buried and forgotten. A silly old English tourist named Euston, who once upon a time worked in the bank beside Dino, recognized him in a restaurant in Naples after all those years—partly from that scar on his cheek, which Euston happened to have given him in a youthful brawl. And this Euston was too stupid and stubborn to be convinced that he could be mistaken. So—perhaps without too much reluctance, after such a reminder of that bygone clout in the chops, Dino had him liquidated. That was when I got interested. And practically everything that's happened since has stemmed from Dino's efforts to buy me off or bump me off."

"But my uncle?" Gina asked bewilderedly. "How does he fit in?"

"Your uncle is dead," Simon said in a more sympathetic tone. "I went back to the mausoleum before I came here, and finished the search we started the other night. Alessandro Destamio did die in Rome of that illness in 1931, as you suspected, and Dino here stepped into his shoes. But the family still had enough sentiment to insist on putting Alessandro's coffin in the ancestral vault. Why they let Dino take his name should only take a couple of guesses."

He had spoken in Italian again, with the calculated intention of including the comprehension of Donna Maria, and now she responded as he had hoped.

"I will answer that, Gina," she said, with some of the old iron and vinegar back in her voice. "Your uncle was a good man, but a foolish one

with money, and he had wasted all that we had. He
was dying when this Dino came to me and offered
a way to keep our home and the family together. I
accepted for all our sakes, with the understanding
that he would never try to be with us himself. But
first he broke that promise and now he will leave us
destitute."

"You should have taken over his loot while you
had the chance, for insurance," said the Saint,
touching the lock on the valise.

The matriarch drew up her dumpy figure with
pride.

"I am not a thief," she said. "I would not touch
stolen money."

Simon shrugged his renewed bafflement at the
vagaries of the human conscience.

"I wish I could see the difference between that
and the money he used to send you from America."

"What she forgets," Cartelli said viciously, "is
that Lo Zio himself was once a Mafia Don—"

"Sta zitto!" shrieked Donna Maria unavailingly.

"—and she had nothing against his support in
those days. And after he had a stroke and was no
more good for anything, Don Pasquale offered him
this deal as a kind of pension, and he was glad to
take it."

"Enough, *vigliacco!* Lo Zio is sick, dying—you
cannot speak of him like that—"

"I tell the truth," Cartelli said harshly.

Then he spoke again in English: "Lookit, Saint,
these people don't mean nut'n to you. When I had-
da give a contract for Euston—yeah, an' for you
too—it was self defense, nut'n else, self defense like
you get off for in court. Nut'n personal. Okay, so

now I'm licked. You tipped off the cops about me, an' even the Mafia won't back me no more after all this trouble I brought on them. But you an' me can talk business."

The Saint's thumb moved against the catch on which it was resting, and the fastening snapped open. The valise had not been locked. He lifted the lid, and exposed its contents of neatly tied and packed bundles of paper currency in the formats and colors of various solvent nations.

"About this?" he asked.

"Yeah. I oughta have left it anyhow—I done without it all these years, an' I got enough stashed in a Swiss bank to keep me from starving now, once I get outa Italy. You take it—give what you like to the old woman an' Gina, an' keep the rest. There's plenty to make up for all the trouble you had." Desperate earnestness rasped through the gravel in Cartelli's voice. "No one ain't never gonna hear about it from me, if you just gimme a chance an' let me go."

Simon Templar relaxed against the table, half hitching one leg on to it to make a seat, and played the fingers of his free hand meditatively over the bundles of cash in the open bag. For some seconds of agonizing suspense he seemed to be waiting and listening for some inner voice to advise him.

At last he looked up, with a smile.

"All right Dino," he said. "If that's how you want it, get going."

Gina gave a little gasp.

Cartelli gave nothing, not even a grunt of thanks. Without a word he grabbed up his coat and huddled into it as he went out.

Simon followed him far enough to watch his flat-

footed march across the hallway, and to make sure
that when the front door slammed it was with
Cartelli on the outside and not turning to sneak
back for a surprise counter-attack. He waited long
enough to hear the little car outside start up and
begin to move away.

He came back into the room again to see Donna
Maria sitting in a chair with her face buried in her
hands, and Gina staring at him in a kind of lost
and lonely perplexity.

"You let him go," she said accusingly. "For his
stolen money."

"Well, that was one good reason," Simon said
cheerfully.

"Do you think I would touch it?"

"You sound like Donna Maria. So don't touch
it. But I'm sure the bank, or their insurance company, would pay a very handsome reward for having it returned. Do you see anything immoral
about that?"

"But after all he's done—the murders—"

From outside, but not far away, they were suddenly aware of a confused sequence of roaring engines, squealing brakes, shouts, a crash, and then
shots. Several shots. And then the disturbance was
ended as abruptly as it had begun.

"What was that?" Gina whispered.

Simon was lighting a cigarette, with the feeling
that this was a moment for rather special indulgence.

"I think that was Dino's curtain call," he said
calmly. "As he told us, he should never have come
back for these souvenirs of that old boyish esca-
pade. But—" he reverted to Italian again for the
benefit of Donna Maria, who had raised her head

in bemuddled but fearful surmise—"I suppose greed got him into this, and it's only poetic that greed should put him out. Digging up this money cost him enough time for me to catch up with him, and then I only had to gain a little more time for the police and the army to catch up with me. We've been having a lot of fun since last night which I'll have to tell you about. A little while ago I managed to take over the fastest transportation, which was mine to begin with anyway because I hired it most respectably; but the head policeman this time is nobody's fool, and I knew he would not take long to guess that this might be the place where I was going."

"The police," Donna Maria repeated stonily.

Simon looked at her steadily.

"This one, Marco Ponti, is not like some others," he said. "I think I could persuade him to let Dino Cartelli be buried under his own name—shot while trying to escape after digging up his share of the bank robbery, which he buried in the Destamio house, where the family had been kind enough to receive him as a guest in his young days, knowing nothing about his Mafia connections. I don't think he will mind leaving Lo Zio to another Judge whom he will have to face soon enough. I think Marco will buy all that—if you will agree not to try to keep Gina here against her will."

"But where will I go?" Gina asked.

"Wherever the sun shines, and you can dance and laugh and play, as a girl should when she's young. You could try St Tropez for a change from everything you've been used to. Or Copenhagen or Nassau or California, or any other place you've dreamed of seeing. If you like, I'll go some of the way with you and get you started."

Her wonderful eyes were still fixed on him in demoralizing contemplation when the jangle of the front door bell announced an obligatory but obviously parenthetic interruption.

WATCH FOR THE SIGN OF
THE SAINT

HE WILL BE BACK!